Realm of Vitalis:
Aislinn's Emergence

Front cover designed by, *Anne Meadows*

First printing: March 2021
ISBN: 978-1-7339577-5-5
M.A.Rose
amazon.com/author/meganrosales

Acknowledgements

I would like to give a big thanks to my family and friends who continually support my passion to write and encourage me to never give up. Also, special thanks to my friend, and illustrator, Anne Meadows, for collaborating with me on the cover design. You helped make my vision come to life.

REALM OF VITALIS MAP

Land of Kalos

Land of the Doulos

Elfspond

Eternal Keep

Land of Agnostos

Valstead

Watersedge

Sea of Thavma

Meadows Clearing

Isle's of Watersedge

Sea of Thavma

E

N   S

W

Chapter 1

"Girls, please be safe tonight." My mother says to my best friend Natasha and I. "We will." We sing in unison, followed by a giggle as we get ready to leave the house. It's been months since I last came home and figured it would be refreshing to do so to celebrate my 25th birthday. We are both giddy with excitement and ready to indulge in a fun night out with some bar hopping and maybe a club or two.

It's my first time home since I broke up with Brad and Natasha thinks it's the perfect time to *get back out there*. I've been missing my best friend and we are long over due for some bonding time. With finals approaching, I've been a little off grid, but like the good friend she is, she understands.

Natasha is like a sister to me and prior to me going off to college, we were inseparable. Not that college has changed our friendship, it has just made me realize how big the world really is. We had both planned to go off to college together, but right before graduation, her mom got real sick. She stayed behind to help take care of her mom and little sister. So, instead, she went to cosmetology school, and then when her mom passed away she took over custody of her sister and has been working her butt off to provide for Kaylee and herself since.

I on the other hand, guess you could say, have it pretty cush. My adoptive parents, Sadie and Everett, have raised me since I was one. They have done everything in their power to provide me with the best life within their means. I sure am grateful I wound up on their doorstep that fateful night. Not grateful in the sense that the person who birthed me, decided to leave me abandoned on a stranger's doorstep one dark stormy night. But, grateful that it was Sadie and Everett's porch that my biological makers happened to leave me on. Dad said it was raining cats and dogs that night, he's not really sure what made him come down stairs to check things out, but when he did, the rain hushed for a brief moment and that's when he heard what sounded like a baby crying. He opened the front door and lo and behold a screaming baby lay on their welcome mat. There was a single note attached to the blanket I was wrapped in and that was it.

Hello,
My name is Aislinn. Today is my first birthday.
Please watch over me.

Dad said he immediately scooped me up and brought me in the house and called for Sadie like a madman. After taking me to the hospital to be evaluated and submit a police report they couldn't bring themselves to hand me over to the system. They said it had to have been a sign, that I was meant to be their little girl. They are the best parents I could have asked for and not a day goes by that I even think about what my life could've been like. Or, who the hell my biological parents are. Deep in my subconscious though, I can't help but wonder. What could a baby ever do to deserve to be dumped like trash? I like to tell myself that maybe they were druggies and just couldn't afford the cost of a baby over their bad habit, but truth is, no one will ever know. I try not to dwell on the past, but for some reason my birthday always takes me down memory lane.

"And don't forget to call if you need a ride. I don't care how late it is." My dad says, snapping me back to reality. "We will. I promise." I tell him with a reassuring smile. He gives me a hug which then prompts mom to give me a hug as well. "It's so good to see you two girls together again. You are just growing up so fast." Mom says as she starts to get teary-eyed. "Mooom." I say with an embarrassed echo. She swats away the tears and dad pulls her into a hug. "You girls go on and have fun. I'll take care of her." My dad says as he kisses mom on the temple.

Only fifteen minutes pass before we see the city lights of Atlanta in our horizon. "Club or bar first?" Natasha asks. "Hmm. I think I need a couple drinks in me before I attempt to dance in public." I say. "Touché." She says and we both erupt with laughter. Once we have our destinations picked out, we park in a place not far from each location and make our way to our first bar.

"To the best friend a girl could ask for" Natasha says as we cheers to our first drink. I take a sip of the citrusy cocktail the bartender surprised me with, and find myself pleased with the taste. "So tell me, how are you? How's Kaylee doing? Any luck with jump-starting the shop? Gosh, I feel like it's been forever."

I ramble. "Kaylee's good. She's so excited that she made it into the honor society this year, plus she's thinking about trying out for the soccer team. It makes me so happy to see her finally getting back into extracurriculars. As for the shop…" Natasha says followed by a long sigh. I give her a frown, "That bad, huh?" "It's like every time I save up enough money to possibly open it solo, something happens and I have to use the money. Or, when I get someone to go in half, they back out last minute. It's just so damn frustrating." She tells me. "Dang, girl. I'm sorry. I wish there was something I could do. Maybe once I graduate and get a job, I can be a sponsor." I tell her. "Ugh, I don't deserve you." She tells me before continuing, "Speaking of, one more month and then you'll be graduated! I can't believe you're going to have your Master's in Psychology!" Natasha says. "I know. It's exciting and nerve wrecking all in one. Do you think I'll make a good counselor?" I ask her. "Um, as if that's even a question? I think you are going to be the best damn counselor there is!" She tells me with a beaming smile. "Thanks Nat." I say as I pull her into a big side hug. "Not to change the subject, but cutie on your ten hasn't taken his eyes off you in the last five minutes." She whispers. "Pfft. Whatever." I say as I try to nonchalantly take a peek over my shoulder, but I don't see anyone. "Are you messing with me?" I say jokingly. She looks past me, "No, I swear! He must've just walked off." She says. I feel my phone buzz and I retrieve it from my pocket only to immediately shove it back in angrily. "Brad?" Natasha says coldly, but also inquisitively. "Yep." Is all I say. "I can't believe the nerve of that guy." She says. "At least he remembered what today is." I say bleakly. "Oh no you don't! You better not be giving him a pass Aislinn or so help me…" I let out a hysterical laugh that cuts her off. "There is no way on this Earth, or any planet for that matter, that I will be giving Brad a single second of my time after what he did." I tell her as the hurt and feelings of betrayal seep back into the front of my mind.

We were high school sweethearts, Brad and I. We started dating sophomore year and had been together up until four months ago when I caught him doing the dirty with some chick in his apartment. It devastated me. We had always talked about marriage, kids, having a future together, all that jazz.

I swore he was the one, I just could never bring myself to take our relationship to the next level and he always seemed okay with it. Of course it's easy to keep from having sex with your girlfriend though, when you just go off and have sex with someone else. Every time we would get caught up in the heat of the moment there was always something telling me, don't do it, wait. I'm glad I listened. Probably saved me from more heartache in the long run.

I've always been blessed with a good sense of intuition. It's helped me out a lot throughout the years. Occasionally, I'll have these trance like daydreams and I can see or hear things and sometimes even feel emotions with them. Then I'll just snap out of it and be left with this nawing sensation until I confront what I saw and then it's like dejavu or something. I've never told anyone about it, not even Natasha. Besides, what would I even tell her? *Hey Nat, just so you know, sometimes I can predict the future.* I scoff in my head at the absurdity.

"Hmpf. Good. He's an asshole and you, my beautiful amazing best friend, deserve so much better and I think tonight, it's time we get you back on the playing field." Natasha tells me. I give her a big smile and just shake my head at her silliness, "Whatever you say." I tell her. Truth be told, it makes me nervous to start darting again. The dating world can be cruel and superficial. Having to meet a new person and hope they like how you look on the outside enough to want to get to know what's on the inside, is terrifying. After six years of knowing somebody and then having to start all over with a whole new person, feels like having your memory card erased on the game you were just about to finish. But hey, no one said life was fair or easy. So, it's time I reset and focus on my future, and what better time to start fresh than on my birthday. I'm still young and so is the night.

Chapter 2

After three drinks, we close our tab and head to Nyx, one of the hottest clubs downtown right now. Once we get our hands stamped we link elbows and make our way into the club. The lights are flashing, the music is bumping, and while there's a good majority of people on the dance floor there's also a good amount at each of the bars socializing. We shove our way to the bar and order a shot followed by a drink we can actually sip on. Once we have our drink, we make our way to the dance floor and let our loosened inhibitions take over. We dance with each other at first and then it's not long before some guys approach us to dance.

After about an hour and a half we work up a good sweat, so we use the buddy system to go to the ladies room. "I think the dark haired one is soooo into you." Natasha says as she gives me a little nudge and I reply with a skeptical side eye. "Do you have a hair tie? I'm so sweaty." I tell her as I fan myself. "Sure do!" She says as she pulls one from her clutch. I scoop my long, now wavy, blonde hair into a ponytail and reapply my pink lipstick and look at Natasha. "How do I look?" I ask. "Sexy as ever. Now go bat those gorgeous green eyes of yours and get some numbers." She says half jokingly, but also half serious.

When we emerge from the bathroom, Natasha leads us back toward the bar. We both order a Bahama Mama and take a seat. "Oh there's the guy from the last bar!" Natasha says excitedly. I look to my left and at the corner of the bar I see a man staring at me. He is indeed a *cutie* as Natasha referred to him. He's tall and brawny with short blonde hair and chocolate brown eyes. He has a little bit of stubble that gives him a rugged, yet sophisticated look. I also wonder how he hasn't collapsed from heat stroke from wearing jeans and a leather jacket in this Georgia summer heat. Something about the way he's looking at me is a little unnerving, but I give him the benefit of the doubt since he might just be shy. I give him a soft smile to hopefully show my interest and he immediately turns his back on me. Alrighty, maybe he's not interested after all. Natasha nudges me, "I think he wants you to make the first move." She tells me. I let out a sigh. "Have I mentioned how much I hate this whole dating thing?" I tell her, "Just go!" She tells me as she practically pushes me out of my seat. I slowly make my way to the man at the end of the bar and I'm about to tap his shoulder when he turns to face me.

"Can I help you?" He says in an irritated tone. "Sorry, I...I, um, just thought you may have wanted to talk." I finally finish saying. "Don't flatter yourself." He tells me flatly. Wow, rude much. Now I am pissed. "Well then how about you keep your eyes to yourself, you creep." I reply. He gives me a smug smirk, "Gladly." He tells me as he turns his back on me once more. I let out another huff and march back to my seat.

"How'd it go?" Natasha asks. "Total, asshat." I tell her as I cross my arms. She gives me a frown, "Sorry, I didn't mean to push you." She tells me. "It's not your fault. Some guys are just straight up self conceited jerks." I tell her. The bartender brings our drinks and I sip my drink as I try and forget my rude encounter. Right as we order our second drink a man approaches Natasha and asks her to dance. She looks back at me and I shoo her away encouragingly. She deserves to let loose and have fun. Last thing I need is her stuck playing wing-woman for me all night. I turn back to the bar to wait for our cocktails when a man approaches me.

"Hi there." He says giving me a pleasant smile. "Hi" I say nervously. "I'm Carter." He says extending his hand out to me. "Linn." I say as I shake his hand. It's not that I don't want him to know my real name, I've just never seen it as a cute feminine name. Plus, most people butcher pronouncing it anyway and I get tired of correcting them. "I hate to be forward, but are you here with anyone?" He asks me. I cock my head in response and I think he realizes my hesitation. He chuckles, "I meant, like with a date." He says. "Ohhh…" I say as I feel myself become flush with embarrassment. Yep, natural blonde right here. "No, no date." I tell him.

We spend the next fifteen minutes chatting about what we each do, what town we grew up in, and so forth. I feel like things are going well between us, when I feel my phone vibrate. I pull it out to make sure it's not Natasha looking for back up. Just Brad again, I see as I quickly glance over his message. Doesn't he have anything better to do? "Everything okay?" Carter asks. I shove my phone back in my pocket, "Yeah, sorry, just some jerk that's not worth my time." I tell him. "Well here, how about you finish your drink and then let's go dance it off." He says as he flashes me a big grin.

I pick up my glass and get ready to down the rest of it when all of a sudden a person comes barreling in between me and Carter. Causing me to spill the drink all over me and the clumsy fool. "What the hell man!" Carter says angrily as he rises from his chair. "I'm so sorry, I must have tripped or something." The man says before turning his attention on me. I'm grateful the club is as loud as it is because when our eyes lock, I let out an audible gasp. He is undoubtedly, the most handsome man I've ever seen in my life. His eyes are baby blue which is complimented by his tan complexion and short black wavy hair. When he finally stands up straight, it's apparent he is at least six feet tall and I can't help but notice how well he fills out his shirt and jeans. He stares at me for a moment and then it's as if he's jolted back to reality as he starts to scramble to gather some napkins and hands them to me. "I'm so sorry my lady, please forgive me." He tells me. I let out a giggle at his outdated choice of words and he looks away embarrassed. "Oh, I'm not laughing at you!" I say reassuringly, once I realize how rude I must have come across. "I've just never heard someone use the term *my lady* in person before." I say as I wipe the sticky cocktail off of me the best I can. "Yeah loser, why don't you get out of here before you make things worse." Carter interjects. "Carter!" I say almost appalled, "don't be so rude. It was an accident." I tell him. Carter scoffs, "Okay Mother Teresa." I scrunch up my face at his attempt of an insult, "Excuse me?" I say. "Whatever, not even worth my time anymore." Carter says and then walks off angrily. I sit there with a shocked look on my face trying to process what the hell just happened.

I turn to the mystery man and watch as he wipes himself off. I notice a tattoo to his right forearm that says *Doulos* and as my gaze trails back up to his face our eyes meet once again, but this time he quickly looks away. "I should be going now. Stay safe my lady." He says without looking at me and tries to walk off. I now realize he isn't just entertaining some medieval vocabulary. He truly has an old English dialect and it has me captivated. "Wait!" I say. He stops in his tracks, but doesn't turn around. "You don't have to go." I add. "I must. I have done my part and now it's time I go." He tells me. "Your part?" I say with a soft chuckle. "That man, Carter. He had spiked your drink. I could not stand by in good faith and let you drink it." He tells me. It's a good thing he's still turned around because my jaw drops open. How could I be so careless and clueless. He must have done it when I checked my phone, now it explains why he was so pissed. I shutter at the thought that crosses my mind if I were to drink the roofied cocktail. "Then at least let me thank you properly. Who knows what would've happened if you didn't intervene." I tell him. I get up from my stool and he turns around hesitantly to face me. "What's your name?" I ask, feeling as if I'm practically begging him. "Jace Galanis-Doulos." He tells me, and I'm not sure if it's the exotic name alone or his accent, but it sure weakens me in the knees. "Well thank you Jace, you are my savior." I tell him. My savior? Good gracious, this guy is already rubbing off on me. "I'm Aislinn by the way." I say as I stick out my hand. Can I be anymore awkward? I think to myself. "You certainly are an Aislinn." He tells me with a smile. Good Lord, the way he says my name, perfectly, makes me want to hear him say it time and time again. "It is my greatest pleasure to meet you." He adds and then takes my hand in his and kisses it softly. When his lips touch my hand, I get an overwhelming feeling of every emotion I've ever felt, all at once. My chest heaves as I become super happy, then laugh, cry, become angry, aroused, frustrated, excited, and then back to stunned all in a matter of ten seconds. I pull my hand away quickly and give him a shocked look and he instantly looks startled. Is it possible that he felt what I did? It was if each emotion I felt I could see flashes of us together. Is this just one of my *see into the future* moments. I never had it feel like that though, this was something so much more, I can't even describe it. "W…what was that?" I ask, starting to doubt my sanity as I look into his eyes and I can tell he is just as confused as me.

"Aislinnnn!" I hear Natasha's slurred words from behind me. Whoops, I almost forgot where I was. I spin around to face her and she throws her arm around me. Partly to steady herself, but also to get the creeper behind her to back off. "Nat, I want you to meet Jace." I say as I quickly turn back around, but he's no longer there. My heart actually sinks a little. I should've asked for his number, but I doubt he would've given it to me. After all, he was quite eager to get away from me after he came to my rescue. "Who?" Natasha says, while trying to maintain her focus. "Uh, never mind. How about we call it a night, I'm about ready to pass out." I tell her. She just gives me a thumbs up. I pull out my phone and call my dad to come pick us up.

Chapter 3

I expect to fall fast asleep when we make it back home, but instead, I find myself tossing and turning. Every time I close my eyes I see Jace's face. It's as if my mind is trying to tell me something, and it's not long before that nawing feeling in my stomach makes itself known. I'm not really sure what my mind or body expects me to do. I don't even know the guy and I'll probably never see him again in my life. It's obvious, I'm not going to be able to go to sleep anytime soon, so I flip back my covers and quietly get out of bed so I don't wake Natasha. I make my way downstairs and head to the kitchen for some late night comfort food.

I make a bowl of ice cream and sit alone as I indulge in the chocolatey goodness. When I'm finished I go to the sink to rinse out my bowl. As I look up, I let out a startled scream. There's a man dressed in all black standing right outside our kitchen window with the most sinister look in his eyes and they are fixated on me. I drop the bowl, causing it to shatter, and make a run for the stairs.

"Mom! Dad!" I yell. My dad meets me at the top of the stairs where I collapse into his arms. "There's a man outside the kitchen window." I say in tears.

My mom joins us and so does Natasha. "Sadie, call the cops while I go check things out." My dad says. "Dad, no!" I say as I start to follow behind him. He turns around and gives me a stern look, "Aislinn, you and Natasha go to your room." He tells me. I've never seen him so serious in my life. My mom pulls me back up the stairs and ushers us into my room.

"What the hell is going on?" Natasha says with a scared look in her eyes. "There was some guy standing outside the kitchen window. He was right there Nat and he had this psychotic look in his eyes." I say as I start to panic. She pulls me into a hug and when she does, I get a sharp pain in my head. "Owe!" I say as I clench my head between my hands. "What is it?" Natasha asks. "Something's wrong. This isn't right." I manage to say. All of a sudden an image of my dad getting stabbed flashes in my head. Next the image of my mom and Natasha's lifeless bodies appear in my mind, followed by another sharp pain in my head. No, this can't be happening. All of my previous visions, I stood by passively and let them play out because I assumed it was destined fate. Not tonight, I can't let this one come true. If I act fast, there's a chance I can prevent all of this. "Get under my bed and do not come out until it's safe to do so." I command. Natasha gives me a terrified look and simultaneously a loud crashing sound comes from downstairs. "Now!" I tell her firmly and she quickly slips under my bed. I then dart to the hallway where I see my moms panic stricken face. I embrace her briefly while I whisper to her, "Go to the hall closet and hide." I'm not sure where this sense of directness is coming from, but I know it's fueled by the distraught images filling my head. "I am not going anywhere until I know you are safe." She tells me. I put my hand on her shoulder and look directly into her eyes, "Mom I love you but, you must go to the hall closet and wait." I demand. Never in my life would I picture myself telling my mother what to do, but there is too much at stake. She gives me a blank stare almost as if she is looking right through me and then makes her way to the closet. I am half shocked that she listened to me, but given the circumstances, I'm grateful she did what I said.

I run down the stairs and quickly find the intruder holding my dad up against the wall, ready to plunge a silver twisted dagger into his chest. "NO!" I scream with every bit of oxygen I have in my lungs and right then the entire house begins to shake. The intruder turns to face me and the corners of his mouth turn to give me a sadistic grin. "Ah, there you are." He says in a spine chilling tone. *There you are.* His words echo in my mind. So the sicko is here for me. "Don't hurt him. If it's me you want, then just take me." I plead as my tears begin to fall. "No Aislinn, run." My dad says, beneath the man's grip around his throat. My eyes dart to the back door and it's as if the man can read my mind. He throws my dad to the ground and then swiftly cuts me off. "Not so fast." He tells me. I peddle backwards as fast as I can until I bump into my dad and he takes his place in front of me. "Listen, we don't have much, but maybe we can arrange something. Please, just leave my daughter alone." My dad says and my heart breaks when I hear the fear in his voice. The man lets out a deranged laugh. "You humans are so emotional, it'll always be your demise." He scoffs and then stabs my dad in the stomach. My eyes fill with horror as I watch my dad fall to his knees. My fear becomes instantly replaced with rage. "You sick bastard!" I scream as I attempt to punch the sick freak. He catches my fist in his hand, and the instant our hands collide we are both forcefully flung in opposite directions. I hit the living room wall hard and have to use it to steady myself. I look across the way at the sociopath in our home as he picks himself up off the floor. He dusts himself off and lets out a chuckle and looks up, "You really think that's going to stop me Demitrius?" He shouts before redirecting his attention back on me. This guy has lost his marbles. I need to get him out of the house before he finds mom and Nat. I make a beeline for the front door and when I fling it open I run into the rude man from the club earlier that night. My mind is running a million miles a second. Is this why he was staring at me all night? Him and his buddy making some sick plan to follow me home and torture me. He quickly pulls me out of the house and pushes me out towards the front yard before entering our house.

I fall to the ground and start to sob and pray that the police show up any minute now. I hear a loud crash and my head turns to the kitchen window and I see the blonde man and the sociopath exchanging punches. Now I'm even more confused than before. I feel a hand on my shoulder and let out a yelp as I quickly turn around and am greeted by the same baby blue eyes I met earlier that night. "J-Jace?" I say, as my voice trembles. My head is starting to ache. What kind of sick game are these guys playing? "I'm not here to hurt you Aislinn." Jace says calmly. "Then what the hell are you doing here? How do you know where I live?" I spout off as I begin to sob some more. "Shh. Everything will be explained, but we have to get you to safety first." He tells me as he tries to pull me to my feet, but I can't move. "My, my dad…" I cry, as I look into his eyes. I can see his face fill with conflict. "We really must go. Xander can hold him off, but not for long." Xander? My eyes flash back to the kitchen and I see the two men now wrestling each other. "I'm not going anywhere until I know the rest of my family is safe." I tell him. He stares at me for a moment and then realizes that I'm serious. He gives a small frustrated sigh as he looks up to the sky. "Demitrius, I call upon you for guidance." Jace says under his breathe and I recognize the same name the maniac shouted just a few moments ago. His blue eyes turn yellow and I let out another yelp as I scramble to get away from him. After thirty seconds Jace lets out a

large gasp and his eyes return to their blue state. "We
have to move quickly if we are going to save them."
He tells me as he extends out his hand. I look into
his eyes and despite everything that has just
happened, I feel that I can put my trust in this utter
stranger. I take his hand and he quickly pulls me up
and leads me to the back yard. "They're both on the
second story, yes?" He asks me. I nod. He picks up
my childhood trampoline and lines it up underneath
the bathroom window. "How did you do that?" I ask
equally amazed and concerned by his strength.
"Come, we must hurry." He demands. We go back
around to the front door and sneak in. Jace tries to
guide me up the stairs, but I can't make it past my
dad without stopping. His breathing is labored and
he's holding his stomach as it continues to bleed. I
fall to his side and take his hand. Jace tries to pull
me, but I don't budge. I look up at Jace with tear
filled eyes and I see him struggling internally. He
kneels down next to my dad, and puts his hand over
his wound. I see Jace start to wince with pain as a
red blot appears on him in the same spot my dad was
stabbed. "Go save the others, and I'll see what I can
do." He says through clenched teeth. I look down at

my dad once more and he gives me a weak smile as he mouths the words, *go.* I give him a nod and then run up the stairs. I quickly pull Natasha out from under my bed and have her follow me to the hall closet to get my mom. I drag them both to the bathroom and open the window. Natasha's eyes practically bug out of her head when she gets what I'm suggesting. "Just trust me." I hiss. Realizing they don't have much of a choice, we each take our turn jumping out the window and onto the trampoline. We make a dash to the front yard and when we round the corner I see my dad hobbling down the porch steps. I run up to him and help him the rest of the way down. I finally hear the sweet serenade of police sirens approaching.

The police take our statements while we are evaluated by EMS. When they check the house, no one is to be found, not even Jace. The only thing they find are the signs of the altercation and the blood from dad being stabbed. Even the paramedics are amazed. They said for the amount of blood dad appeared to lose, he should have something much deeper than just a superficial wound.

I have so many questions. If Jace was trying to save me, why did he flee? Who is Demitrius? Better yet, who was the sociopath after me, and why did the rude guy from the club come to my defense? How did him and Jace even know I was in trouble? And how did Jace heal my dad? None of this seems real, if I didn't know any better I'd think tonights events were from a sci-fi movie. I am just so confused, but I guess I should be grateful that we are all alive and safe.

Chapter 4

By time Monday rolls around, I'm relieved to be back at school. I'm worried about my mom, dad, and Natasha, but if that sick freak was after me all along, then the best thing is for me to be away from them. When I get out of my second class of the day I get a text from Natasha. *How you holding up?* I wish I could tell her the truth. I'm constantly looking over my shoulder in fear. Not to mention, every person I've come across since that night, I've been able to feel their emotions and see things about their life that I'm not even sure are real or not. I feel as if I'm going crazy or losing my mind. I keep getting these headaches and I'm not sure if it's from being over stimulated or what, but I think I'm on the brink of a breakdown. *Hanging in there, you?* I reply.

I decide to head back to my dorm room for lunch, because I don't think I can handle feeling the emotions of hundreds of people right now. When I make it to my building, I see a group of people pile into the elevator and quickly opt for the stairs. As I round the third flight of stairs, there at the top stands the same blonde asshat that came to my rescue Saturday night. This can't be a coincidence.

"Xander?" I say, trying to see if my assumptions are correct. His eyes narrow and I can tell that is indeed his name. "What do you want from me? I've done nothing to you." I tell him. "You need to come with me." He says. "I'm not going anywhere with you. I don't even know you, and quite frankly every time you're around, something bad happens." I tell him. "Don't be so cynical." He tells me before continuing, "what's at stake is so much bigger than you and I. It's my job to simply make sure you aren't harmed and arrive safely to Vitalis." "Arrive safely? Vitalis? What are you even talking about? Am I being pranked?" I sputter. He gives me a flat stare, "I assure you, I do not prank. Now if you would please gather your things so we can get going." Xander tells me. I open my mouth to ask more questions, but quickly decide not to since I doubt he would answer them anyway. I make my way past him and he follows me to my room. I get out a duffel bag and start to pack some clothes as he watches. I can't believe I'm actually packing a bag to go off to some place I can't even remember the name of, with a total stranger. Is this even real life? I feel like I should be scared out of my mind. Like I should be finding a way to notify security or call the cops, but I don't. I have this indescribable sensation to trust Xander and I don't know why.

"Look, since you're going to be kidnapping me and all, I feel the courteous thing to do is at least get to know one another." I say as I pivot to face him. I don't realize how close he is to me, so when I turn we find ourselves mere inches away from one another. We stare at one another for a brief moment before I quickly turn back to continue packing my bag. "My names Aislinn, like Ace-lynn." I say, as I enunciate it for him. "I know who you are." He tells me. "Oh really?" I say sarcastically. "Aislinn Somerfield. Abandoned on Sadie and Everett

Somerfield's porch on May 9th 1998. They took you in and adopted you. You…" "Stop!" I say cutting him off as I officially start to freak out. How does this man know my most personable secret, yet all I know is first name? "Look, I don't who you are or how you know me, but you better start explaining or I'm not going anywhere with you." I demand. He doesn't say anything and just continues to stare at me. I cross my arms and sit down on my bed to show my protest. He lets out a grunt and rolls his eyes. "We don't have time for this." He mutters as he proceeds to pick me up and sling me over his shoulder. "Put me down." I shout as I pound my fists into his back. I give up quickly when it's apparent my fists are taking more of a beating than his back is. "Hope you grabbed everything you wanted." He says as he picks up my bag and carries us back to the stairwell. "People are going to be suspicious when they see you carrying a flailing girl over your shoulder." I tell him. "Then I suggest you cooperate so no one will have to get hurt." He tells me. "Fine." I say angrily and he sets me down at the bottom of the stairs. "Now let's go. We are already a whole day behind schedule, because Jace couldn't just stick to the plan." My ears perk at Jace's name.

"So, you and Jace are working together?" I ask as I follow Xander. "Well, we were." He says gruffly. I let out a gasp, "Oh my gosh, is Jace okay?" I ask. "Hard to say. It depends where he's at." "What does that even mean?" I ask, frustratedly. He whips around to face me and stops me in my tracks. I can see his brow furrow with frustration. "I am not some oracle, here to answer all of your questions. I am a Laskaris, which means I am of soldier blood. Do you understand what I am saying?" He says, practically fuming. My bottom lip begins to quiver as I shake my head. I don't understand anything that's happened in my life these past three days and this strange man yelling at me sure doesn't help. When he sees how distraught he has made me, I see the tension in his face soften a little as he takes a step back and lets out a long exhale. "I'm sorry that I don't have a single clue as to what is going on. In the past three days, my whole world has been turned upside down and filled with a bunch of things that I can't even begin to wrap my head around and then to make matters worse I have you yelling at me, telling how stupid I am for not knowing what you're talking about." I say breathlessly. "I never called you stupid." He barks defensively. "It was insinuated! Hell, every time you look at me, I feel insignificant, as if I'm the most annoying, helpless thing in the world." I tell him. For a change, I can tell that I've made him uncomfortable as he rubs the back of his neck, unsure of what to say. "Look, I don't mean to come off so brash. I am a solider and a protector and right now, I am ordered to protect you. My objective is to get you to the Realm of Vitalis and then Diona Kosmo can hopefully answer all of your questions." Xander tells me, only making my head buzz even more. "This can't be real." I tell him, flabbergasted. "I know things don't make sense right now, but they will. We need to keep moving though, before anymore of Stavros's warriors find us." He urges me. I give him a nod and we both continue our way to wherever the hell it is he is taking me.

"So that's who was at my house that night? One of Stavros's warriors." "Yes." "But why? I'm just a nobody, trying to get by like everyone else in this world." I tell him. "Maybe in this world, but you are far more then, a nobody, in the Realm of Vitalis."

Xander tells me and for a brief moment I see a hint of compassion in his eyes, but it quickly fades as he directs his eyes back on course. "Which makes you a threat to Stavros and his plans to create the Neophere." "Does this have anything to do with the dumb little visions I have?" I ask. "Ah. So you aren't totally in the dark." Xander says in almost a teasing tone. "I take that as a yes then." I say, before continuing. "If he would've just left me alone. I would've had no idea any of this stuff existed, and he could've just done what ever it is he is planning without dragging me into the middle of it." "There's two problems with that Aislinn. One, if Stavros destroys Vitalis, life is over for anyone rooted to its Realm. I know that may not mean anything to you right now, but it will." Xander tells me. "And two?" I ask. "Two, he wants you as his prisoner, because he needs your powers to make him the Ultimate Deity" Xander says. I give him a wide eyed look.
"But why me? Surely, there's another person in your world who can see visions and do whatever it is he is wanting." He gives me an unsettling look. "There is, but no one has seen him since Stavros started killing off all the Seekers. Now you and Dru are the only

ones remaining." "So, I'm a Seeker?" I reiterate to be sure. "I sure hope so. Otherwise this is all for nothing." Xander tells me. I shoot him a glare and he gives his best attempt at an apologetic half smile. "But why now? How come he didn't he just come get me when I was a baby?" I ask. "Because you have now reached the Age of Revelation." He replies. "What the heck does that mean?" I ask baffled. "Unless a being is raised practicing their powers, their powers are repressed until their 21st birthday. So, now that you are 21, your powers are emerged, making Stavros able to track you." "Um, news flash, but I just turned 25, so that can't be accurate." "That's not exactly true. An Earth year consists of 365 days, but in the Realm of Vitalis, our years are 435 days long. So, you are actually younger than what you have been led believe." He explains. My mouth falls open. "This, so can't be real!" I say frantically, trying to convince myself that this is all just some really weird immersive dream. "I'm sure this is a lot to process, but Stavros would have come after you years ago if you were actually 25." Xander says, as if that should convince me that I'm actually 21. "Okay well what if I don't use my powers? Then will he still be able to track me?" I ask. "Well, unless your parents left an instruction manual on how to control your powers then I'd say we are a bit out of luck." He tells me. *My parents.* Now my mind fills with many more questions.

"Alright, wait here." Xander commands. I hadn't even been paying attention to where we were going this whole time, but now as I look around, I notice we are in the middle of some woods not far from my school. I watch him disappear into the woods, leaving me alone. How in the hell is this even possible? I think to myself. Growing up and reading stories and watching movies that portray these fantasies, just to find out that it might actual be real. It's enough to make a person question their sanity. A normal person would be freaking out right now, claiming this is all ludicrous. Maybe that means I'm not normal after all? Because deep down, there's a part of me that can sense the truth in what Xander is saying.

After about fifteen minutes, Xander returns with a bunch of wood and some rocks. "Are we setting up camp already? I thought you said we have a lot of ground to make up." I tell him. I can't believe my ears when I hear Xander let out a chuckle. "What's so funny?" I ask him. "And how exactly do you think a person gets to the Realm of Vitalis from Earth?" Xander asks me with a smirk. I throw my hands up in the air, "I don't know. I thought maybe you had a spaceship and you would fly us there." I tell him. He lets out another laugh. "Do you realize how outrageous that sounds?" My jaw drops open, "Me, sound outrageous? You're the one that's spent the past hour telling me about this whole other world filled with people with special powers and some bad guy who's after me because he wants me to be his evil minion." I tell him. Xander gives me a smirk, "At least I know you've been listening." I return the smile as I shake my head. "I guess if you could enlighten me on how we are supposed to get to the Realm of Vitalis, that would be great." I tell him. "Simple. We make a portal, offer our blood and then ask for passage." He tells me. I raise an eyebrow, "Excuse me, what? What part of that is simple." I tell him. "Well, simple compared to how it use to be done. Before you needed a sorcerer or sorceress on both ends, very complex and expensive." He says gruffly. "Ah, yes. Well, I'm so glad they could simplify portal travel for you guys." I say mockingly. He rolls his eyes as he continues placing the rocks in a circular ring. I watch him carefully, as this may be a skill that will come in handy in the future. Next he draws a familiar star-like symbol in the dirt. "Why does that look familiar?" I ask him. "It's the eight cardinal directions. One for each of the regions in the Realm of Vitalis." He points to the North end, "That's Eternals Keep. Only the immortal deities, like Diona and Demitrius reside here. North East, is the Land of Kalos, which means land of the good hearted. Only those with the purest intentions and a good heart are capable of living here. East is Elfspond. As you can imagine, only the Elves are allowed to live there. South East is Land of the Doulos, which means land of the slaves. The Realm of Vitalis does not believe in imprisonment, so those who are criminals and have done wrong are punished with indentured servitude and are forced to live here. South is Land of Agnostos, which means land of the unknown. Those who don't really have powers or a calling typically reside here, but now it's turning more into an overflow for Meadows Clearing, which is South West. This is where most of the general population lives. West is Watersedge. Those who have to live in water or whose powers fueled by water typically live here. And lastly, North West is Valstead. Those with valor, courage and honor live here, so mainly the soldiers of Realms Guard and other warriors and hunters." He finally finishes explaining and looks up at me. "Wow, that's a lot to take in." I say. "I'm sure it is, but you seem like a fast learner." He tells me. I can't help but blush at his form of a compliment. "I take it you live in Valstead." I say. "I do." He replies stoically.

As I'm going over the regions in my head, the word Doulos dawns on me, I've heard it before, but where? My mind flashes to Jace and then I picture the word tattooed on his arm. "Jace Galanis-Doulos…" I say slowly. Xander peers over at me and raises an eyebrow. "So Jace lives in the Land of the Doulos… which means he's a slave." I say as if I just discovered the world's deepest secret. "That is correct." Xander says. I try to hide my dismay. I'm not even sure why it bothers me so much anyway. "So your name is Xander Laskaris-Valstead?" I ask in hopes of covering my sudden interest in Jace. "No, it's just Xander Laskaris. The reason Doulos is added to Jace's name is because it's not just a Region it's a brand. Addressing himself with Doulos is part of his punishment." Xander tells me. "How would they even know if he did or not?" I ask curiously. "When a person is branded a Doulos, they are given the mark of Doulos. That mark is what gives their Overseer the power and control over them. The scope of what each Doulos can and can't do is set and enforced by their Overseer." He tells me. I remain silent as I ponder the meaning of all this. Jace seemed so kind, how could he be a criminal?

I notice Xander place a stick at each of the eight points and then angle them inwards as if he is making a teepee. "So which Region are we going to?" I ask him. "Ultimately, Eternal Keep, but right now the place is crawling with Stavros's men because they are expecting us to bring you to Diona. For now, we are going to Elfspond. There's always a high amount of magic circulating there, so, Stavros shouldn't suspect anything out of the ordinary." I nod as if I'm actually comprehending all of this. "How come the Realms Guard doesn't just fight them off?" He lets out an aggravated sigh. "The day

Stavros proclaimed that he was destined to be the leader of what he calls, Neophere, or the New World, he ordered a preliminary massacre upon Valstead. We never even saw it coming, and although they didn't wipe us out entirely, it sure thinned us out." Xander says and I can hear the hurt and anger in his voice. "I'm so sorry Xander." I say as I rest my hand on his arm. He quickly pulls his arm away and moves to the other side of the ring. "I don't need your pity. We were fools to be unprepared. A soldier should always be ready." He snaps. I can tell his anger towards me is just an outward reflection of the pain he is feeling on the inside. "Besides, the gods and goddesses don't need protecting, the people of Vitalis do. So, those that remained were assigned to each of the seven other regions to serve and protect." "How come the god's and goddesses don't just come together and put an end to Stavros crap?" I ask. Xander gives me a defeated look as he throws the rest of the sticks down. "Because technically Stavros, is a god, thanks to the trinities Balance." He pauses before continuing, "every year ending in a 3, a random inhabitant in the Realm of Vitalis is gifted with three powers from the gods or goddesses. For that entire year, that individual gets to rule as a god or goddess with the power of three immortals, making them the most powerful being. It also doesn't help that whoever's powers they are given, are then rendered useless until the year is up. After that, the three deities regain their powers and the inhabitant resumes their life as a mortal and the balance is restored." He tells me. "Alright, hold up! First of all, that has got to be the *dumbest* form of checks and balances that I have ever heard of. Who in their right mind, would grant a mortal, who mind you, has probably been pissed on by immortals for their entire life, the power of three immortals for an entire year. Please tell me, in any world, how that sounds like a good idea." Xander actually cracks a big smile followed by a laugh, which allows me to notice what a nice smile he has. "And secondly, what does any of that have to do with me?" I say. Xander shrugs his shoulders, "I'm not entirely sure, but I'm betting Diona will be able to answer that."

Xander then marks an X on the East Region of his mud-drawn cardinal star before lighting the sticks on fire. "That should do it." He says as he takes a step back and admires his handiwork. "Um, that's it?" I say, feeling a bit skeptical. "Almost. Can I see your hand?" He asks as he pulls out his knife. I hesitantly stick out my hand, and when he takes it I feel a strong sense of pain and sadness, that knocks me to to the ground and makes me cry out in pain. Xander kneels beside me and I can see his face fill worry as he's unsure how to help. "What's wrong?" He asks. Almost a minute passes before I can gather my bearings. "W-when I touched you. I was consumed with so much sadness and pain. It felt as if I was being tortured or something." I say between tears. He gives me a shocked look. "That's impossible. Seekers can't channel the emotions of a Laskaris. It's too much grief and death for a person to be consumed with at once, so the powers at be, made Seekers immune to a soldiers touch." "Well I don't know what to tell you," I say, still trying to recover from the pain I felt. "I mean it didn't happen when I touched your arm earlier, and I was actually being sincere then." I add. "How do I know when I'm going to use my power or not?" I ask. "I'm not sure since I'm not a Seeker, but it's all the more reason we need to get you to Diona, and fast." He tells me. He then retrieves his knife and makes a cut to his palm and then lets the blood drip into the fire. "Your turn." He says as he hands me the knife. He watches me as I take the knife and mimic what I just saw him do.

"I Xander Laskaris, call upon the Realm of Vitalis to welcome us. We seek passage to Elfspond and so graciously ask for your permittance Hermes. Please, accept our blood as a sign of good faith." Xander says with his hands outstretched over the fire. After five seconds of nothing happening, I start to question if it worked. Then all of a sudden a loud roar erupts from the fire and the flames rise nearly ten feet tall and the flames turn blue. I become mesmerized by the blue abyss before me as I watch it shimmer between every shade of blue imaginable. "Ready?" Xander asks. Now that the reality of the situation is sitting right in front of me, I become nervous and scared. I turn to Xander, "What about my mom and dad? And Natasha? How will I be able to get ahold of them? What if something happens to me and they are just left wondering if I'll ever come back home?" I ramble off as the panic starts to settle in. "They will be fine. Demitrius is watching over them and has placed them under a trance to keep them from worrying. As for you Aislinn, I'm not going to let anything happen to you, I promise." He says followed by a swoon worthy half smile. I simply nod to show that I'm now ready to accept my fate. "What do I do?" I ask. "Just walk into it." He says. I try to get myself to move, but my legs won't listen to my mind. I turn back to him, "But, Xander I'm scared." I say. "I'll be right behind you." He tells me reassuringly. "Can we do it together?" I ask. He gives me a nod, "Sure." I hold out my hand and he gives it a leery look. I give him a soft smile, "It's alright, I think it'll be ok this time." I tell him. He takes my hand, and we take our steps in unison until we fade into the blue abyss.

Chapter 5

At first we are surrounded by a dark blue emptiness. As we make our way deeper into the vastness before us, the hint of blue becomes lighter and lighter, until finally we enter into a bright white light. I have to shield my eyes with my free hand as Xander leads us on. Next thing I know, we are standing in the middle of a clearing. I look around and take in the beautiful site of tall trees, lush green grass that is scattered with pink, purple, and yellow flowers. In the distance, I can see a sparkling turquoise waterfall that cascades into a pond beneath it.

My admiration is soon interrupted, by the need to vomit and I quickly turn away as I throw up what feels like the entire contents of my stomach. When I finish I wipe my mouth and turn back to Xander. "I'm so sorry, I don't know what overcame me." I tell him slightly embarrassed. He gives a small chuckle, "Don't worry. There's always a side effect on your first portal travel. You should be good from here on out though." He tells me. "Well, that's good, I guess." I say before turning my gaze back on the world around me. "So this is Elfspond?" I ask. "Yep." Xander replies. "It's beautiful." I comment. "You should see Valstead." He says boastfully.

All of a sudden somethings catches my eye as it flies past my head. I quickly turn to see what it is, but now it's flying in circles around my head. I start to swat at it, but Xander grabs my wrist. "Careful. It's a fairy." Xander tells me. My eyes grow big with bewilderment. This is all still so surreal. "An actual fairy, how cool!" I say. The buzzing around my head ceases and now I can finally see, hovering in front of my face is a fairy. She's probably a good six inches tall and emits a bright yellow aura. She has flawless porcelain skin, hazel eyes, and her clothes consist of two small leaves covering her breasts and a skirt made out of flower petals. As she flutters in front of me I give her a smile to hopefully show that I mean no harm. She gives me a smile and holds out one of her hands with her palm facing upwards. Something tells me to copy her, so I put out my hand. When I do so, she lands on the edge of my hand and walks to the center of my palm. She then looks into my eyes and stares at me. "Hello, I am Ella Kouris." I hear in a sweet delicate voice. I didn't see her lips move, but something tells me it's her. Is she communicating telepathically? It wouldn't be the craziest thing I've seen today, so I decide to give it a shot. "Hello." I say inside my head. She gives me a bright smile and I see her wings shimmy with excitement. "So it's true, you are a Seeker. We all have been looking forward to your arrival." She tells me. "How do you know for sure I am a Seeker?" I reply. "Only the deities, Elves, and Seekers can communicate with fairies. It requires a certain level of thought transference that only we all are capable of." She says. "So Xander can't hear anything that we are saying?" I ask. "That is correct. Which means you will need to translate for me." "Okay, what do I need to tell him?" "Elfred, or the Wise Elf, wants me to bring you to him. He has a message from Diona regarding her new whereabouts. Stavros has officially infiltrated Eternal Keep, so she had to flee into hiding." I give her a nod and then look at Xander.

"She says Stavros has infiltrated Eternal Keep, so Diona had to go into hiding. Ella will lead us to the Wise Elf who has a message for us regarding her whereabouts." I tell him. Xander lets out a low growl. "Very well. Let's be on our way then." He says. I look back at Ella and she gives me smile as she starts to flap her wings. I cautiously lower my hand as Ella begins to levitate in front of me. "Follow me." She says.

We follow Ella as she leads us into a nearby forest. As we start our trek through the forest, I now notice other fairies lingering in the trees as they watch us walk by. I offer them a smile and a small wave and they wave back ecstatically. The forest is crawling with friendly wildlife, but it's only the fairies that appear to be of magical nature so far. "Can you still hear me?" I ask Ella in my mind. "Of course." Ella responds. "So, are we just reading each others minds?" I ask her. "Not quite. You have to want me to hear what you are saying or thinking, otherwise I won't hear anything. It's just like talking aloud, you just have to direct what you are saying to whoever it is you want to hear it, but they have to be in the nearby vicinity." She says. "That makes sense. Not that I don't mind if you are able to read my mind, it's just, sometimes that could be a little embarrassing." I tell her. I hear her give a small laugh, "Yes, indeed. Some things should remain private." She tells me. "So, I don't want to be a nuisance, but do you mind if I ask you some questions?" I ask Ella. "Not at all. I'm sure you are quite curious as this is all new for you." She says. "Well, I keep being told I'm a Seeker, but I don't even know what that means. Like what does that entail? What are my so called powers?" I ask. "Seekers are special beings who originated from a forbidden love between an angel, Malakhi Alma and a great oracle, Ragna Akeem. Malakhi was from the Land of Kalos. He was one of the kindest and most compassionate angels in the Realm of Vitalis. Of course Malakhi had the typical angelic powers. Such as being able to fly, guardianship over those under his care, and being able to grant miracles to those he felt most deserved them. However, Malakhi was not your average angel. He could sense and feel people's emotions, which allowed him to read a person's true intentions and nature. He also had the power to alter or take away peoples feelings, and was often sought out by those who had trouble controlling their emotions. Ragna was, who at first, seemed to be just another oracle. Meaning she could foresee the future and speak of prophecies to be fulfilled. It was later discovered that she also held the power of psychometry, which is the ability to attain information about a person or item simply by touching a person or an object owned by that person. So she could read a person's past, present, and future, and was able to tell them what actions they needed to take in order to change the outcome of their future. People flocked to her in hopes of seeking a new destiny. Her powers were not just limited to the mortals though, she could read the deities as well, which was a rare phenomenon. No mortal, let alone immortal in the history of mankind has been able to foresee an immortals destiny, with the exception of Ragna. While a few of the deities saw this as a blessing, the rest saw it as a threat and feared that one of the deities may seek Ragna's counsel to become what they call, the Ultimate Deity. To prevent this from occurring they forbade Ragna from practicing her powers and even had a sorcerer put a spell on her, so if she were to ever foretell a prophecy or speak of a destiny again, she would lose her voice. They also took away her ability to bear children to prevent anymore of her kind from reoccurring. Ragna was heartbroken and sought the counsel of Malakhi to overcome her grief and depression. As you can imagine, Malakhi helped Ragna channel her emotions and in the process they grew fond of each other. The deities frowned upon the couple, as an angel's duty is to the people and they are not supposed to have intimate relationships because it is thought that it interferes with their work and clouds their judgement. However, their love for one another was so strong that they had always managed to find their way back to each other. They decided not to fight fate anymore and saw each other in secret. One day, one of the goddesses fell witness to one of their secret encounters and had no choice, but to order Malakhi to be executed. As breaking the angels oath is punishable by death, because an angel is no longer considered pure. What they didn't know was that Malakhi's dying wish was to grant Ragna the miracle of having their child. Thus, the line of Seekers was born when Ragna gave birth to their son, Edin. Edin had the powers of both of his parents, to an extent that is. Mind you, Edin was not an angel, so he could not fly, grant miracles, or serve as guardian, but he could feel and sense the emotions and true nature of others, but could not alter or take away peoples emotions like his father. Like his mother, he was able to see peoples past, present, and future and could see the actions needed in order to change the outcomes. Unlike his mother, his powers were limited to only mortals, thankfully, or when the deities finally learned of Edin they would have killed him. Being a breed of his own, the deities deemed him a Seeker, given that his powers were used to seek prophecies, answers, truth, and peoples feelings. From then on, every offspring that came from Seeker blood has wielded those powers. Which means, one of your parents was a Seeker, and that my friend is how you came to be one." "Wow. I don't even know what to say." I tell her. "I know it's a lot of information, but I think it's important to know your history and where you come from." Ella says. "No, I appreciate it. It's all very interesting, it's just every time I get the answer to one question it gives me so many more questions." I say. "It's okay, that's how you learn." She tells me. "So, I take it you wouldn't know who my biological parents are?" I ask Ella. "No. Unfortunately, I do not and if I may be brutally honest, I doubt they are still alive. One of Stavros's prophecies had foretold that a Seeker would be his demise so he put an order out to kill all of the Seekers. It wasn't until one remained that Stavros learned, a Seeker was required to show him how to become the Ultimate Deity, thus making him permanently immortal and becoming the ruler of Neophere. Stavros has been turning over every rock in the Realm of Vitalis and threatening to kill anyone who is helping hide Dru, the only other remaining Seeker. That is until a few nights ago when your powers were activated and gave Stavros a new target. Diona was informed by one of her allies of the prodigy on Earth and sent people to retrieve you and bring you back to Vitalis for protection." Ella tells me. "I just hate that you all are risking your lives for me. I can't even control my powers, so it's only a matter of time before Stavros finds me." I tell her. "Please do not feel bad. Everyone helping you, knows what is at stake if Stavros becomes the Ultimate Deity. We are willing to do whatever it takes to keep you safe Aislinn." She tells me. "Is there someone who can at least train me? That way my powers aren't just running rampant all over the place." I ask her. "The problem is, only a person from the same line can truly train another on how to wield their powers." Ella says. "Which would be Dru...who is apparently the champion of hide-n-go-seek." I say depressingly. "Indeed, but we do have plenty of people willing to help you. Some have worked closely with Seekers and can maybe offer some tips and good advice." Ella tells me before coming to a halt.

I hadn't been paying much attention, but now before us stands a large sparkling medieval looking castle that appears to be surrounded by a moat. Across the way I can see two armored guards at the entrance and they instantly become on the defensive as we approach. "You two wait here." Ella instructs me as she flies closer to the castle. "She wants us to wait here." I relay to Xander and he just gives me a nod. I sense that he's aggravated and I'm not sure why. "Everything okay?" I ask him. "Yeah. Why wouldn't it be?" He says. "I just feel like something is bothering you." I tell him. "If you must know, I don't really like being in Elven territory. They are condescending and like to flaunt their powers in people's face. I'm quite surprised they are even helping, they usually ostracize themselves from the rest of the Realm and keep to themselves." He tells me. "Oh…well, that is very reassuring to know before meeting them for the first time." I say. I see his brows furrow as if he feels guilty for saying anything. "Did you get some of your questions answered?" He asks trying to change the subject. "How did you know I was asking her questions?" I ask. "That was the longest I had heard you go without talking since I met you, so I knew you had to be talking her ear off." I give him a playful glare, "Ha, ha, very funny. But to answer your question, yes I did. I learned some very interesting things."

"Good." He tells me before I see him stiffen back up.

I turn my attention back on the castle and see Ella fluttering back towards us. Simultaneously, I notice the guards start to lower the bridge. "We may now enter!" She tells me. We all three, make our way to the bridge and I can't help but gawk in awe as we enter the castle walls. It's as if the entire castle is covered in glitter as it sparkles in the sunlight. There are many more guards on the inside and they are all wearing the same metallic green and silver armor while carrying a sword on their hips and holding speared staffs. If these are Elves, they are not short at all like some myths portray, in fact they are all at least six feet or taller.

Two guards greet us at the entrance and lead us into the castle. They bring us to a large dining hall and instruct us to wait here and then leave the room, closing the large elegantly carved double doors behind them. I take this time to explore the room before me. Theres a large elaborate wooden dining table in the center of the room that is set for fourteen people. A large jeweled chandelier hangs above the table and gives it more of a fine dining atmosphere.

As I look around I take notice of some of the tapestries along the wall, but I'm unable to read what the words say as it appears to be a foreign language to me. At the far end of the room is a large painting on a wall by itself. As I approach it, it appears to be a portrait of a man, but all of a sudden the painting changes into that of another man. I blink excessively, to try and refocus my eyes as if they are playing tricks on me. The painting then transitions into that of a woman. All of these people have similar features that must be partial to Elves. Emerald green eyes, pointed ears, and majority of them have platinum blonde hair. As I'm watching the painting transition between the different people, Ella flutters over to me and plops down on my shoulder. "Who are these people?" I ask her. "These are all the appointed Wise Elf's throughout the history of time. When they die, they honor them by keeping a portrait of each one as a reminder of each one's legacy." "So there's only been like fifteen Wise Elf's?" I ask a bit shocked. She lets out a soft chuckle, "Fourteen. Elves, may not be immortals, but they can live a very long life as long as long as they stay out of harms way." She tells me. "What if they get sick?" I ask. "It's very rare that an Elf becomes severely ill. They are naturally a healthy species, with a very strong immune system. They also do not age like most mortals do. Each of these Elves you see here, were in their prime, so about 150 to 200 years old when these portraits were done." "Holy cow, they look so young though." I tell her. "Yes. Elves are certainly blessed with good genetics. They are some of the most beautiful people here in the Realm of Vitalis, which is why their allure and charm are considered as part of their powers." She tells me. "What other powers do they have?" I ask her curiously. "Elves, are highly intelligent, quick thinkers, who are also very agile and physically gifted. Despite how lean they are, they are very strong, precise, and swift fighters. Of course they are also capable of performing magic. Much like a sorcerer or sorceress, but with the exception that they cannot perform dark magic, or magic that is intended to harm others." Ella says.

"Unless it's for protection purposes." I hear a man's voice say. I turn around to see a tall lean fair skinned man, standing in the door way. I now realize what Ella was talking about, there is a certain sense of appeal that this man holds. His straight long blonde hair falls to the midst of his chest and I can see his ears protruding through his hair. He gives me a charming bright smile as his green eyes twinkle. "Hello, I am Elfred." He says aloud as he makes his way closer to me. "I'm Aislinn." I say as I offer out my hand. He looks at my hand and gives me a closed smile. "On a normal account, I would love to take your hand. However, you my dear, are a Seeker who is unable to control her powers at the moment, so I must politely decline." Elfred says. "Oh…right." I say as I give a small nervous chuckle and withdraw my hand back to my side. "Please, join me at the table. I'm sure you must be starving." He tells me. I follow him over to the table as me, Elfred, and Xander take a seat while Ella remains on my shoulder. "Would you care for some wine?" Elfred asks us. Xander shakes his head no, but I feel inclined to take his offer. "Yes please." I tell him. I see Xander roll his eyes. Elfred snaps his fingers which prompts, his and I's glasses to fill with a red wine, while Xander's fills with what appears to be water. More Elves emerge from a door at the other end as they start to bring out some food.

"So, Aislinn, how are you liking the Realm of Vitalis so far?" Elfred asks. "Well, I've only seen Elfspond so far, but it sure is beautiful. Nothing like I've ever seen." I tell him. "Ah yes, you will need to see the rest of the Realm for a true testament, but I must say, Elfspond is certainly the best of the Regions. Then again, I could be biased." He says giving me a wink. I offer a small chuckle before taking a sip of my wine. I then feel Ella walk down my arm and then onto the table. I watch her walk over to a platter of fruit that was laid out in front of us and take a strawberry and bite into it. I can't help, but smile to myself at the realization that this all a reality, and not just some dream. "Any burning questions?" Elfred asks me. I look across the way at Xander and he gives me a smirk as if my un-relentless questioning is now an inside joke between us. "As a matter of fact, I do." I tell him. "By all means, ask away." He tells me. "How old are you?" I ask. "I am 172 years old." He replies. "And what makes you so special? Like why do you get to be the Wise Elf?" I ask. My blunt question causes Xander to choke on his drink, as he is half shocked but pleased by my bluntness. Elfred gives a small chuckle before answering. "When the previous Wise Elf dies, a tournament is held to determine who should take over the Reign. The tournament consists of three categories that the Elf must demonstrate mastery of. First is sorcery. Each contender is assigned three spells that they must learn and master in a matter of twelve hours before they have to present to the council. Those who are able to do so move on to the second round, which is intellect. Before passing, the Wise Elf creates a highly challenging and mentally strenuous quest that is utilized to narrow down the top three contenders. The first three Elves who complete the quest are then sent to the final round, which tests physical agility and strength. The three Elves are subjected to trial by combat and the Elf left standing becomes the Wise Elf." Elfred finishes explaining. I let out a gasp, "So you just kill the other two Elves?" I ask in shock. "Heavens no." He laughs before continuing, "A true Elven warrior, must be so swift that they could kill if needed too, but also be able to show restraint at a moments end. So essentially they are defeated by submission." He tells me. "Oh. Well that's a relief." I say and then fall silent. "I may not be a Seeker, but I can tell you have a kind heart, full of compassion Aislinn." Elfred tells me. I blush, "Thank you." I tell him. "Now, enough questions for the time being, let us eat." Elfred says as he motions to the table. I look back to the table and it is now covered with tons of food, from different breads, fruits, and vegetables. I don't see any meat and it makes me wonder if they even eat meat here. Not wanting to disrupt the silence that has fallen amongst us, I decide to ask Ella.

"Ella, do they not eat meat?" I ask. She looks up at me and gives me a smile, "Here in Elfspond, we do not eat meat. We believe in feeding ourselves with what the soil provides, as we feel our powers are driven by nature." I give her a guilty look. "Don't feel bad Aislinn. Just because our beliefs differ does not make you a bad person. Besides, majority of the rest of the Realm consumes meat. In a way it serves as balance." She tells me. I give her a smile to show my understanding and then fill my plate with some food.

After lunch, or dinner, not really sure what time it is here or if they even keep rack of time, Elfred leads us to another large room. This room appears to be a library or study of some sort, as every wall is covered with shelves of books and scrolls. The wall in front of us has a fireplace and in the middle of the room is a round table with chairs that is surrounded by some chaise lounges. There laying along one of the chaises is a beautiful Elven woman. Her skin is practically glowing and her long blonde hair is scattered with sections of braided hair with flowers intertwined. She has on a long décolleté lavender dress that flows into multiples slits. She rises from her seat with much poise and gracefully strides over to us. "Hello, I am Fraeya." She tells me followed by a warm smile. "Hi. I'm Aislinn." I reply and then her eyes flicker to my right. "Hello Xander." She says softly. I glance in my peripheral and I can sense the unease radiating from Xander. "Hello Fraeya." He practically mutters with distaste. "Shall we?" Elfred says, interrupting what appears to be an awkward reunion between Fraeya and Xander. He motions for us to sit at the table in the center of the room and we all do so. Once at the table, Elfred and Fraeya hold their hands up to the sky and close their eyes. They stay like this for about thirty seconds and it's not until they open their eyes and put their hands on the table that I notice we are encapsulated in what feels like a bubble. I look over at Xander, but he doesn't seem phased by this at all. I turn to Elfred and Fraeya, "What's going on?" I ask, trying to remain calm. "We have created a force of solitude, so we may speak freely without risk of exposing our secrets." Elfred tells me. I nod to show my understanding. "Fraeya, if you would." Elfred says. Fraeya nods, "Diona is currently hiding in the Land of the Doulos. She asks that you bring Aislinn to her. She is residing in a cottage just North of the Drunken Woe's tavern." She tells us. Xander lets out a grunt, "Why would she go there and risk being sold out by any Doulos willing to exchange their freedom for her location?" He says. "She is not there as herself. She is disguised and living as a Doulos for the time being." Fraeya tells him. He teeters his head back and forth as if he is judging her decision. "If she's disguised, how will we know if it's really her or not?" I ask. They all laugh as if I just told a hilarious joke. "Trust me, you will know." Fraeya tells me. "Oh, okay." I say bashfully, not wanting to make a bigger fool of myself. "Anything else?" Xander asks. "That was all she had relayed before going silent." Fraeya says. "Very well. Then we'll be on our way." Xander says as he rises from his seat. "Must you go so soon?" Fraeya asks. "Yes." Xander says flatly. Fraeya quickly glances at me and gives me a soft smile, "Forgive me, but you can't go trekking through the Realm dressed like that. You will stick out like a sore thumb." I look down at my shirt that displays my favorite rock band and my shorts and realize she's got a point. "You know I'm right." Fraeya says to Xander. He lets out an annoyed sigh and rolls his eyes. "Whatever. Do what you see is fit, but I will be waiting elsewhere." He says gruffly. Fraeya turns to me and gives me a look of excitement. "Do you mind?" She asks me. I shake my head, "Not at all." I tell her. "Great, let's go!" She says as she stands up and swipes her hand across the air, causing the force of solitude to disappear.

I follow Fraeya upstairs and she leads me to another room as she excitedly barges through another set of double doors. I stand in the doorway as I take in my surroundings. To my left is an elegant four poster canopied bed, across the way has a door that leads to a large bathroom, in the far right corner stands a tall armoire accompanied by a mirror and ottoman, and to my right is a set of glass doors that lead out to a balcony. "Over here!" She says as she waves me over to the armoire. I make my way over to her and instantly become self conscious as she circles around me, looking me up and down. "Hmm. I'm feeling a pink or yellow. What do you think?" She says. "Um. I'm not sure. Whatever you think I'm fine with." I tell her. She flings open the armoire and flicks through the hangers, before pulling out a dress. She turns to me with a big smile, "This one will suite you well." She says as holds out the dress for me to see. It's a light pink half sleeve A-line dress that falls just below my knees. The top half is a sheer lace while the skirt flows out into a satin material. I hesitate to take the dress from her. "Fraeya I can't take your dress." I tell her. "Don't be silly Aislinn, I insist." She says as she fully extends the dress out to me. I take the dress and she lets out a squeal. "Go try it on." She tells me as she ushers me into the bathroom.

Once in the bathroom, I shed my last bit of Earthly existence and slip on the dress Fraeya bestowed upon me. Overall, the dress fits me well, but it's a little loose in the bust due to Fraeya being slightly bustier than me. I emerge from the bathroom and Fraeya gives me a bright smile. "You look lovely!" She tells me, "How does it fit?" She asks. "A little loose in the top, but not too bad." I reply. "Easy fix." She says and then waves her hand and mutters something unintelligible. I instantly feel the dress hug me a little tighter and it's apparent that she used her magic to have the dress altered to me. "Um, thanks, that's better." I say. "No problem. Now sit." She urges me as she points to the ottoman. I take my seat as she goes behind me and starts braiding my hair. "You don't have to do all this." I tell her. "I know, but I want too." She tells me. We both fall silent for a moment, before I gather the courage to ask her what's been weighing on my mind. "So, if you don't mind me asking. What's the story between you and Xander?" I ask. In the mirror I can see her give an almost nostalgic smile. "It's not a very pleasant story, but it might be good to get it off my chest." She says before continuing, "Two years ago, I was doing what we call Roaming. Basically I was spending time in each of the Regions, gathering a sense of the different cultures within each. After all, to be a member of the Wise Council, one must not only have an in depth amount of knowledge about Elven history and practices, but also a broad knowledge of the other Regions. I had not shown an interest in being on the Wise Council until later in my life so I had some quick making up to do. My last Region before returning to Elfspond and requesting my spot on the council, was Valstead. It was during my time there that I happened across Xander, and despite his ruggedness, I grew quite fond of him. I wanted him to like me back, but Laskaris's are not susceptible to Elven charm so I had to wait. It was two weeks before Xander finally admitted his mutual fondness and allowed our relationship to bud. For the next few weeks we were inseparable and radiating of love. Even though we knew ultimately we could never be mated, we still wanted to revel in each other's company as long as we could. When it came down to the time for me to leave, Xander had asked me to stay, to give up my spot on the council so we could stay together. I counter offered him to give up his spot in the Realms Guard and come stay with me in Elfspond. He asked me to give him a day to consider the option. Despite knowing that if I waited another day, I could potentially loose my chance for a spot on the council, I waited. Only to have him tell me that he couldn't give up his livelihood for something that would only be temporary. I angrily left and rushed back home, to then discover that mere hours before my return, the seat I was so eager to attain was already pending a claim. Luckily, I was still within the time frame to submit a rebuttal on why I felt I would make a better member of the council. After hearing me out, the council asked me one final question before making their decision. They asked me if I were able to share something that could in anyway sway the council in my favor." She pauses for a moment as a sullen look falls upon her face. "I shared with them a secret that Xander had entrusted me with. It was foolish of me, but I had wanted my claim to the council and I knew his secret would guarantee it. After I told them, matters got out of hand and word had gotten back to Xander. He was so enraged with me, and I don't blame him. He told me I would be the reason he would never love or trust another being and that he never wanted see or hear from me again. It broke my heart to see him so angry and hurt, especially since I was the cause. So, up until today I had respected his wishes and I had not seen him since." She tells me. Unsure of what to say, I remain silent. "I hope this does not make you think differently of me. I am not an evil person. If anything, I have learned a lot from the experience and it has made me a more level headed person. It was a terrible selfish decision, that I did not think would ever be acted upon, but I realize now, a person with true integrity, will always uphold their promise." Fraeya says. "I don't think you are a bad person. It was an unfortunate situation for the both of you and I'm sure it didn't help that your emotions were heightened because of the feelings you two shared." I tell her. She gives me a soft smile as she makes her way back in front of me. "You are certainly right Aislinn." She says before cocking her head at me. "What?" I ask. "Ah, I know what you're missing!" She says. She goes to the armoire once more and retrieves a flowery halo and places it on my head. "Perfect, take a look!" She says with excitement as she steps out of the way. I approach the mirror and I have to admit, I definitely look like I belong here now. "Thank you so much!" I tell her before adding, "I could hug you, but…" I trail off. She gives me a big smile. "Your gratitude is plenty. Now let's go rejoin the men." She tells me.

As we make our way back down, I can't help but wonder. What was Xander's big secret? I know better than to ask, but it has to be deep. When we make it back to the study, the men are taken by surprise. Elfred's mouth falls open and I see Xander avert his gaze to the floor once I catch him staring. "My, my Aislinn. If I didn't know any better, I'd say you were that of Elven descent." Elfred tells me and it makes me blush. "Thank you." I say bashfully, and then look over at Xander. It's apparent he has changed too and I'm not sure if this is his typical wear or this is what Elfred loaned him. Either way, I'm not complaining. Xander is now shirtless, but has two brown leather straps criss-crossed over his chest that hold two swords on his back. He has a red and brown leather pteruges covering from his waist down to just above his knees and some brown leather sandals that wrap up along his legs. "What happened to your clothes?" I say, trying to mask my gratification. "This is the attire of a Laskaris." Xander tells me. I give him a soft smile and then

Fraeya interjects, "A mighty fine Laskaris indeed." She says. He just purses his lips at her, "I think it's time we were on our way." Xander says. I give him a reluctant nod. I know it must be hard for him to be here, but I have actually enjoyed my time here and still have so many more questions that I know he won't be willing to answer. "Where's Ella?" I ask and I instantly see here fly over from the window seal. "Here I am." She tells me. "Will you be coming with us?" I ask her. I see her brows furrow before responding, "I hadn't really thought about it. I've never been out of Elfspond before." She tells me. "It's okay, I understand." I tell her. "But, there's a first time for everything." She tells me, and I give her a big smile in return. "Are you sure?" I ask. "Of course!" She tells me. I then notice Xander shake Elfred's hand. "Thanks again for the assistance and cooperation." Xander says to Elfred before making his way over to me. "Ella is coming with us." I tell him happily, he just gives me a nod and walks out the door. I turn to Fraeya, "Thanks again." I tell her before turning to Elfred, "And thank you for your hospitality. It was a pleasure meeting you both." I tell them. "It was an honor. May our paths cross once again." Elfred says.

Chapter 6

I follow Xander as he leads us back to the castle grounds where we are met by another set of guards awaiting with two horses. One guard hands Xander the reigns to one of the horses while the other guard pauses before handing me the reigns to the other horse. "Elfred has offered this horse as a parting gift to hopefully make your journey more bearable. Please accept it, as it'll be your very own." The guard tells me. "Um, wow, okay. That is very generous, tell him thank you." I reply. The guard nods and finally hands me the reigns. As he steps out of the way, he reveals a beautiful white horse with purple eyes and a silver mane and tail. I approach her and rub the bridge of her nose. "Hi pretty girl." I tell her and she lets out a neigh. The guard then retrieves a saddle and places it atop of the horse. "Safe travels." The guards say in unison before walking away.

I look over at Xander and see him tightening the straps to his saddle. "I can't believe Elfred gave me a horse." I say. "It's cause he likes you." Xander tells me grumpily. "Well I wouldn't go that far." I reply.

"Please, he was ogling you the second he laid eyes on you." Xander says. "It was still very generous of him. Besides, what does it matter if he *likes* me anyway?" I say. "It doesn't, but I'd be leery of their kind." He mutters. It dawns on me that he's probably alluding to his past with Fraeya, so I decide to leave it at that. He mounts his horse to signify that it's time for us to get on the road. I look at my horse and grab the horn of the saddle and try to hoist myself up, but immediately fail. I fall to the ground very ungracefully and immediately pick myself up, trying to hide my embarrassment. Xander dismounts his horse and comes over to me. "May I help?" He asks. I give him a nod and he gets down on one knee and interlocks his hands. I grab the handle once more and step into his hand. He lifts me up and I swing my other leg over my horse and steady myself. "Got it?" He asks me as he stays at my side. "Yes, thank you." I tell him as I look down at him and give him a smile. He just nods and walks back over to remount his horse. Ella then flies in front of me, "Can I ride with you?" She asks. "Of course." I tell her. She then plops down on my shoulder once more. "You should give her a name." Xander says cordially, as he nods at my horse. I give a big smile, "I was thinking Lila. Short for lilac, like the color of her eyes." I tell him, giving Lila's mane a stroke. She lets out a pleased neigh. "Nice choice." He says as he takes his reigns and pulls them toward the right. I mimic him and follow behind as we start our journey to the Land of the Doulos.

For the first hour we all three remain quiet. Each of us probably trying to gather our thoughts and feelings toward the uncertainty that lies ahead. I'd be lying if I said I wasn't nervous. The thought of Stavros or one of his men finding me and taking me prisoner, has me on edge. From the sounds of it, if I were taken, there's no one who would be able to save me, leaving me trapped as his prisoner for who knows how long. I only pray that we can make it to Diona and come up with a plan before I can be discovered.

"How long should it take us to get there?" I ask Xander. "About 10 hours." He replies. "So are we gonna have to stay the night or camp out somewhere?" I ask. "Yes, but it'll depend where we are before the sun goes down." He tells me and we fall silent again. "Can I ask you a question?" I ask.

"Do I have a choice?" He replies. Feeling disheartened I remain quiet. "Aislinn, I'm joking. What is your question?" He says. "Who is Demitrius? Stavros's warrior was practically cursing him at my house that night and then I heard Jace ask him for his help, so who exactly is he?" I ask. "Demitrius is one of the gods, or deities as we call them. He in particular, is the lover of Earth." Xander says. "So, he's the god over Earth? Like the one who created us, or well, the humans." I clarify. "No. Earth has their own God who created the humans, Earth, and its surrounding solar system. Unlike our deities, Earth's God does not live amongst his people, instead he over watches from a divine plane. No one here in the Realm of Vitalis knew He or Earth existed, until the day the original sorcerers started experimenting with portal travel. One day, one of the sorcerers ended up on Earth and was then quickly pulled into the divine plane where God resides and was questioned. They both informed each other about their worlds and in the end, God told the sorcerer that the people of Vitalis were welcome to visit Earth and coexist amongst His world, but under no circumstances would they be allowed to corrupt His world or be able to use their powers on a large scale basis. He also forbade our kind from mating with his humans, so it would not disrupt the balance between the two worlds. In return, God would not wreak havoc amongst the Realm of Vitalis and would keep His people from infiltrating our world, as humans tend to try and take over things they don't understand or have control over. Therefore, God and the sorcerer agreed that a deity would be appointed to oversee Earth from our Realm, to ensure that we uphold our end of the bargain. Thus, Demitrius was selected, and he has watched over Earth and has kept the line between the two worlds in order ever since." Xander tells me. "Wow. That is mind blowing." I tell him. "So the two worlds just exist separately? They aren't interconnected at all?" I ask. "As far as we know. They exist parallel to one another, but how is not really known. Our deities have tried traveling past the palace in the clouds in hopes of finding answers, but all that surrounds our atmosphere is a vast abyss of nothing." He tells me. "The palace in the clouds?" I say inquisitively. "It's the true home of the deities. From what I hear, it's a large golden kingdom that sits amongst the clouds and is home to the gods and goddesses. However, mainly the great deities like Zeus, Poseidon, Athena, and so forth are the ones who get to live there. While the others, reside in Eternal Keep to rule over the realm directly until their heirs become fit to rule." He says. "Oh my gosh! Zeus, Poseidon, Athena, they're all real?" I reiterate. Xander chuckles, "Of course. I mean, none of the mortals in this lifetime have interacted with them, but some of the Elves can attest to their existence. They usually don't interfere with the mortal world, unless they have to." He says. "I guess that makes sense." I reply. "Any other questions?" Xander asks me. "Um, only a million." I say sarcastically. He lets out a chuckle, "Alright then, fire away." He tells me. "So, are you a soldier because your parents gave you the name Laskaris? Or because you were born with the powers of one?" I ask in confusion. "Surnames are that of a complex nature here. While most people's surnames describe what and who they are, not everyone's does. Typically, when a child is born, the parents who can afford a visit to an oracle, will take their child for a reading. The oracle will then tell the parents what their child is fated to be. More times than not, the child will take the powers of one of their parents, or they will inherent their own, but it's rare to see them take after both parents. My father happened to be a Laskaris, and when my parents took me to the oracle she had foretold me to be a *mighty protector,* and said I would be a Laskaris just like my father. Thus, my parents gave me the surname because it signifies who I am and what I am capable of." He tells me. "But what about those who can't afford the oracle? They just have to wait and see what powers their kid develops before they give them a last name?" "Not quite. Usually they will treat them the same as an individual whose powers are delayed. Meaning they'll just assign them a name based on physical characteristics or personality traits." He replies. "Well that's not such a bad thing. What's the big deal in having a set surname then?" I ask him. "Knowing the true surname helps the parents and individual be aware of who they are and allows them to start training at an earlier age. Which in turn allows them to develop control of their powers a lot sooner." He says. "So, it's basically like a brand then?" I say. "For a lack of better terms, yes. The surnames essentially describe either what our origins are and what we are capable of or they describe something about us." He tells me. "Hmm. Okay." I say as I mull this new information over in my head. "Take me for example," I hear Ella say, "my surname is Kouris. It means someone who lives in the forest." "Ah, I see." I tell her, even though I know that it's going to take me forever to learn the context of what all these different names mean. My mind then wanders to Jace and it makes me wonder what his name means. "Do you know what Galanis means?" I ask Ella. "It means, one with blue eyes." She tells me. "Oh." I reply. That is quite fitting for him, I think to myself. "So what exactly is a Laskaris's powers?" I ask aloud to Xander. "We are mighty strong individuals with armor like skin that is hard to penetrate or cut. We have a very tactical mindset and hardened emotions to prevent our feelings from interfering with our tasks and keep us from feeling the guilt of our kills and decisions. Our sense of fear is nullified and is replaced with great amounts of valor and we are driven by honor and honesty, making us incapable of lying or abandoning our mission." He tells me proudly. "Wow, that's pretty intense." I tell him. "Do you ever get to just have fun?" I ask. "What do you mean?" He asks. "You know, do something that is exciting and fun. Something you actually enjoy." I tell him. "I'm having fun right now. This journey is very exciting, wouldn't you agree?" Xander tells me and I can tell his tone is serious. "Uh, yeah, if you consider fleeing for your life to avoid being caught by the strongest power hungry god there is right now then sure, this is totally exciting and fun." I tell him. Ella lets out a snicker while Xander gives me a flat side eye. "I'm just saying, there's plenty of things I'd rather be doing right now." I tell him. "Do you not like learning about who you truly are and the place you come from?" Xander asks curiously. "Don't get me wrong, this whole ordeal is surreal and phenomenal. I just don't get why a person can't ever find out that they're magical or special without such drastic circumstances." I say. "Fair enough." Xander says coming to a halt.

"We should stop here for the night. This is a popular location so we won't seem out of place. There's a stream nearby and plenty of trees for cover too." He says as he climbs off his horse and makes his way over to me. I swing both legs to one side and Xander outstretches his arms to help me down. "Thank you." I tell him softly as our eyes lock for a brief moment before Xander quickly turns away. I turn to retrieve the satchel hanging from Lila's saddle and begin inspecting the contents inside. There's a small pan, a canister, a blanket, a couple of oranges and apples and a few pieces of bread. I smile at Elfred's generosity and thoughtfulness. It's almost overwhelming how kind and helpful everyone is being towards me.

"Why don't you and Ella go fetch us some water while I find us something to eat." Xander says. I want to tell him that we have some fruit and bread that Elfred gave us, but as I look at him and take in his brawny muscular physique, I realize he probably needs more than that to fuel him. I give him a nod and I follow Ella as she leads us to the stream. "Will this water be safe to drink?" I ask Ella. "Well of course. Why wouldn't it be?" She replies. "I don't know, it's just, where I come from, the water needs to be treated and cleaned before we drink it." I tell her. She cocks her head at me, "That sounds tedious. How do you even clean water?" She asks me. I tap my chin as I try to think of how to explain it. "To be honest I'm not entirely sure. There are people who do it for us since it is their job." I tell her. "Interesting. Well, here in the Realm of Vitalis we just drink the water freely. We have never had a problem with it." She tells me. I kneel down next to the stream and scoop up some water into mine and Xander's canteens. I watch as Ella twirls the water and it levitates and forms into little beads that she then sticks into the pouch hanging off her hip. "That is so cool." I tell her. "She gives me a smile, "Would you like to see something else?" She asks me. "Of course!" I tell her excitedly. "What's your favorite color?" She asks me. "Pink." I reply. She lands amongst the grass and puts her hand to the ground. Seconds later, multiple pink flowers appear all around her as she rises back up. "Wow, you are amazing!" I tell her. She gives me a big grin. "Thank you. I'm still working on mastering my powers, I haven't quite reached maturity yet." She tells me. "What do you mean?" I ask her. "A fairy cannot harness the full extent of their powers until they are sixteen." She replies. "And how old are you?" I ask. "Technically I am 15." She tells me. "Technically?"

I say rhetorically. She offers a small laugh, "Faeries do not age like most everyone else. While you grow older each each year, faeries grow a year older every two years." She tells me. "So, *technically*, you've been alive for 30 years, but really, you are only 15 years old." I say. "That is correct." She tells me. "Do you mind me asking what the average lifespan of a fairy is?" I say, afraid of what the answer might be. "A fairy lives well into their thirties. However, the oldest fairy to have lived was 41! So you never know!" She tells me with a perky attitude. "Ah, I see. And what exactly is the extent of a faeries powers?" I ask her. "Well, we are basically guardians of nature. We can control and alter the forces of nature and its land. We enforce that the land, its waters, and its inhabitants are not taken advantage of or abused. We also can communicate with the creatures of the land, sky, and sea." Ella says. "So is your magic what makes you glow?" I ask. Her glow gets brighter as she gives me a warm smile. "Not quite. Our glow as you call it, is our aura. The color we emit can tell what emotions we are feeling and also how lively or sick we are. The brighter our glow the healthier we are. The duller our glow… well, it's usually not so good, and when a fairy no longer has an aura it means they have passed away. " She says "Yours has been yellow since I met you. What does that mean?" I ask her. "She rubs her wings together, making them shimmer. "It means I am happy and positive." She tells me. I give her a smile, "How wonderful!" I tell her. "Should we head back, so Xander doesn't start to worry?" Ella asks nervously. I let out a huff as I take in the serene scene of the stream and surrounding bright green grass, now equipped with the pink flowers, courtesy of Ella. "Yeah, probably so." I tell her as I give the sunset one last look before we both make our way back.

As we approach our makeshift campsite, I see Xander roasting what appears to be rabbit over a fire he has made. "I was just about to come looking for you two." Xander says. "Sorry, we got caught up talking." I tell him, "Here's your water." I add handing him his canteen. "Thanks. You hungry?" He asks as he offers me a skewer of rabbit meat. I give a conflicted look between Ella and Xander. Ella puts her hand on mine. "It's okay Aislinn. I won't be upset." She tells me. I give her a nod followed by a soft smile as I take the skewer from Xander. "Thank you." I tell him. As we sit around the fire, we eat in silence and it's not till I finish eating that it hits me how tired I am. "Where are we going to sleep?" I ask. "Right here." Xander replies. "Here in the open?" I say skittishly. "Yes, where else would we sleep?" Xander asks me. I look at Ella and she stares blankly at me. "I don't know, at least somewhere covered. What if it rains?" I say. "Then I'm sure Ella will cover us." He says as he looks at Ella and she gives him a big nod with a beaming smile. "Oh, right…" I say. I go over to Lila and feed her an apple as I retrieve my blanket from my satchel. Well this is a first, I think to myself. I take my blanket and plop down on the grass. I watch Ella as she flies over to a nearby tree and covers herself with a leaf and quickly falls asleep. I stare into the smoldering fire as I ponder over everything that has happened today and I wonder what all this means for me. Eventually I am going to have to decide to stay here, or go back to Earth. There's so much I have to learn though, I haven't even started learning my powers or how to control them. Who knows how long that will take. Not too mention, how long I'll have to be in hiding to avoid Stavros. His powers are only good for a year, but how much of this year is left? So many questions, so much to learn. Can I really go back to Earth and pretend like I don't have a magical heritage and belong in a parallel universe?

"You alright?" Xander asks, interrupting my thoughts. "Um, yeah. Just processing today." I tell him. "Anything you want to talk about?" He asks. "Not really. I'm just trying to come to terms with everything." I reply. He just gives me an understanding nod and lays back and closes his eyes. "Where's your blanket?" I ask him. Without opening his eyes he replies, "Apparently Elfred doesn't think I'm cute enough to send with a care package." He says as a smirk spreads across his face. I suddenly feel guilty. "Don't worry about me. Laskaris's are immune to the elements. It's not like battles stop because of weather." He tells me, as if he can read my mind. "Oh, right." I tell him. We fall silent and I start to look around. I'm supposed to just lay on the ground? Where do I lay my head? What if a bug crawls in my hair? I shutter at the thought of bugs crawling all over me. I look over at Xander and he seems to be just fine laying on the ground. I lay back and close my eyes as I try to get comfortable. After about three minutes I raise back up. This is going to be a long night. "Something wrong?" Xander asks without moving a muscle. "I just, can't seem to get comfortable." I tell him shamefully. I can't help but feel like some prissy princess, throwing a tantrum about sleeping outside while others are sleeping just fine with less. He lets out a sigh, "Fine. Come over here." He tells me. I get up and plop down next to him, waiting for him to reveal his solution. Without opening his eyes he just pats his stomach. I hesitate for a moment. There's no way he is indicating what I think he is, is he? He opens his eyes and peers up at me. "Well, are you going to lay down or not?" He asks me. I give him a nod as I lay perpendicular to him and place my head on his stomach. After about a minute I can feel myself starting to doze off. "Is that better?" Xander asks me. "Yes." I murmur. And that's the last thing I remember before falling asleep.

Chapter 7

The next morning, I slowly awaken to the bright shining rays of sun. Man I had the craziest dream, I think to myself. In my sleepy daze, I reach my hands above my head to stretch and then rollover onto my side and bring my hand up to fluff my pillow. That's when my hand is met by Xander's sculpted abs and I am quickly reminded that it wasn't a dream after all. My eyes fling open and I swiftly sit up.

"Well about time." Xander says half playfully, but also half serious. "Sorry, you could've woke me up." I tell him. "Yeah right. Wake a new untrained Seeker up from her sleep? No thanks." He tells me. I give a half chuckle, "Good point." I reply. I get up and make my way over to Lila to put away my blanket. "How much further from here?" I ask Xander. "About four hours give or take." He replies. "Wow, we are almost there." I say partially excited, but also equally nervous. "What's going to happen to me once we get there?" I ask. "To be honest, I'm not entirely sure. We didn't think we'd make this far." Xander tells me. I give a gulp. "Oh, well, that's reassuring." I say. "Me and Jace were lucky we found you before that warrior did or you wouldn't even be here right now." Xander says. My eyes grow big, "You're so not helping ease my mind right now." I tell him. However, now I've become distracted by thinking of Jace. "Do you think we'll see Jace once we get to the Land of the Doulos?" I ask. Xander shrugs, "I don't know and I could really care less, he's not essential to the mission any more." He says gruffly. "Why don't you like him? He was your partner after all." Xander puffs out his chest defensively. "I don't like him or dislike him, but he is a Doulos and they can't be trusted. There's a reason they are a Doulos and there's hardly ever a good excuse as to how they ended up as such. You'd be crazy to think anything good could come from one." He says. I let out a gasp. "That is so prejudice. You don't even know him, or any of them for that matter. You can't just sit around assuming they are all evil. As a matter of fact, I know Jace means well, otherwise he wouldn't have saved my father or kept me from drinking a spiked drink." I say defensively, followed by a large huff. I might as well have the word *obsessed* tattooed on my forehead while I stand here defending some guy I barely know. Xander lets out a scoff, "Well that explains it." "Explains what?" I say with an attitude as I cross my arms. "Why Jace got recalled. I thought maybe he tried to flee, but turns out he just broke the rules." He tells me unfazed. "How did he break the rules? You two were there to help me." I tell him matter of factly. "Yeah, we were there to help *you*, not anyone else. Large scale magic is forbidden on Earth and especially practicing on humans. So, when Jace healed your dad, that was a big violation, which I'm sure he has been paying for since." Xander tells me. I become distraught. The fact Jace knew he'd get in trouble for healing my dad, but did it anyway, only justifies my notion that not all Doulos's are bad. It makes me want to find him that much more and tell him how grateful I am. Now my mind starts to wonder what would've happened if Jace wasn't there. "So you're telling me that you wouldn't have saved my dad, because it wasn't part of the mission?" I snap angrily. Xander just stares at me and I can see him tense up as he tries to refrain from answering. "I asked you a question." I say sternly, knowing he can't lie. "Yes." He says through clenched teeth. I let out a scoff and throw my hands up in the air. "Unbelievable! You can think what you want about Jace, but for someone who is supposed to have all this valor and honor, you sure don't have any regard for human decency." I tell him. I can tell I struck a nerve as his face turns red. "Even if I wanted to save him, I couldn't. I'm not a healer like precious ole Jace. I am a soldier, my duty is to serve and protect, so excuse me for not being well rounded in compassion and empathy. Never mind the fact, that if I wasn't there, you would've been taken and everyone else would've been killed." Xander tells me with fury in his eyes. It dawns on me that there is some truth to what he is saying, and I realize how ungrateful I probably sound. "Then why would they even send a healer in the first place?" I say manically. Xander approaches me as he frustratingly runs his hands through his hair, "For you! Everything is for you Aislinn. I can only protect you so much. If anything were to happen to you, Jace was supposed to there to help you. So yeah, forgive me if I'm not Jace's biggest fan, doing what he did, jeopardized your safety and if something were to happen to you, I don't know what I'd do with myself." Xander says breathlessly and I suddenly realize how close he is to me as I stare up at him. I see his anger simmer and his eyes soften the longer he stares back at me. As the silence between us grows longer it makes it harder for me to think of what to say in response. "If you care about me at all, you should also care about the ones I love. Without them, there's really no reason for me to go through all this." I tell him. He gives me a nod. "Very well, I'll try to keep that in mind." He tells me before we both fall silent again. Neither of us have yet to move and I'm sure it's because we are both basking in the proximity of one another and our heightened emotions are just pulling us together like magnets.

"Is everything okay?" I hear Ella's voice ask. I clear my throat as I step back from Xander and watch as Ella flies over to us. "It's fine, we were just having a heated discussion, but we are good now." I tell her. Xander returns to his horse's side. "You two sure looked heated alright." Ella says teasingly. I flash her a stern side eye. "It's not like that, trust me." I tell her. "We should get going, we don't need to burn anymore daylight." Xander says and I give him a nod. This time I successfully manage to get on my horse without his assistance and we begin the rest of our trek towards the Land of the Doulos.

As we make our way through the forest, the silence has only given me time to think of more questions. I know better than to ask Xander any more questions about Jace, so I resort to asking Ella.

"Ella are you familiar with healers?" I ask. "Why yes, of course." She tells me as she takes a seat between Lila's ears. "What exactly are their powers?" I ask her. "Well, pretty much like the name says, they heal people. Unlike sorcerers, they don't need potions or spells to facilitate healing. They are natural healers and heal people by transferring their energy onto those in need. Although, nature always has a balance. Therefore, whatever they heal the person of, is reflected onto them and is then taken on by the healer." Ella tells me. "So, essentially they are trading places?" I ask reluctantly. "Exactly." She tells me. My mouth falls open, but I quickly gather myself. That explains why Jace began to show blood on his stomach. He healed my dad by taking on his stab wound. I couldn't imagine voluntarily taking someones pain onto myself in order to heal them. That's a lot to ask of someone, and the fact Jace would do it for me makes my heart flutter. Now that I think about it, my dad's wound was fatal, so does that mean... Jace died? "What if it was a fatal injury? Like the person they were healing would have died if they didn't intervene. Does that mean the injury they take on will end up killing them instead?" I ask frantically. "Not necessarily. Healers have a natural ability to not only heal others, but also heal themselves. Although, they can heal others instantly, healing themselves is a slower process. They also can't effectively heal significant wounds or multiple people unless they are entirely well. Many healers have died from trying to heal too many people, or a large wound by themselves, before they are fully recovered. It's important they don't try to heal more than what they can handle. Otherwise, trying to heal a fatal wound can kill them." My chest becomes heavy, I sure hope Jace was at his best when he healed my dad. "I see. So, can they bring back those that have died then?" I ask out of curiosity. "No. Once a person has passed away, there's nothing a healer can do. Their powers are strictly limited to the living, so long as the person is still technically alive, then there is a chance a healer can save them." She tells me. "Wow, so they are pretty much a doctor." I say. "What's a doctor?" She asks me curiously. I give a soft chuckle, just as I hardly know anything about this world, she hardly knows anything about where I came from. "They are basically like the healers you described, but they do not have the power to heal people instantaneously. They have to use, erm… like medicines and devices to help heal and even then it's not guaranteed if it'll heal them." She gives me a puzzled look. I guess I haven't realized how difficult it is trying to explain things that have always just been second nature to me. Now I realize how annoying all my questions must seem. "It's a bit complex to explain, you'd have to see it for yourself." I say. "Ah yes. I'm sure you feel that way about some of things we have told you." She tells me reassuringly. However, that's not exactly the case, everyone has done a great job of explaining everything to me. I seem to be grasping most everything, it's just remembering it all is the issue. My brain feels fried with how much information I've had thrown at me in just a day and a half.

A sudden cold breeze blows and makes me shiver done to my bones. I hadn't really noticed till now, but as I look around, our surroundings have grown gray and cold. "What happened? Is it about to storm?" I ask aloud. "No. We are just entering the Land of the Doulos. It's a cold dark place, which is why they designated it for the Doulos's ." Xander says. "Well I'm freezing." I say as my body starts to shiver. I start to regret letting Fraeya talk me into such scant clothing. I retrieve my blanket from the satchel and wrap it around me. "How is this even possible? It was sunny and warm just a few miles back." I express my frustrations aloud. "Not everything has an answer Aislinn. This is the way things are and always have been." Xander replies, and I'm not sure what's colder, his tone, or the air. I decide to remain silent, it's apparent he is still upset with me.

After a few more miles, I start to hear some voices in the distance. I see Xander's whole body stiffen. He slows down his horse and takes his place at my side. "I need you to remain calm, up ahead are two of Stavros's men. They do not know what you look like so please try to act as natural as possible and hopefully they will let us pass without any issues." I take a hard swallow and give him a small nod. "Ella you may want hide so we don't seem suspicious." He tells her and she quickly slips into my satchel. I take some deep breaths and let them out slowly.

"Woah, now where do you two think you are going?" One of the men say as they cut us off on their horses. I start to have flashbacks of the warrior that was at my house. If one of them was that strong then I can't imagine what it would be like to take on two of them. "We are venturing to the Land of the Doulos, obviously." Xander says. His annoyed tone makes me tense, the last thing we want to do is piss these guys off. "We can see that, but what's your business here?" I see Xander tense his jaw as he remains silent. "Are you deaf soldier? He asked you what are you doing here?" The other man says as he hones in on Xander, while the other starts to eye me suspiciously. I then realize that Xander is struggling because he is unable to lie. I make Lila force her way in between Xander and the man. "Please, stop. It's my fault." I say as I let a look of embarrassment fall on my face. "Don't." Xander says seethingly. "I look up into the eyes of Stavros's men, "It appears that I cannot seem to bear children." I say and pause to bury my hands in my face and offer some sniffles for added effect. "We have been unsuccessful thus far and I am seeking guidance from my Doulos to see if there is anything we can do." I give Xander an apologetic gaze. "I feel like such a failure." I add with a few more sniffles. I can tell the men have become uncomfortable as they slowly start to back away from us. I look at the men, "So, if you could so kindly let us be on our way, and spare us from anymore embarrassing heartache." I say, giving them a pleading look. They look at one another for a moment and then look back at me. "Have you considered that you have been unsuccessful because you are mating outside of your species?" The bigger one says to me. I can feel the anger fuel my body. Even if this is all a lie, it still shouldn't matter. Why does every world that exist have to be consumed by such bigotry. "I believe you have bigger issues at hand than to be worrying about which species seems to be mating. I only hope one day you may find women that will love you despite your cold harsh ways." I snap. The other man opens his mouth to talk, but I cut him off. "I encourage the next words to come out of your mouth is to be that of wishing us luck and merriment and bidding us on our way, or so help me that I pray that all the might of the great deities reign down on you." I tell them. They give an astonished look and the taller man then moves aside and the other man quickly follows suit. "Thank you and good day." I say as I give them a parting nod and lead us onward.

Once we are out of earshot, Xander takes his place at my side and I can feel him staring at me. I glance over at him and see an astonished look on his face. "What?" I ask him. "I don't know where that came from, but that was the most fascinating thing I think I have ever witnessed." He tells me as he continues to stare. I blush, it was pretty bold of me. I don't know what overcame me, but it felt good. It made me feel like a badass. Glad, the drama class I took freshman year finally paid off. "I saw you struggling to keep from lying and wanted to help. I'm glad it worked though, because if they would've started a fight I would have been useless." Xander lets out a small laugh and we finally make eye contact. He gives me a soft smile as to signify an apology for early and I give him one back. I feel Ella plop down on my shoulder.

"That sounded like quite the spectacle you put on. I wish I could've seen their faces." Ella tells me. "Me too, it was quite funny. I'm surprised I didn't laugh and blow the whole thing." I tell her. She lets out a giggle. As I look around, I gather that we have officially made it to the Land of the Doulos. There a many poorly built cottages crammed together in small proximity. It makes me wonder exactly how many Doulos's live here and what they would do if they ran out of land to harbor them? As we trudge through the muddy path, we gain the attentions of some of the Doulos's as a couple of the men let out a catcall. I can see Xander become tense as he follows closely at my side. We pass by a shop were I see a blacksmith working and then a few feet away a woman trying to sell her handmade crafts. If I didn't know any better I would just assume this was a poverty stricken area filled with misunderstood people just trying to get by, and just like every bad area you have those who aren't afraid to do horrible things.

Almost on cue with my thoughts, I hear a woman cry out, "Stop let me go!" Without realizing it, I guide Lila towards the direction of the plea for help. "Aislinn, stop. It's not of your concern." Xander hisses. I round the corner into an alleyway and see a man pinning down a woman. "Stop!" I command. The man doesn't move, he just looks up at me with a mischievous grin. "Are you volunteering to take her place?" He asks, sending chills down my spine. "Watch your mouth Doulos."

Xander says as he catches up to me. "What's it to ya, this isn't your business anyway." The man tells us. "He's right it's not our place. Besides, I don't have jurisdiction here." He tells me with a conflicted look. "That's right, so move along unless you want a free show." He says as he turns back to the woman as she continues to writher about. Anger courses through me, in one swift motion I hop off Lila and shove the guy off the woman. He looks up at me startled at first, but then gives me a twisted grin, realizing I am now on his level. Before he has a chance to get up, I land a punch to his face and then put him in a head lock and tell the girl to run. The girl gives me a grateful nod and scurries off.

Xander hops of his horse and is ready to come to my defense, but I tighten my grip around the mans neck. I grit my teeth as I start to feel even angrier, dark, and twisted, and then I realize his emotions are transferring onto me. I decide to try and use my powers against him. I use the anger he is giving me to transfer onto him the feelings of what it's like to be scared, helpless and violated against his will. I try to channel the feeling of fear, weakness, and remorse onto him, but by this point I can't hold on anymore and I let him go and we both fall to the ground. He gives me a horrified look as he pats his body and realizes it was just emotional torture he was subjected to. I try to catch my breath and when I finally manage to stand up the guy flinches. "Stay away from me witch." He says in a disgruntled tone. "Then I suggest you stay away from women who don't want you near them." I say looking him sternly in the eyes. I see him take a hard swallow and give me a nod before scrambling to get up and scurrying off.

I remount Lila and look at Xander. "What has gotten into you?" He asks, now with a hint of concern. "Me? How could you just sit by and be okay with letting him violate her? That doesn't require having a certain jurisdiction Xander, that just calls for having basic human decency. It doesn't matter if she's a Doulos, nothing a person does warrants them to be sexually assaulted." I tell him. "I didn't say that it was okay, I just said there wasn't anything I could do." He tells me. "There's always a choice Xander, choosing to do nothing is like being accomplice." He looks away, embarrassed at my words of insight. I know it's hard for most guys to understand something when they haven't gone through it themselves. Quite honestly, I doubt Xander has ever been afraid a day in his life. He certainly doesn't act like it. "We should probably keep going, now that you've used your powers the magic is going to show up on Stavros's radar." He tells me. Shit, I forgot about that. "Are we still that far away?" I say, trying to clear the air. "No, just about another mile down the road." Xander says as he gets on his horse and leads us back to the path. "For what it's worth, I think you were very brave." Ella tells me. "Thank you." I tell her.

We remain silent until we arrive outside of the tavern. A wooden sign dangles from the roof and it reads DRUNKEN WOE'S TAVERN. We get off our horses and Xander hitches them to the designated post outside. I can smell the aroma of bread and beer coming from the tavern. I suddenly become nervous. I kept telling myself not to worry about it until we got here, and now that the time has arrived, I am freaking out. What is Diona's plan? And whose to say if it'll even work? Not too mention, I am about to meet a Greek goddess. No pressure or anything.

"Follow behind me and stick close. You too Ella, some of these guys would love to get their hands on a fairy." I see Ella's eye grow wide as she moves from my shoulder to Xander's and I have to refrain from laughing. Not because I think it's a funny situation, but from the sight of a bright delicate fairy sitting amongst the hard rugged Xander Laskaris. I give a nod and follow Xander has he leads us into the tavern. I instantly feel uncomfortable when I feel dozens of eyes fall on me. I try to channel the courage I had earlier and reassure myself that Xander is here to protect me. When we make it to the bar, the bartender approaches us. "Well to what do I owe the pleasure of having three upstanding citizens in my tavern?" The man asks. Xander looks at me as to signal for help. "We were meeting my Doulos and couldn't pass up the smell of fresh bread and the thought of a good beverage." I reply. "Very well. Find ya a place to sit and I'll bring ya my finest bread and ale." He tells us.

Xander leads us to a small table in the far back corner and we take our seats. We sit silently as the fellow bar patrons continue to exchange glances in our direction. After a few moments a plump busty brunette comes by to give us a plate of bread and our drinks. Disregarding me, she gives Xander an overly-friendly smile and he lays out some coins. "Why thank you." She says as she collects the coins and trails her finger up his arm as she walks off. I look at Xander as he continues to stare blankly ahead. "Doesn't any of this phase you?" I ask him. "Not really." He replies. Of course it doesn't. I take a piece of the bread and actually find it to be quite delicious. After a few pieces I decide to give the ale a taste. As the bitter ale hits my tongue, I do my best to choke it down. I can't believe people are drinking this stuff willingly. I look over at Xander as he takes a sip of the ale without even a grimace.

"How will we know when…" My question is cut off when the door flings open and a frigid breeze sweeps through the tavern. Everyone directs their attention on the beautiful woman standing in the doorway. I become mesmerized by the tall slender woman with long wavy black hair and her golden eyes. She scans the the room and then her eyes land on us. She gives a tight smile before making her way towards our table. I can't stop watching as she gracefully glides over to us. The torn ratty clothes look misplaced on the woman and then it dawns on me that this must be Diona. The feelings of insecurity start to creep into my mind.

When she reaches our table, she takes a seat across from Xander and stares at him for a moment, but I can see that he is doing his best to direct his gaze away from her. After a moment she looks at me and gives a smile. "Hello Aislinn." She tells me and if her beauty isn't enough, her voice is also that of a melodic tune. "Hi." I say weakly. "Shall we head to my cottage? I know you both have traveled far and I don't want to waste anymore of your time." She says to us. Xander just lets out a grunt and I give her a nod. We follow her outside and she watches us as we mount our horses. She gives Xander a domineering look, "Surely, you won't mind letting me hitch a ride? It's a couple miles up the road." She says. Xander lets out a huff, "Very well." He says as he extends an arm out to her. She grasps his arm and he pulls her up onto his horse with him. She then wraps her arms around his waist and I have to look away because the sight makes me slightly uncomfortable for some reason. "Just take a left and head straight down this path." She says.

After about fifteen minutes, we arrive to a secluded cottage on the brink of a forest. We tie up the horses once more and go to follow her inside, but we are stopped at the door. It's as if there is an invisible shield preventing us from entering. "Ahem." Xander says. She turns to face us, "Oh I almost forgot." She says before continuing, "You three may enter." "Clever." Xander says as we now pass through the threshold. "Can never be too safe." She replies. "Agreed." I feel myself say and it's as if she is reminded of my presence. She makes her way over to me. "Let me introduce myself." She says. She snaps her fingers and her tattered clothes turn into a white flowing dress and gold bands appear on each of her arms and her hair is pulled into an elegant updo. "I am Diona Kosmo, goddess of order." She tells me as she offers me a friendly smile. I give an awkward smile back. "I would introduce myself, but it's as if you know more about me than I do." I tell her. She lets out a laugh. "You are witty, that I could not have known. However, yes I do know a great deal about you Aislinn." "Does that mean you know who my biological parents are?" I ask in high spirits. She gives me a frown, "I apologize, but my powers are not that great. I'm afraid I do not know who they are, but what I do know is that, it's apparent they knew you would need protecting from an early age. They must have foreseen the disruption Stavros would cause during the Trinities Balance. Which I'm still trying to figure out how they could foresee it so early on." Diona tells me as she taps her chin trying to puzzle together an answer. "Sorry I can't be of much help." I say at first and then continue, "But, what's going to happen to me? What's the plan?" I ask nervously. "Please sit, we will go over everything." She says as she motions towards the chaise lounge behind me. We all take a seat across from one another and Ella rests on my shoulder.

As you know, Stavros is currently under reign due to the Trinities Balance, are you aware of what that is?" She asks me. "Yes, and I know he is wanting to become the Ultimate Deity and needs me to figure out how to make it possible." She gives me an affirming smile. "You catch on quick." She tells me. "I just don't get it though, he's just that power hungry or what?" I ask. She lets out a sigh, "Yes and no. Prior to this year, Stavros was a Doulos. He's the first Doulos to be granted the Trinities Balance and it has caused quite an uproar. Stavros's father was a sorcerer and his mother was an oracle of which she had prophecies of him one day being a powerful ruler. Even though, Stavros did not wield any powers at first, his father had taught him dark magic throughout the years, to hopefully aid in his success as a ruler. On his 21st birthday, Stavros's powers emerged and he was indeed a sorcerer. By this time, his parents had already filled Stavros with a sense of entitlement, that when he got his powers he abused them. Here in the Realm of Vitalis we forbid dark magic unless there is a justified cause. Stavros, used dark magic to try and poison a girl who broke his heart. The deities agreed that Stavros was still young and didn't know better. They deemed it his parents fault for corrupting him, so, they were sentenced to death. In turn, Stavros went on a rampage killing anyone in his line of sight. We then called upon the great deities to strip him of his powers and make him a Doulos. Now it's rumored he wants to become the Ultimate Deity so he can be the true ruler that his parents always seen him to be and kill all of the deities in the process as revenge." Diona states. "But if the deities knew what he was capable of, then why would they grant him the Trinities Balance?" I ask dumbfounded. "The deities have no control over who is selected during Trinities Balance. Some other force is at play when it comes to selecting who is awarded the Trinities Balance." She replies. "Ah." I say softly. "So as you can see, it's important that Stavros does not get ahold of you. Our job is to hide you and protect you to the best of our abilities." She tells me. "But where will I hide and for how long?" I ask. "The year is halfway over, so a little over 217 days." She says, before adding, "and until you can control your powers, we've come to an agreement for you to reside in Elfspond with Elfred. The magic emitted there is already high on the radar and they have their very own powerful militia. And, now after seeing you, it looks like you will blend right in at Elfspond." Diona says followed by a charming smile. "You can't be serious?" Xander says, professing his objection. "Did you have a better plan?" Diona questions Xander. The corner of his mouth curls up into a snarl. I'm sure his feelings towards Fraeya are hindering his judgement. "It's not like you would have to stay with her. Once you make sure she has arrived safely to Elfspond, you are relinquished from your duties and are free to go back to Valstead." Diona tells him. He just gives a brisk nod and looks away. This news actually makes me slightly unhappy. I had gotten use to having Xander around and the thought of him not being around anymore makes me sad. At least I'd still have Ella. I look over at Xander to catch him staring at me before he quickly looks to the ground. "Who can train me to control my powers? I was told the only other Seeker was in hiding." I say. "This is true, but there are sorcerers and oracles who worked alongside Seekers that can maybe offer some guidance. Of course, we will have to screen them first to ensure they don't have ties to Stavros. It is a dark time right now. The Realm is normally a friendly place, but lately people are fearing for their lives and their families so, be careful who you confide in." Diona says. I give her a nod. "Now, it's almost dark, so, you two can stay here for the night and start your journey back to Elfspond in the morning." Diona tells us. "Thank you." I reply while Xander just rolls his eyes. "Xander can I speak to you for a moment." Diona says as she rises from her seat. He lets out an aggravated growl as he stands up. "Excuse us for a moment. Please, make yourselves at home." She tells Ella and I. I watch her and Xander disappear into a room as I remain seated.

Ella flutters in front of me. "Shall we see if there's any fruit in the kitchen?" She asks. "Sure." I say as I get up and we make our way to the kitchen. Sheesh, there must be some kind of spell on the cottage, because the looks of the cottage on the outside, does not match up to what's on the inside. The kitchen alone is the size of what the cottage appears to be on the outside. As Ella indulges on some grapes that she found, I begin walking around the house. I head back into the living room and approach the door that Xander and Diona went in.

I put my ear to the door and I can faintly make out their muffled voices. I know I shouldn't be eavesdropping, but I can't help myself.

"Will you stop it, now is not the time." Xander says frustratingly. "How dare you turn me away. Have you found another lover?" Diona questions. Xander scoffs, "No. I am on a mission and you know I don't have time for such things when there's a task at hand." He says. "Yes, but right now there is only time to waste until you can travel in the morning, why not put it to use." She coos. "Because there is too much on my mind at the moment." Xander replies. "Like what?" She asks. "How could you just put her with the Elves?" He says angrily. "You know good and well that is the best place for her. I don't know why you are acting this way." She tells him. "Because you should've seen the way he looked at her the whole time we were there. By the time this is over, Elfred will surely have tried to wed her." Xander says. "Ah, so you've grown fond of her and now you are jealous?" Diona says. "No, of course not." Xander says defensively. "Then kiss me." Diona tells him. I hear Xander give a defeated sigh and then the air falls silent. I can only assume it's because they are now kissing and I quickly walk away. I can't believe this. I thought mortals and immortals weren't allowed to be together or is that something I just made up? Who knows and what does it matter anyway? Of course I think Xander is attractive, but he's been a jerk to me and has made it abundantly clear he isn't interested in me. Not like I care if he is, I have much more important things on my plate at the moment. But, now I am curious as to where I fall on the beauty scale in this Realm. On Earth I am probably a solid eight when I'm dressed to impress. Here though, I'm finding it hard to compete with beautiful Elves and Greek goddesses.

I preoccupy myself by looking around the rest of the cottage and find two extra bedrooms, a bathroom and then a locked door. Interesting. I wonder what's behind the closed door. I put my ear up to it and I hear the low hum of what sounds like electricity. I twist the knob once more, but it doesn't budge. I know it's not my place, but something is telling I need to see what's on the other side of this door. I scurry back to the kitchen and retrieve a knife and make my way back to the door. "What are you doing?" Ella asks me as she follows me back to the door. "I don't know why, but I have this strong urge that I need to get this door open." I tell her. I slide the knife where the lock meets the door frame and drive a wedge between the two until I manage to get the door open. When I enter the room, Ella lets out a gasp and my mouth falls open at the horrific sight before me.

Chapter 8

There lying on the ground inside an electric cage is Jace. He is only wearing a pair of shorts and I can see burns nearly all over his body. "Jace!" I say as I rush to the side of the cage. I try to put my hand through and it shocks me. I let out a yelp as I pull my hand back. Jace groggily raises his head as he peers up at me. "A...A...Aislinn?" He mutters before fading out of consciousness once more. "Yes, it's me. I'm here Jace." I tell him soothingly. I begin searching the room for the cord so I can unplug this sick torture device, but to no avail I don't see one. It must be magic. The cage then emits a shock and I see Jace writher in pain for a moment before returning to a barely conscious state. I fall to my knees in front of the cage as I start to become sick to my stomach. This is all my fault. He's being punished because of me.

Wait a minute, I think to myself. This must mean, that Diona is Jace's overseer. I can feel my blood start to boil. "I'm gonna get you out of here." I whisper to him. I stand up and march my way over to Diona's room. "Aislinn, proceed with caution. Remember, she is a goddess." Ella says trying to reason with me. "Yeah well, I don't care who she is. This is wrong on so many levels." I say.

I don't even bother knocking I just barge in her room. "Good gracious. Do they not knock on Earth?" Diona says. "You!" I say as I point to Diona and try to overlook the fact they are naked in her bed. "You are absolutely horrific. I can't believe you." Diona gives me a perplexed look. "Sweetie, we were just having some fun, I assure you that if you have feelings for Xander…" She says, but I cut her off with a disgusted scoff. "I could care less who you trap into sleeping with you, but what I do care about is, how you are keeping Jace locked in an electrical cage that is shocking him as we speak." I say angrily. I see Diona's body go tense and the playful look from her face falls. Xander sits up and looks at her and then at me. "Is this true Diona?" Xander asks. She ignores his question as she keeps her eyes locked on mine. "That room was locked for a reason. Clearly you don't know your boundaries." Diona tells me. I raise my eyebrows in astonishment, "Don't you dare turn this on me, like I'm the monster here." I sputter. "You dare call me a monster?" Diona says as she snaps her fingers to clothe herself and gets out of bed. She approaches me and gives me a smug look. "You may have people fooled with your beauty and charm, but I should've known. Just like any person with power, you are a corrupt, horrible person." I shout. "I never claimed to be a good person, but I am a goddess and you shall respect me as such." She demands and I can see the flicker of rage in her eyes. I have no idea what she is capable of doing to me, but I stand my ground. "I will respect no one, who has not first deserved my respect." I tell her firmly. I see her brows furrow and her lip squirm as it's clear no one has challenged her like this before. She vanishes and then appears behind me putting me in an arm lock. "Diona!" Xander says as he goes to jump out of bed. She flicks her hand up and Xander becomes frozen still. "I think it's time you learn your role here. You may be able to disrespect your God on Earth, but that is not permissible in the Realm of Vitalis." She tells me before continuing, "And to make matters worse, I am trying to help you, and this is how you repay me?" I wiggle my hand free and manage to grab her arm and squeeze it tight, in hopes of making her let go.

When I grab her arm I instantly feel scared, angry, and hurt. Is this what Diona is feeling? I then see flashes of her and Xander in bed, her seducing Jace, her and a few other men in bed and then lastly I see her in bed with a man as another man enters the room with some flowers. He looks hurt. "I thought what we had was special..." He tells her angrily. "Hunny we were just having some fun. You're a mortal and I'm immortal, it would've never worked." She tells him. "But, I told you, one day I will be the most powerful ruler there is and together we could rule it all." He says in a heartbroken tone. She just laughs, "Right, cause your mommy and daddy said so." She tells him. You can see the heart shattering look on his face as he throws the flowers to the ground and storms out. I then see a vision of Diona at a feast when she begins to choke on some wine. I see Jace rush to her side as he starts to heal her. I want to see more, but it's too exhausting. I go limp in Diona's arms and she lets me fall to the ground as an astonished looks crosses her face. I look up at her with a horrified look.

"It was you." I whisper. "How?" She says as her voice quivers with fear. I then remember Ella telling me that no one other than Ragna has been able to read a deity. Xander helps me to my feet and I push him away angrily. "Don't touch me." I say as I give him a look of disgust. "Aislinn…" Xander pleads before I cut him off. "You knew she was Jace's overseer and you didn't think that would be important to tell me?" I snap. They both stand there staring at me as I continue to make a scene. "Does he know?" I ask Diona, motioning toward Xander. "Aislinn, please." She begs me, "You have to understand, I didn't mean for any of this to happen." She tells me. "Tell me what?" Xander asks curiously. I can see the pleading look in her eyes as I now hold what must be her deepest secret. It's apparent no one knows how true the rumor about Stavros is, however, it was Diona who triggered the wrath of Stavros. I clinch my jaw as I hold back the truth. As I think it over, I realize I can use this as leverage. "She advanced herself on Jace." I tell him, and I see a wave of relief wash over Diona's face. Xander gives a disgusted snarl, "So? That's not surprising at all. What's the big deal?" He says. "Oh dear." Diona says as her mouth falls open and looks as if she's had an epiphany. "She's imprinted on him." She says. Xander gives a deer in headlights look. "Excuse me? What are you talking about?" I say sternly. "I believe that you have imprinted on Jace." She says. "And what does that even mean?" I ask impatiently. "You two are soul mates. Making you linked to one another." Diona says. I let out a gasp as I look at Xander to see if this is true and he won't even look at me. "How do you know?" I ask her, after all, it's not like I can trust her. "Possessive behavior, thinking about him constantly, strong urges that you can't explain, the burning desire to be with him." She tells me. My head starts to spin as I process what she is saying. Could it be? "I, I didn't mean to." I stammer. "How could I even do that? I've only seen him twice and I didn't even know what I was then." I say in a panic. I don't want to come off as some obsessed freak. It does make sense though, all my irrational thoughts that somehow always led back to Jace. My inability to get him out of my head, even before he saved my father. "It's not something attributed to a Seeker. It occurs when two souls cross that are fated to be together. Typically the two souls share a strong initial connection and it creates the imprint on each other so that destiny can bond the two together. Quite a rare phenomenon, but it seems to be the year for such." Diona says. I become baffled and distraught. "Can you please just let him out of there." I beg, and then cover my mouth as if only to prove the point further. She gives me a nod and waves her hand in the air.

I rush past her and back to the room Jace was in. I cautiously put my hand up to the cage to ensure she wasn't just tricking me. I breathe a sigh of relief when my hand grabs ahold of the cage. I fiddle with the locks until I have them all open and fling the cage open. I go to pull Jace out of the cage and suddenly a large wave of pain consumes me. As I cry out in agony, Xander quickly enters the room and pulls me away from Jace, allowing me to feel some relief. "Please Xander, get him out of there." I beg. He picks Jace up and carries him to the main room and lays him on the chaise lounge. Diona emerges from her room and I shoot her a glaring look. She gives me an uncomfortable, apologetic look in return. I turn my attention on Jace as he now lays peacefully in a comatose state. My heart breaks at the horrific sight, but swells just at the mere sight of him. I feel Diona's looming presence as I look up at her.

"Can we talk?" She asks me. I look at Jace and I see Ella take her place next to him, "I'll watch after him." She tells me. I give her a nod and then follow Diona to her room. When she shuts the door, she turns around and I can see how nervous she has become. "Well, start talking." I tell her as I fold my arms across my chest. "You have to believe me, when I tell you that I never meant for any of this to happen." She says. "Quite frankly, I don't have to believe anything you tell me, but I'm curious as to what you have to say for yourself." I reply. She lets out a sigh. "I realize now that, you were right. I am a monster and I have let my power go to my head. I did not use to always be this way. Believe it or not, I was in love once, with a mortal man. I loved him dearly and I would've given up my powers if it meant that I could be with him." She says longingly. "However, matings between mortals and immortals are forbidden. As, the concept of demigods put the world at an imbalance. So, when Zeus had found out about my mortal lover he had him killed. I was angry and heartbroken. In horrible fashion, I went out in retaliation and started sleeping with every mortal man I saw fit. I did not think about the consequences at the time. When I came across Stavros, I did fancy him, he was a good lover, so unlike my other single night retaliations, I found my way back into Stavros's arms a couple times. When he found me with another man, I reacted foolishly because I did not want to admit that I could find myself falling for another mortal. There has not been a minute since then, that I wish I could go back and change what I did, even more so now. Stavros was angry and heartbroken so when he had me poisoned, I was not surprised. People are always trying to poison deities. That's why during the big feast we always have healers as our taste testers. The night of the feast, Jace was my taste tester and he had played it off that the wine was fine. When I started to choke, the guilt overwhelmed Jace and he ended up saving me and confessing his part in the plot. I know he did it out of spite for advancing myself on him earlier that day. Unlike most mortals, Jace was able to refuse me, so I had used my powers to convince him to sleep with me. He was the victim, not me, but I felt betrayed and enraged. I told the deities what he had done and they allowed me to brand him as my Doulos as punishment. I'm not proud of what I have done and I am ashamed of the way I have treated you tonight. It was a horrible first impression for you to have of not only me, but all of the deities." She tells me. I stare at her for a moment as I ponder what she has said. "So, you're sorry?" I ask her. She is taken aback by my question at first, but then gives me a nod. "Then I need to hear you say it." I tell her. She gives a hard swallow, "I'm sorry Aislinn." She tells me and I can tell she is being sincere. "And I think Jace deserves an apology too, once he's coherent again that is." I say snidely. She gives me another melancholy nod. "I know how awful I may seem to you now, but I hope you can see that I'm the good guy here, I am on your side." She tells me. "Whether you're the good guy or the bad guy, is all based on perception. You may think you're the good guy because you're fighting for what seems right, but Stavros believes what he is fighting for is the right thing too. So, your allegiance isn't what makes you a good or bad, your morals and choosing to do the right thing, no matter what it costs, is what makes you the good guy." I tell her. I see the guilt spread across her face, "You are exactly right." She tells me. "And to be quite honest, you and Stavros are both in the wrong. What sets him apart, is that he has killed a bunch of innocent people and now wants to kill all of the deities. Regardless of whose side you are on, that is wrong and he needs to be stopped." She looks up at me and gives me a nod. "So, if we are going to stop him, we need to be honest with one another and treat each other with respect and work as a team." I tell her. "You are wise beyond your years Aislinn." She tells me, while giving me half smile. I don't what overcomes me, but then I do what any compassionate person would do, I give her a hug. I startle her at first, but then she hugs me back and I can sense the good intentions radiating from her. It makes me all the more eager to control my powers so I can read people much better and know for sure what I am sensing or feeling.

"Are you going to tell anyone?" She asks me skittishly. "It's not my place, but I think you should. Maybe not right now though, we all need to be on the same page and I'm afraid that kind of news will separate people from you." She gives me an understanding nod. "Thank you for opening my eyes." She tells me. "We all need it every once in a while." I tell her and give her a reassuring smile. She gives me a big smile in return and loops her arm around mine and escorts us back to the main room.

I'm not justifying what Diona did, but we are all beings who hurt, love, cry, and laugh and sometimes it can get the better of us. She may be immortal, but she's just like the rest of us brought into this world, or I guess worlds. If only it were this easy to talk to Stavros, then maybe we could avoid this whole world domination ordeal. I mean I don't think anyone's tried, but I have a feeling it wouldn't go so well.

As we remerge into the main room, I can see the confused look on Xander's face as we enter the room, arms looped as if we have been besties all this time. Jace lets out a groan and I'm reminded of the harsh reality. I unlink arms with Diona and quickly go to his side. "What can I do to help?" I ask. He blinks a couple times as his blue eyes finally focus on me. "Aislinn, what are you doing here?" He says dreamily. "Wait. Where am I?" He asks as he looks around. His eyes then land on Diona and he instantly tries to sit at attention and fails miserably. "It's okay Jace." She tells him warmly. "I'm sorry for the way I've treated you and it's not going to happen anymore." She tells him. I help him sit back against the arm rest and he gives me a dazzling smile despite his rough state. "This is definitely a dream, but apparently one of the best." He says as he reaches his hand out and cups my face. I can't help but blush. Xander lets out a disgusted scoff and Jace looks over and sees Xander sitting in a chair to his left. Jace quickly pulls his hand off of my face. "Oh dear, this is not a dream after all." He says as he looks away embarrassed. I let out a small laugh. "What's going on?" He asks confusion.

"Maybe we should give them some privacy." Diona comments as she looks at Xander and he reluctantly gets up. I watch as they leave the room and I even see Ella flutter towards the kitchen, leaving us entirely alone. He looks at me for a brief moment before looking away again. "Is something wrong?" I ask. "Aside from having no clue as to what's going on, no." He replies. "Then why won't you even look at me?" I ask. He looks up at me reluctantly, "Because a Doulos isn't supposed to look a non-Doulos in the eyes my lady. It's considered an offense due to our unworthiness." He explains. I can't believe what I'm hearing. "Jace, I consider it an offense if you don't look me in the eyes." I tell him. He gives me a warm smile that nearly makes my heart melt. "Now that we got that established. I should probably let you know that we are in Diona's cottage in the Land of the Doulos. She is hiding out here and perpetrating as a Doulos because Stavros has invaded Eternal Keep. Xander brought me here from Elfspond, which is where we portaled to. It was pretty cool, but it made me sick which is supposedly normal since it was my first time. Anyways, Elfspond is where I meet Ella, the fairy that is with us. And I also met Elfred, the Wise Elf, who is really nice, so much so, that he even gave me a horse. I named her Lila because of her purple eyes. I also met Fraeya, who is on the Wise Council and she gave me this dress so I could blend in since my human clothes would've been too noticeable." I tell him and then pause to catch my breath. "Sorry, I think I'm rambling, you probably didn't need to know all that. I'm just a bit nervous." I tell him. He gives me another smile, "You have nothing to be nervous of. I could never grow weary of listening to you." He tells me. I find myself blushing once again. "However, it does concern me that you are here dressed like that." He says with a frown. I look down at my dress. "You don't like the dress?" I question. He gives a soft laugh, "I think you look stunning, but that is the problem. The people around these parts, won't hesitate to um, well…" His voice trails off. "Ah, I understand. I've handled myself fairly well surprisingly. Plus, I had Xander with me." I tell him reassuringly. "Ah, yes. Well, rest assured, nothing will happen in his presence." Jace says. "Hopefully when I get back to Elfspond, Fraeya can lend me something a little less revealing." I say. "When you get back to Elfspond?" Jace reiterates. "Yes. Diona said that since a bunch of magic is generated there continuously, it'll be the best place for me to hide out until I am able to control my powers." I tell him. He remains quiet as he looks up to the ceiling. "What's wrong?" I ask. "Nothing, I just didn't realize that was now part of the plan." He tells me, but I can tell something else is bothering him. "Why did Diona let me out of the cage and why is she being so nice to me?" He asks faintly and I can tell it's because he is still afraid of her. "Well actually while her and Xander were, um preoccupied, I was wandering about the house, when

I stumbled upon the room you were locked in and something kept telling me to get the door open. When I did, I saw you in there and I was so upset, that I went right up to her and demanded she let you out." Jace winces at thought of me doing such a bold thing. "And she listened to you, just like that?" He asks, slightly astonished. I let out a half laugh. "No, we had a bit of a tussle followed by a deep heart to heart before she caved." I tell him. He gazes into my eyes and I feel as if he's sucking every breathe of air I have from my lungs and it's absolutely invigorating. "I can't believe you would do that for me. You must not know what I am." He says disappointingly. He looks away once more as I see the shame overcome him. I put my hand to his face and I feel a wave of warmth and love consume me and I try to concentrate on transferring those same feelings onto him. He reaches his hand up to meet mine and grasps it. When our hands meet, the emotions I am feeling start to grow stronger and our faces draw closer. The urge to kiss him starts make itself known and the stronger the urge gets, the dizzier I become and I have no choice, but to let go before I pass out. "You are truly exhilarating." He tells me. "I could say the same about you." I smirk. He shakes his head, "I do not deserve your affection my lady. You deserve someone of high esteem with a respectable nature." He tells me. Is this when I tell him, *oops too late, we are soulmates?* How do you even tell a guy that you barely know that you claimed him as your soulmate? I try to imagine feeding that line to some guy back on Earth and him laughing in my face. Diona said that it only happened when the two souls were fated to be together, so why am I so hesitant to tell him? Maybe he already knows and can feel it too. "Whose to say you aren't those things? Besides, I know what you did." I tell him quietly. His face grows pale and he buries his face in his hands. "I'm so ashamed, it was a moment of weakness." He mutters. I crouch down in front of him and try to pry his hands from his face. His eyes meet mine, "How can you even stand to be near me after knowing what I've done?" He says tensely. "Because I know that there's two sides to every story. What you did was wrong, but what Diona did to you was wrong too. She just had the power to make you pay for it. I also know that, anyone willing to save the person they intended to kill, probably isn't that bad of a person. You're a pretty terrible accomplice, now that I think about it." I tell him and we both start to laugh.

As his laugh subsides, his face falls serious and he gives me an intent stare. "It brings me much relief to see you have arrived safely. I would never be able to forgive myself if something were to happen to you and I wasn't there to help you." Jace says. I give him a reassuring smile, "Hey, it all worked out. I also realized that helping my dad was a big risk for you, and I can't thank you enough for saving him anyway." I say with a big smile. "Of course. I would do anything for you." He replies. I look into his hypnotizing blue eyes and try to maintain my focus on the conversation and distract myself from how handsome he still looks despite his noticeable injuries. "I was really worried when I found out that healing someone while you were hurt could kill you. Or that it would cause you to undergo such cruel punishment. If I would've known what I do now, I never even would've asked. It's just, seeing the ones I love hurt, is my weakness." I say in a sullen tone as I look away. Jace uses his finger to gently turn my head to face him. "It appears that my logic escapes itself when I'm with you. I guess that makes you, my weakness." He tells me. His sweet words make my heart flutter. Our heads start to gradually drift toward each other and I can feel my heart start to beat uncontrollably. I have never felt so much desire to kiss someone until this moment. I close my eyes once our lips are shy of an inch apart and prepare myself for what kind of impact this may have on my powers and emotions.

"Ahem." I hear Xander say as he clears his throat. We become so startled, Jace and I bump heads and slowly turn to see Xander standing in the doorway. I feel my face become flush with embarrassment. How long had he been there and how much did he hear? "Hello Xander." Jace says. "Jace." Xander says with a nod. An awkward silence then falls amongst us, until Diona emerges from her room. "Jace I have fetched you some clean fresh clothes. How about you go wash up and get changed." Diona says in her peppy demeanor. Jace gives a nod as he rises from his seat and avoids making eye contact with her. "Thank you very much." He says as he takes the clothes from her. She gives him a nod. "Down the hall to the left." She tells him. I watch Jace disappear around the corner, leaving me, Xander, and Diona alone. I start to wonder if Diona's mercy toward Jace is only a facade, that of which will wear off once I leave tomorrow.

"So, what now?" I ask curiously. "Well for starters, I should notify Elfred of our new discovery. He will need to know the extent of your powers." Diona says. "Does that really make a difference?" I ask. Xander gives both of us a puzzled look, "Did I miss something?" He asks. Diona lets out a nervous chuckle as she looks at me. "Yes, yes you did." She tells him. "It appears Aislinn is capable of reading deities." Xander's jaw drops open as he turns to face me. "But, that hasn't been possible since…" Xander's voice trails off. "Since the time of Ragna. I know. This is certainly an anomaly that I did not foresee." Diona says. "Hold on, anomaly? So you're calling me a genetic freak?" I say defensively. "No, on the contrary. This is a rare occurrence, your ability hasn't been possessed, but two times in an eternity. Once, by Ragna the mother of the original Seeker, and now you. Therefore, the extent of your abilities may not really be for certain." She tells me.

"Well great. It was already going to be hard enough trying to train my powers in the first place, and now we don't even know what powers I really have." I say frustratingly. "I'm sure Elfred will be able to think of something. Elves are excellent history keepers, so I'm sure they can find the full account of Ragna's abilities." Diona says. "Surely this can't be a coincidence." Xander says. "It's hard to say. It's been 150 years since Ragna has passed. So, it could just be time for another occurrence, or, it could serve as a counter balance for the Trinities Balance." She says. I let out a groan, "Either way I'm screwed. If Stavros doesn't kill me once he's done with me, the deities will kill me, just like they did Ragna." I say. The room falls silent.

"We don't know that yet." Diona says softly before continuing, "I will vouch on your behalf that you mean no harm. My vote tends to weigh a little more heavily since I am the goddess of order." "Well, I would appreciate that. You can also tell them that my idea of a good time does not consist of sitting around reading deities. In fact, I don't think I ever what want to read another deity again." I say as I shudder at the thought. "Duly noted, in the meantime, I say we keep this secret amongst us and Elfred. We can deal with the aftermath, once the Trinities Balance is over." Diona says. Me and Xander give her a nod. "Very well. If you'll excuse me I am going to try and summon a thread to Elfred." She says before retreating back to her room.

"What's a thread?" I ask Xander. "It's one of the first styles of long distance communication, which uses older magic. Instead of teleporting or sending a hologram, a person will try to establish a connection by channeling an object to communicate." He says. I cock my eyebrow to show my incomprehension. "For example, if she foresaw Elfred sitting at his desk she would channel her energy onto a piece of paper and write out her message. It would appear on the paper before Elfred and he would get her message. If he wanted to respond he could simply write a response to her message and she would receive it telepathically." He explains. "Ah, okay. I think I get it now." I say. We both fall silent, just staring at one another.

"Well it seems you and Jace aren't wasting time fulfilling your destinies." Xander says in a snarky tone, disrupting the silence. "Shh!" I say in a panic.

"I haven't exactly told him that we are imprinted, or bonded, or whatever the hell it is. I am waiting for the right time." I tell Xander. "I am confused. Are you saying the right time would be after you two kissed? Because if you tell him after, then wouldn't it seem as if you only kissed him because you felt like you had to? You should kiss someone because you want to, not because you're obligated to." Xander says and his sudden words of *insight* irritate me. He has no idea how I feel when I'm with Jace. Although, yes I have the undeniable urge to kiss Jace, but that doesn't mean the desire isn't there along with it. "What do you know about how I feel?" I snap. "I know that you shouldn't be kissing someone you hardly know." He tells me. I'm filled with embarrassment and frustration. "Coming from the guy who seems to jump into bed with every woman he comes across." I say harshly. I can tell I've struck a nerve. "That is not what I do. You may not understand the politics here just yet, but, like I said there's a big difference between doing things because you want to and doing things because you have to." He says. "Really? So you just had to jump into bed with Diona." He clenches his jaw in frustration, "In a way, yes." He replies. I roll my eyes, "Whatever. The point is, why should I listen to you, when you don't even follow your own advice?" I say snidely. "Maybe because I'm just trying to look out for you and I don't want you to get hurt." He says heatedly and then quickly turns away as he realizes the sensitivity behind his outburst. I crack a small smile at the revelation that the tough and callused Laskaris before me is actually showing emotion. I step to the side so I'm facing him directly, "I care about you Xander, but you shouldn't worry so much. Jace is a good guy." I tell him. "That's what I'm afraid of." He mutters, but before I can ask what it's supposed to mean, Jace enters the room. I can't help, but become captivated by his appearance. Now that he has showered his hair appears jet black which only makes his blue eyes pop even more. He now wears an off white cloaked tunic shirt with some tight brown pants, which overall gives him a Robin Hood vibe. It truly is unfair how attractive some of these people are, I think to myself.

I watch as he makes his way over and takes a seat in one of the chairs. "What have I missed?" Jace asks. "Where should I start?" Xander scoffs. I elbow him in the stomach, which, to no surprise, doesn't even phase him. "Nothing really. We were just talking about tomorrow." I say quickly. "Ah, yes. Your journey back to Elfspond." Jace reiterates sadly. "Yes, but Diona says I only have to stay until I get my powers under control." I tell him matter of factly. He gives me a polite smile, but I can still see the sadness in his eyes. "I'm a fast learner, so it shouldn't take long." I say reassuringly and I'm not sure if I'm trying to convince Jace or myself. "You should take as much time as you see fit. Your powers are not something you should rush." Jace tells me. "But you guys think I can do it though…right?" I say as I look at both Xander and Jace. They look at each other and I can see them both hesitate to respond. My head starts to fill with doubt. I haven't the first clue how to channel my powers, let alone use them. If it's anything like the movies back home, then this could take years for me to learn. "It definitely isn't going to be easy." Xander says. "But it's doable. You just have to believe in yourself." Jace adds promisingly. I give them both a smile, it's almost hilarious the contrast between the two of them. They are both right though. I need to start taking this stuff seriously and focus on learning my powers. I then notice Ella hovering meekly in the distance. I hold out my hand to acknowledge her and she flies over and lands in my hand.

"Have you been eating strawberries this whole time?" I ask in amazement. She lets out a giggle, "Not quite. I came back once to see you and Jace having a rather intense moment and then another to find you and Xander having another tiff." She tells me. I let out an embarrassed groan, "Ugh, I'm sorry you keep laying witness to my awkward social encounters." I tell her. "No worries. I can definitely see why you were so obsessed with Jace though." Ella says with a snicker. I start to blush, even though I know Xander and Jace can't hear what we are saying, it's still nerve wrecking to be discussing this in front of them.

"It's getting late, we should head to bed. We have another long journey back tomorrow." Xander says. "It's so not fair. We just got here." I reply frustratingly. I could care less about spending time with Diona, but more upset with the fact that I'll have to leave Jace. "Trust me, you do not want to stay in the Land of the Doulos." Jace tells me.

"Exactly. See we both agree on something." Xander says as if that should be all the convincing I need. I let out a huff, "Fine."

"Diona said you can take the room down the hall." Xander tells me. "And where will you be sleeping?" I ask spitefully, even though I already know the answer. His eyes narrow on mine, "Somewhere you won't be using me as a pillow for. Now, goodnight Aislinn." He says with a smirk as he retreats to Diona's room. I quickly glance at Jace and see his brows furrow. "It wasn't like that." I blurt out. "We had to sleep outside and I'm not use to that so he offered to let me rest my head on him." Jace looks at me, "Aislinn, it's okay. You don't have to explain yourself to me. You are your own person, who can do as they please. If you fancy Xander then that's all there is to it." He tells me as he does his best to give me a convincing smile. I can practically feel my stomach churn at his words. I can't believe he doesn't see that I have feelings toward him. Why isn't it as obvious to him as it is for everyone else? "But I don't *fancy* Xander. I fancy you." I tell him softly as our gaze locks. Then all of a sudden Jace pulls me to him and kisses me. When our lips meet, it's as if every nerve fiber I'm made of emits warm jolts of electricity, making every part of me come to life. I didn't know it was possible to feel such exhilaration and desire with just a kiss, all I know is, I didn't want it to end. His lips are soft and savory as they meet with mine, and I can finally take a deep inhale of the musky sandalwood aroma that makes him all the more inticing.

My emotions become so overwhelmed between love and lust that it makes my heart throb uncontrollably and I start to become dizzy. I push him away as I clench my heart and try to catch my breath. Jace looks hurt as he immediately looks away. "My apologies my lady, I hope you forgive my intrusive behavior. I don't want this to change your thoughts of me." He says remorsefully. I take his hand in mine and I can sense the feeling of rejection. I suddenly realize that he's not aware of how sensitive my powers are. "It wasn't you at all. I quite enjoyed it actually. It's just right now with my powers out of control, my feelings and emotions are severely heightened. So, it's not that I didn't like it, I just figured it would be best to stop before I passed out." I tell him. He gives me a grin, "So, it's okay that I kissed you then?" He reiterates. "Very much so." I say as I feel myself blush. "In that case, I will be looking forward to when you have your powers under control." He tells me. I give him a bashful smile, "Goodnight Jace." I say followed by a kiss on the cheek. "Goodnight my lady." He says as he steps out of my way. I make my way to the room and as I shut the door I feel a weight on my shoulder. I look to my right and see Ella sitting on my shoulder.

"Ella, hi." I say awkwardly. I'm curious where she has been this whole time. It seems as if this isn't a very private place after all. "Do you mind if I stay in here with you?" She asks. "Of course not, we can even share the bed." I tell her. "Oh wow! Thanks." She tells me excitedly as she flies over to the bed and lets herself fall onto to the pillow. I make my way over to the bed and plop down myself. It seems like it's been an eternity since I've laid in a bed, and boy is it a welcomed feeling. As I lay in bed, I replay mine and Jace's kiss over and over again in my head. Just the thought alone keeps giving me butterflies and sends me to sleep with a big smile on my face.

Chapter 9

The next morning I awake to a loud banging and some indistinctive shouting. Ella and I jolt up and give each other an alarming look. "Who is that?" I ask her. "I'm not sure, I don't recognize the voice." She tells me. All of a sudden, Diona bursts through the door. "You must go now, Neophenian soldiers are here." She says in a hushed frenzy. "But, but..." I sputter, but can't come up with any words. "Go out the window and when I let them in, grab your horse and ride straight back to Elfspond. Me and Xander will try to distract them as long as we can." I start to panic, "I don't know my way back, what if I get lost? What if I run into more soldiers?" Almost as if on cue, Jace appears in the doorway with a bag. "Jace will be going with you. Now go before they start trying to break down the door." Diona says. I open the window and let Ella fly out and then I climb out as Jace follows behind me. We scale along the cottage and wait until we can hear Diona let them in. "About time." One soldier says as Diona opens the door. "It's so early, to what do I owe the intrusion?" "Silent Doulos. You have a high amount of magic radiating from your residence and we are here to make sure you aren't harboring a Seeker." Another soldier says. "Thats preposterous, your leader killed all the Seekers, but please, by all means have a look around." Diona says. Once we hear them enter the cottage, we send Ella ahead to make sure the coast is clear. When she waves us on, we make a dash for Lila. Jace swiftly mounts Lila and pulls me up onto the saddle with him and we quickly make our escape.

After we put about fifty miles between us and Diona's cottage we finally slow down so we don't draw any unnecessary attention. I then loosen my grip around Jace, after realizing I'm still holding onto him for dear life. "Well that was a close one." I say trying to break the tense silence. "Indeed it was. We are fortunate that they even knocked." Jace says. "So, who are the Neophenian's?" I ask in confusion. "It's just what Stavros and his followers call themselves. It's the name of those in support of the new world, or Neophere, that Stavros intends to create." Jace tells me. "What about the people who support the Realm of Vitalis? What are we called?" I ask him. "Vitalisans." He replies. "Ah. Got it." I say and then we fall silent. "Can I ask you something else?" I ask Jace. "Always." He says. "Did you only work as a taste tester for the deities?" I ask him. "No. I primarily worked in an infirmary with other healers, sorcerers, and sorceresses. When we work together it does not drain as much of our powers and lessens the time it takes for us to heal. We also work on discovering new remedies. However, our treatment facility is located in Eternal Keep so the deities have a say in who lives or dies. We only serve as taste testers during the annual eclipse festival, then we go back to our daily lives." Jace says. "Eclipse festival?" I say with a sense of intrigue. "Every year on the first day of summer, a lunar eclipse occurs, but it stays that way for the entire day, and then the following day, a solar eclipse takes its place for the entire day. On the third day, everything returns back to normal. During these three days, the deities hold a feast and celebration for everyone in the Realm, except for the Doulos's. The Eclipse Festival is what marks the start of a the New Year. During the year of the Trinities Balance, this is when the selected mortal gains their powers." Jace explains. "Interesting. So, then, how do you keep track of the days and time here?" I ask curiously. "The Realm does not have constraints of time within a single day. When the sun comes up it marks a new day and if we should have to hold a meeting we schedule it in accordance to the location of the sun or moon. Our days are numbered by the season, of which we have four seasons. Summer, Fall, Winter, and Spring. Each season offers 100 days, except Summer which has 135 days. Thus, our years are 435 days long and we just count up from the day of the lunar eclipse which marks day one." He finishes explaining. "Wow, I am definitely not on Earth anymore." "I know it's all much different from Earth, but I promise to help you every step of the way so you don't feel lost." I tighten my grip around him as a makeshift hug. "Thank you." I tell him. "Of course. I couldn't imagine what you must be feeling. It all must be so overwhelming." He replies. "Well, it's definitely been chaotic, but I think I'm starting to get use to it. Besides, having you, Xander, and Ella as my guides, make it all the more worth it." I say. Ella flashes me a big smile. "I'm certainly glad you feel that way. I must admit, since I have met you, my life has been the least bit of boring." Jace says. I take a hard swallow, maybe now I should tell him about our imprint on each other.

"Can I ask you a personal question." I ask Jace. "Of course." He replies. "How long have you been a

Doulos?" "Two years and two hundred and fifteen days." He says and I can feel a slight bit of sadness emit from him. "How old were you then?" I ask. I don't know why I don't just ask him how old he is since that's what I really want to know. "I was twenty-two at the time I became a Doulos." He tells me. "So you are twenty four now?" I ask in a relieved tone. I'd be lying if I said I wasn't afraid Jace was like a century old or something. "That is correct." He says. "Wait, are you actually twenty four or do you only age every so many years or something crazy like that?" I say in a skeptical tone. Jace lets out a chuckle, "I am indeed twenty four years old." He says. "Good." I reply before adding, "not that it'd be bad if that were the case. I just figured that since I'm technically 21 in this Realm and if you were like a hundred years old it would make the whole dating thing a bit awkward. Not that we are dating, I just mean that if you were a hundred, I'd still like you, it would just take some getting use to. Oh my gosh what am I even saying? I'm going to just stop talking now." I say as I finish my rambling. Luckily his back is to me so he can't see my face turn red with embarrassment. Jace gives a small laugh, "Aislinn, my attraction to you is undeniable, and I would want nothing more than to be with you, but unfortunately the laws here will not allow it." "What do you mean?" I ask. "I am a Doulos, we are not allowed to marry or have families. So unfortunately, the thought of us being together is not a reality." Jace tells me. I can feel myself becoming upset. "Seriously?" I say angrily before continuing, "How can they even do that? Why would fate even let two people imprint if they can't even be together?" I pause at the realization of what I just said and Jace brings Lila to a halt. "What did you just say?" He asks. Great, this is not how I wanted to tell him. He looks back at me, waiting for me to answer. "Sooo, Diona believes we have imprinted on one another. Which I guess means that fate has bonded us as soulmates." I say followed by a nervous laugh. Jace opens his mouth to speak, but then stops. "I know that sounds crazy, but I want you to know that my feelings aren't being forced. I truly am attracted to you for who you are." I say. Jace remains silent. "Please say something." I beg. "I'm sorry. I'm just trying to process this. I knew I felt strongly for you, more than I have for anyone, since the moment I bumped into you, so it definitely makes sense. I just can't believe I am lucky enough to be fated to you." He tells me as he gives me a big pearly white smile. My heart practically skips a beat, "So then you feel it too?" I say. "Indeed. It's undeniable, I am yours and you are mine." Jace tells me. I can feel the love and joy channeling onto me from Jace. He then pulls my face to his and gives me a long sensual kiss before pulling away. "I'm sorry, I know your powers aren't under control, but I just can't help myself. It's almost painful to resist the urge." He tells me. "It's okay, I know exactly what you mean." I tell him. Jace gives me a warm smile and then turns back to the reigns so we can continue our journey.

As I rest my head on Jace's shoulder I notice Ella perched on the horn of the saddle and instantly feel awkward. "Ella I'm so sorry you had to witness that. I feel so embarrassed." I tell her. "Don't be. Love is a part of life, and it is quite an honor to witness a fated love. It does not occur very often." She tells me. "Since it's such a rare occurrence does that mean we would be allowed to be together?" I ask Ella. "I would believe that is the case, but it's never happened with a Doulos before, so I can't say for sure." She says. "But who can deny fate?" I say rhetorically.

Over the next few hours, I teach Ella and Jace the game twenty questions and we occupy our time by playing a couple rounds. It was a fun way to start getting to know one another. When the sun begins to set, we pick a good place to set up camp and settle down for the night. After munching on some snacks Jace had packed, we then take our spots on the ground and Ella takes her place in a nearby tree. Jace pulls out a small pillow and blanket and hands it to me before he lays back in the grass.

I lay down a few feet from him and lay on my side as I watch him stare up at the sky. I roll onto my back and look up to notice the deep purple sky illuminated by the stars. I've never taken the time to admire the night sky before and I find it truly mesmerizing. I start to wonder what else the universe holds. Back home we always flirted with the idea that there was other life forms out there, but nothing was ever certain. Now, here I am in a parallel world, living proof that there is. So, who knows what other mysteries are still out there? I look back over at Jace and soon find myself admiring his sharp jaw-line and the way his silky black hair shines in the moonlight.

"What are you thinking about?" I ask him. He doesn't move as he continues to look up at the sky. "I'm thinking how I should be thanking every single star for leading me to you." He says as he rolls onto his side to face me. I become entranced by his soft, but masculine baby blue eyes. The longer I stare into them, the more vulnerable I feel, as if he is staring right into my soul. "Do you really think fate has a play in this?" I ask him. "Well it was certainly out of my control. After all, I am a Doulos. I'm not even allowed to look people in the eyes. So, for something good to work in my favor, lets me know that some greater power has a part to play in this." He tells me. "I guess you're right. I keep asking myself *what if,* but I guess that's the the whole point of fate. What ifs don't matter, because what happened has happened, there's no changing it." I say. "Exactly. You can't preoccupy yourself with trying to think of what could've been, otherwise you'll let everything in front of you slip past. Trust me, there's been plenty of days I have sat around thinking what if, but it doesn't change the past." He says reflectively. I frown, "I'm so sorry you've been treated so poorly, my heart breaks at the thought of it." I say. He outstretches his hand and rubs his thumb over my cheek. "I would go through it all over again, if I knew this is where I'd end up." He tells me. I grab his hand and he entwines his fingers with mine. We rest our hands between one another and that's how we stay as we drift off to sleep.

Chapter 10

The next morning I can feel the sun beaming down on me and I hear the faint sound of birds chirping in the distance. I can still feel my hand wrapped in Jace's and it makes me smile. I slowly open my eyes so they can adjust to the bright sky and while doing so I take in it's beauty. I see the silhouette of what could be a moon or another planet, but who really knows at this point. I have the feeling someone is watching me, but when I look over at Jace he is still sound asleep. I scan the tree across from us to find that Ella is sleeping too. I then hear a twig snap and I quickly rise to my feet.

"Whose there?" I shout as I foolishly take a fighters stance, but there's no reply. "Aislinn what's wrong?" Jace says as he quickly rises to his feet.

"I…I had this feeling someone was watching us and then I heard something from over there." I point to the border of the forest entrance. Jace takes his place in front of me. "It's okay. We don't mean to intrude, we are just passing through." Jace proclaims as he starts to slowly make his way toward the tree line. "If you could so kindly point us in the right direction, we will gladly be on our way." Jace says reassuringly. However, just as he is about to approach the nearest tree, we hear frantic rustling and then from afar I see a shadowed figure take off into the depths of the forest. "Hey wait, stop!" I hear Jace say as he goes to take off after the mysterious figure. "Jace, don't!" I shout. Jace immediately comes to halt and turns to face me. "Let's just go." I say nervously. He gives me a nod and then looks back at the forest once more before jogging back over to our campsite. Ella is now awake and it's apparent she is spooked.

"Did you see who or what it was?" Ella asks me. "No. All I could make out was a dark figure." I tell her. "Did you happen to get a better glimpse?" I ask Jace. "I didn't see anything at all, but it definitely sounded like they were running on two feet. Which makes me think we are dealing with a who rather than a what." "So, what does that mean?" I ask. "It means, they could be assigned to spy on us. They could be tracking us so they can monitor our location, or they just happened to stumble upon us accidentally. Who knows, but it's best we not wait around to find out." He says. "Agreed." Ella chimes. We quickly gather our things and continue on to Elfred's Castle.

After what feels like a few hours, I start to notice some familiar sights, reassuring me that we are almost there. Just as we are making our way through the last bit of the forest, I see Ella fly ahead of us. As we get closer, I see her embrace another fairy. I see her glance at us when we start to pass them and she gives him another hug before quickly retaking her place on my shoulder. "Who was that?" I ask Ella. "Oh, him?" Ella asks as she gives a nervous chuckle, "that's just Alvin." She says. "Uh-huh. And is Alvin *just* a friend?" I ask her. "Aislinn!" she says bashfully. "What? You're the only one who can give someone a hard time about boys?" Ella gives me a playful side eye. "I guess there's no denying that we are fond of each other, but courting isn't permitted until a fairy turns 16." "Then I can't believe I'm saying this, but I guess it's a good thing you're 15." I tell her. She gives me a flat smile, "Yeah I guess so." She says sadly. "Wait, what's the matter?" I ask her. "Well, it's just that once a fairy turns 16 they are to be betrothed within 180 days or they will be unable to mate. Which at that point, they are seen as unfit and are exiled to another region. "And I take it Alvin is older than you?" "By exactly 150 days." She replies. "Then what's the problem?" I ask confused. "There's this other fairy, Melantha, who makes it well known that she fancies Alvin. While most fairies are respectful of the bonds that some fairies form, others use this time frame to their advantage." "Yeah, but you will still have 30 days before Alvin has to make a decision right?" "Only if Melantha hasn't proposed a marriage by then." Ella says sullenly. "Can't he say no?" I ask. "Yes, but it is considered a bad omen to deny a marriage request. The elders see it as a sign of defying fate and questioning the work of the gods and goddesses." She tells me and I notice her aura fade to a bluish hue and I can only assume it means she is feeling sad. "Well how about you use this time to go catch up with Alvin. I think me and Jace can handle it from here." I tell her. She looks up at me and I can see her start to shimmer again. "Really are you sure?" She asks. "Yes, of course." I tell her reassuringly. She shoots up and gives me a bright smile, "Very well, but I will be by to check on you!" She says. "No rush, go have some fun." I tell her followed by a wink and before I know it she is off in a flash.

"Where is she off to?" Jaces asks. "I told her to go spend some time with her friends. I don't want her to feel like she has to stay at my side the whole time ya know?" "Fairies are a very caring species, it's in her nature to want to help you." He says. "I know. I just hate that all this attention is on me, and to make matters worse, I have no idea what I'm doing. I feel useless." "You are the least bit useless. You are more important than you realize, you just don't know how to channel your powers yet, but in due time you will learn." He tells me just as we approach the castle. "Wow, I've never seen it up close before." Jace states in amazement. "It sure is amazing." I comment.

"Halt, stay where you are." One of the guards shout. Two guards then approach us cautiously. "Who is your traveling companion?" One guard asks as he eyes Jace suspiciously. "This is Jace." I reply. "We were informed that you would be traveling with a Laskaris." He states. "There was an issue at the cottage, so she sent me instead." Jace replies. "Mind your tongue Doulos, you should know better than to speak out." "Don't talk to him that way." I say sternly. "Well we didn't ask him, we asked you." The guard says, now focusing his attention on me. "Then I guess I will waste my breath to re-inform you, that an issue arose, so, Xander had to stay back while Jace took his place." The guard narrows his eyes on mine before looking Jace over once more. "What are your powers Doulos? Are you taking advantage of this woman's naivety?" The other guard questions Jace. "What? No! My name is Jace Galanis-Doulos and I am a healer." "Then remove yourself from this horse so you can be escorted in separately." The guard demands. "What? This is absolutely appalling!" I say angrily. The guards ignore me and I try to hold onto Jace as he slides off Lila. "I demand to speak to Elfred right away." I snap, as I watch the other guard bound Jace's hands behind his back. "As you wish. I am ordered to take you to him right away." The guard says as he takes Lila's reigns and guides us within the castle walls.

"You must tell them to release Jace at once." I shout as I enter Elfred's office. "Well hello to you too Aislinn." Elfred says. I give him a sharp nod of acknowledgement and then remain silent to express how serious I am. "Give us a moment" Elfred says as he waves off his guards. After they shut the doors, Elfred makes his way around to the front of his desk and motions for me to sit in one of the chairs. "I don't feel like sitting." I tell him firmly. "Very well." He says before taking a deep breathe and letting it exhale slowly. "Aislinn, you must know that our main priority is to keep you safe and out of the hands of Stavros. In order to do this, you must be inconspicuous in everything that you do. We still do not know the extent of your powers and it seems you possess more than the average Seeker. So, until you can get a handle on things, it is in your best interest to be entirely focused so that you avoid generating a high profile and making yourself visible to Stavros." Elfred tells me calmly. "I just don't understand how keeping me from Jace and treating him poorly affects my chances of being found." I reply. "There is no denying that Elves do not take kindly to those outside of our species, especially those branded a Doulos. I will see to it that Jace is not mistreated amongst the castle members, but I'm sorry I cannot allow you two to be together until you have control of your powers. There is a high amount of magic that is emitted when those of an imprinted love are in within a hundred yards of each other. Now you add a Seeker who doesn't know how to differentiate her emotions from her powers and you are practically begging Stavros to come find you." Elfred tells me. I remain silent, unsure of what to say. What Elfred is saying makes sense, but I also know that my urge to be with Jace is like a raging fire that I can't seem extinguish. "How can I go on each day feeling like this though." I say frustratingly as run my fingers through my hair. "It will get easier the longer you are apart. It also helps if you preoccupy your time on your studies and with other people." Elfred says. "Studies. Other people. What are you talking about?" "There are now 215 days until the Eclipse Festival. Until then you are to blend in amongst us. The best way to do so is to make sure you attend lessons that will better acquaint you to this Realm, practice controlling your powers, and socializing with other Elves. If anyone outside this castle asks, you are of Elven heritage, but your parents were free lancers who were exiled. Since their recent passing you have returned to Elfspond to seek the roots of your true heritage." Elfred says before continuing. "Everyone inside this castle is sworn to secrecy, so as long as you are within these castle walls you are safe, but that does not mean you can always speak freely. Any high risk matter must be discussed within a secret chamber or a force of solitude." I give a nod and then look around the room. "Don't worry, when the doors are shut, my office becomes a secret chamber, so everything we have discussed is confidential." I give another nod as Elfred claps his hands, triggering the doors to his office to open. "Now, if you would forgive me, I have some council matters to tend too. I will have one of the guards show you to your wing of the castle. Dinner is at sundown in the main dining room. Fetch one of the guards if you need help finding something." He says matter of factly as he makes his way past me. He stops and gently raises my hand to give it a kiss before making his way out of the office. "Show her to the West Wing and see to it she gets whatever she desires." Elfred tells one of the guards. "Yes sir." The guard says. Elfred turns and gives me another smile before vanishing into thin air.

"This way Miss Aislinn" The guard says as he directs me down the hall. He leads me down another long hallway and up about two flights of spiral stairs. When we reach the top of the stairs I am nearly out of breath, but my exhaustion is quickly replaced with astonishment. The entire room from floor to wall is covered in a glistening rose marble and is offset by a silver ceiling with an elegant crystal encrusted candelabra hanging in the center of the room. I look to my left and see two large silver doors that open into a balcony. Across the way I see a lovely clawfoot tub poised in the corner of the room accompanied by a beautifully crafted changing partition. Adjacent to the partition is a walk in closet that is filled with different sandals and every type of dress imaginable in nearly every shade you can think of. In the opposite corner is a floor length mirror and a vanity that holds a hairbrush and different bottles of what seems to be perfume. The far wall contains a door that opens into a small room that contains what must be the toilet, a bucket, small rags, and a table holding a basin and some goopy white paste and what I'm guessing is my toothbrush. I pick up the carved piece of wood that has bristles of, who knows what, attached to it. I set the brush back down and give the guard an awkward smile.

"Is something wrong Miss Aislinn?" The guard asks. "No, everything is, um, great." I reply. "I do have a question though. The guard raises an eyebrow. "How do I turn the sink or the tub on? I don't see any knobs." I say. "What do you mean?" He asks quizzically. "How do I get water into the basin or the tub?" I ask. "Ah yes, your handmaid will fetch you some water, shall I summon her for you?" "No. It's okay." I reply. "Wait, actually yes please. Not for the water though, I just have some questions for her." He gives me a bewildered look before giving me a nod and walks off. I listen until the sound of his clinking armor disappears before I go plop down on my bed.

I realize that this is the first time, since coming to the Realm of Vitalis that I am by myself. Although, I'm sure someone would be here in a matter of seconds if need be. I'm not sure if that is a refreshing thought or if I find it hella overbearing. It is certainly a lot to embrace and process. In a matter of days, I have discovered that I belong to a magical realm filled with other magical species and I happen to be the one who holds the fate of the Realm in their hands, literally, no big deal. I have a vengeful power hungry bad guy after me that only wants to use me for my powers, which, I don't even know how to use or control, which apparently some of the powers I possess, the deities don't appreciate and killed the last person to wield those powers. Oh, and let's not forget that all the while I have supposedly found my soulmate. So, I can see this going three ways.

One, our plan fails. Stavros finds me, takes me prisoner, uses me to get what he wants and then kills me so it can't be undone. Two, our plan works. The deities find out about my true powers and then they kill me to prevent the same thing from reoccurring. Or three, the plan works, the deities are cool with me being a bad ass and then me and Jace get to live happily ever after. I let out huff and sit up on the foot of my way oversized four poster bed. I trace my fingers over the sheer pink material that cascades down each post, creating a canopy over the entire bed. I can't believe this is mine, at least for the time being. I feel like a princess, a literal medieval princess. You would think a magical world full of magical species, run by gods and goddesses would have a better concept of plumbing though. What do I know. Not like I even have a clue of how most things on Earth operate.

I get up from the bed and walk over to the doors to the balcony. I open the doors and step outside. The sun is setting in the horizon, but I can still see the greenery of the meadow and the forest in the distance. To my left is a shimmering emerald green pond that stretches out further than I can see. To my far right, I see what I think to be mountains, and it suddenly hits me that there is still a whole Realm out there for me to explore. I've only seen two Regions so far, which means there's still six Regions I have yet to see. Will I ever get to see the other regions? Hell, will I ever get to see my mom and dad, or Natasha again?

I become so lost in my thoughts that when I hear a delicate voice say, "Pardon me," I nearly jump out of my skin. I quickly turn to see a tall, slender, fair skinned woman with sleek red hair that flows down to her waist. Her red hair makes her green eyes pop and unlike most red heads I've known, this woman does not have a single freckle. Then again the Elves are known for their flawless skin. It's now apparent my lack of response has made her uncomfortable. Even though her ears protrude through her hair, she nervously tucks her hair even more so behind her ears.

"I'm sorry to have frightened you my lady." The woman states. Her choice of words instantly make me think of Jace. "No, it's quite alright. I was lost in thought and hadn't heard you come in." She gives me a polite nod and then curtsey's before speaking again. "My name is Ariti. I am to be your handmaid." "Nice to meet you. My name is Aislinn." I reply. "Pleasure to meet you my lady. Is there anything I can do for you?" She asks. "Please, call me Aislinn. And yes, I have some questions that I hope you can help answer." "I will certainly try my la…I mean, Aislinn." She says carefully. "So, I take it you know who I am?" I ask her. She gives me a timid look, "Yes, yes I do." "Then you must know, I am not from here and I do not know a lot of things about this world." I tell her. She nods meekly. "Well then, let me apologize in advance for all of my questions." I tell her followed by a friendly smile. "No need to apologize, that is what I am here for." She replies followed by a polite smile.

I make my way back into the room and Ariti follows me at a safe distance. "If you don't mind me asking, how old are you?" I ask Ariti. "I am 92." She tells. I try to hide my amazement, as it still blows my mind of the age differences. "Wow, I hope to look as good as you at 92." I say jokingly and I finally see Ariti give a big bashful smile. "Thank you, I'm sure you will look just as beautiful." She replies. Now it gets me thinking. "Actually, do you know how long a See..I mean, I, how long I should live?" I ask her. "The average lifespan of your kind, is 99 years old. The oldest ever being 110." She tells me. "Interesting. And I age every year?" I ask. "Correct." Well, at least it's reassuring to know that I could live a good long life, as long as Stavros or the deities don't kill me in the meantime.

"And please don't laugh, but how do I go to the bathroom?" I ask her. She cocks her head in confusion, "I'm not sure what you mean. This is your own bath," She tells me as she points to the tub. "There should be no need for you to go to the public bathing room." She adds. Learning the different terminology is going to be the death of me. "My mistake." I say as I walk over to the separate room with the toilet and open the door. "What do you call this room?" I ask. "That is your personal privy." She tells me. "I see. And how do I use it?" I ask dumbly. "Once you have finished...um, doing your business. You use the clean cloths provided and then dispose of them into the bucket you see there. You can then ring your bell to summon me and I will take the bucket of soiled linen to dispose of and I will return with a bucket of water to pour into the hole to ensure everything flushes out." She explains. I put on my best poker face as I try not to gag. They definitely never showed that in the movies. "Oh wow, that is embarrassing. I can just do it myself. If you could just show me where everything is though." I say. Ariti's eyes widen as she seems taken aback by my proposal. "I do not think Elfred will appreciate me letting you tend to your own privy. Rest assured, it is my job and I do not mind it." She tells me. "Right... fine then, but I will be asking Elfred about this, because it would definitely make me feel much more comfortable." I reply.

"Now, tell me Ariti, what does your name mean?" I ask abruptly to keep her from protesting. "It means friendly." She tells me. "I find that fitting." I tell her and she gives me a toothy grin. "And what about Aislinn?" I ask, and quite frankly am surprised I haven't asked anyone sooner. "It means, like a dream or a vision." She replies. "Which I find fitting as well." Ariti adds as she gives me another smile. I smile back at her kind words. Simultaneously, it makes me think of the time Jace told me, *You certainly are an Aislinn,* and it makes me smile even harder. Ugh, quit thinking about him, you are only going to make this harder on yourself.

"So, what am I supposed to do in the meantime?" I ask. "Well, many Elves like to spend their time reading, studying, socializing, sparring or practicing their magic to keep their minds and bodies sharp and ready. It is also important to spend a good amount of time with nature, whether it be taking a stroll or going for a swim. Being around nature grounds us, as we believe it is Mother Nature who gives us our abilities and fuels our powers. In return, we respect and take care of our designated land, and all of its inhabitants, to show our gratitude." Ariti explains. "Wow, I have a lot to learn." I say. "In due time." She tells me. Ariti then looks toward the balcony. "The sun is nearly set, which means dinner should be almost ready. Do you need me to show you the way?" She asks. "That would be awesome." I tell her.

After walking through what feels like a corn maze, we arrive to the same dining room I ate in when I first met Elfred. Ariti walks over to the table and then pulls out a chair at the far end of the table. I walk over and take a seat in the chair. Ariti then goes to leave the room, but I quickly stop her. "Wait, where are you going?" "The hired hands do not eat with the Elites. If you need something, either the butlers or servers can assist you." She says before giving me a bow and walking off. I sit in an awkward silence for a few minutes and then I hear some voices approaching the dining room that cause me to sit up straight. Elfred and Fraeya then enter the room with smiles on their faces.

"Aislinn, how wonderful to see you again." Fraeya tells me. "Likewise." I tell her with a smile. Elfred then takes his place at the opposite end of me and Frayea takes her place along the right side of the table. "Are you excited to be staying in Elfspond?" Fraeya asks. "Yes and no." I reply. She gives me an inquisitive stare, "Do explain." She says. "I am excited to be here and to learn about Elfspond. It's just that I would like to see the rest of the Realm and learn about the other Regions as well." I say as they both stare at me. "I understand your curiosity and if it didn't pose such a great risk I would encourage you to see the rest of the Realm. Maybe after the Eclipse Festival perhaps." Elfred replies promisingly. "I understand, that's why I am just going to make the most of my time here in Elfspond." I say cheerily. "Now that's what I like to hear." Elfred says as he raises his glass. When doing so, it causes all three of our glasses to fill with wine. "Here's to making new friends and learning new things." Elfred toasts. Me and Fraeya then raise our glasses before we all three take a sip.

Elfred then cues the servers to start bringing out the food. "Have you had time to explore the castle?" Fraeya asks. "No, not yet. I spent most of my time in my room." I reply. "I see, and which room are you staying in?" She asks. I look to Elfred for the answer. Without taking his eyes off me, he proudly replies, "The West Wing," as he gives me a charming smile. His alluring look, suddenly makes me flush. Out of my peripheral I see Fraeya give Elfred a sharp look, before resuming her composure.

"My, the West Wing. It is certainly is the loveliest room in the castle, aside from the Wise Elf's chambers that is." Fraeya states and I can hear the spite in her tone. "The loveliest room, for the loveliest woman." Elfred says. At this point, I have to break eye contact otherwise I feel like I might burst into flames. "Thank you." I say sheepishly as Fraeya lets out a forced awkward laugh. What has gotten into me? Elfred has to be using his charm on me.

I look down and start to fill my plate with grapes, cheese, bread, nuts, and some assorted fruit. "I take it you have met Ariti then?" Elfred asks. "Yes, she is very nice and has been quite helpful. I just feel bad that she is just there waiting on my beckoning call." I say before adding, "Which reminds me, I would like to clean my own privy." Elfred and Fraeya both choke a little on their food. "Oh my." Elfred exclaims, as Fraeya snickers and gives him a smirk. "Do they find this as appropriate table talk on Earth?" Elfred asks in astonishment. I hadn't thought about how such a topic would seem inappropriate to discuss over dinner. "Uhhh…it really isn't an issue, but then again on Earth, the methods of doing such aren't as outdated, as they are here." I say cautiously. Elfred rubs his temple, "I advise against it, but you can do as you please. Just do not tell me of your decision and I beg you not to speak of this matter to anyone else." He groans. I give him an understanding nod and then decide not to bring anything else up.

"She has much to learn." Fraeya comments. "Indeed." Elfred agrees. "You will start your lessons with Cicero tomorrow at high noon." Elfred tells me directly. I give him another nod. "And if you could see to it that you teach her some proper etiquette, maybe take her for an outing with Sarris and Rosi, so she can see how some other Elves socialize."

Elfred tells Fraeya. "But Elfred…" Fraeya starts to say, but then her words cease as her and Elfred stare blankly at one another. Which, I can only assume they are communicating telepathically. "I mean, yes Wise Elf, I would be happy too." Fraeya finally says as she gives me a perky, forced smile. "Great, I am confident if you work hard and stay focused, you will be plenty ready in five days time." Elfred says.

My ears perk at his words. "Wait. Ready for what in five days?" I ask. "The Wise Council has demanded an audience with you. They have suggested throwing a ball in your honor, so they can meet you and determine if they should grant you Elvenhood. Fraeya lets out a gasp. "But I'm…" Elfred holds a finger to his pursed lips as a means to silence me.

"Keep in mind, we are not in a force of solitude nor a secret chamber." Elfred tells me telepathically. "How am I going to pass as an Elf? There's no way five days is enough time." I respond frantically. "Nonsense. I know you can do it. Besides, I know you will do your best to convince the council so they will agree and allow you to say." Elfred replies.

"Stay? What do you mean? I thought that was already determined?" I tell him.

Fraeya clears her throat to interrupt our thought transference and reestablish her presence. "Elfred this is madness! The council is really considering letting a self proclaimed, estranged child of exiled parents claim Elvenhood? This goes against everything we stand for." She says hysterically. "As far as the council is aware, she did not know about her true heritage until her parents death. And with her just recently becoming the age of revelation and still being unwed, they do deem her eligible to seek her birthright as an Elf under the claim of plausible deniability. That is, as long as she proves herself and abides by the stipulations the council sets forth." Elfred says sternly. "We agreed that she would be safest here, did we not?" Elfred says. "I agreed we could safely harbor her here as a guest. Not by passing her off as one of *us*." Fraeya says angrily. I suddenly start to feel uncomfortable as the conflicted tension only grows. I could now see the pridefulness in Elves that Xander loathed, unfold before me.

It was apparent Fraeya was prejudiced against non Elves, just as Xander was toward Elves. "If only the council knew who she really was." Fraeya says in a challenging tone. Elfred swiftly rises from his chair, now towering over Fraeya with a fierce look in his eyes. "I urge you to choose your words wisely Fraeya." Elfred says in a coarse tone. Fraeya throws her napkin on her plate and rises from her chair. "We will discuss this at a later time." She says coldly, before flatly adding, "now if you'll excuse me."

We both watch Fraeya storm out of the room, before Elfred returns his attention back on me. "I do apologize for Fraeya's offensive manners." Elfred tells me. "It's not your fault." I reply flatly. I would be lying if I said Fraeya's words didn't get to me. Up until just a few minutes ago, I considered Fraeya as one of the few people I could trust here. I can't be too upset though, she is right after all. Elves seem to be a very proud species who take their heritage seriously, and then I come along and make a mockery of everything they stand for.

"May I escort you to your room?" Elfred asks, bringing me back to reality. "Uh, yeah. sure." I say solemnly. He quickly vanishes and reappears at my side. He puts out his arm for me, but I give him a wary look. "I thought you said you didn't trust me touching you?" Elfred gives me a smoldering look, "The second I knew we would be spending more time together, I knew it would only become harder to resist your touch. So, I've been practicing some power suppressing spells." He says. I can't help but blush as I hesitate to loops my arm around his. "Are you sure?" I ask him. "Only if you are." He says encouragingly. I quickly loop my arm around his and brace myself for what I might experience.

After a couple seconds pass without anything happening I peek up at Elfred. "It worked!" I say excitedly. Elfred gives me a big smile, "It appears so." He says in a relieved tone. As we walk to my room, Elfred uses this time to reassure me that it's okay I am here and that this is the right thing to do.

"Elves are very conventional. We tend to stick to our traditions and are very conservative in our thoughts and actions." Elfred says. "That sounds awfully closed minded." I reply. Elfred laughs, "I can see how you may think that, but it's not always a bad thing to respect the values and beliefs an individual holds, especially if the entire species' way of living is rooted in those values, and has been since the beginning of time." He says in a very wise tone. "However, some of us do agree that we should try to be more progressive in our ways and advocate for what is right. I just never thought I'd find myself breaking the rules like this, it certainly puts me in bit of a rebellious predicament." He tells me teasingly. I give him a playful smile. "But you are the Wise Elf, doesn't that mean that whatever you says goes?" "I am honored you think so highly of me, but no, that's not how it works. Although, I do indeed rule over Elfspond and my word is of the highest authority, my decisions and actions can always be overturned by the Wise Council if they unanimously disagree with my ruling. This keeps the Wise Elf from becoming a tyrant. In fact, if the Wise Council discovered our secret, they could charge me with treason and sentence me to death."

I stop in my tracks to show my dismay. "This is just great, another person's life I am responsible for. Why would you even agree to help me if you knew the cost?" I say frustratingly. Elfred cups my cheek in his hand. "Sometimes a punishment is worth every risk if the heart sees fit. That's why from the moment I saw you, I knew that not even the fear of death itself could keep me from helping you." His affectionate words leave me speechless and cause my heart rate to rise. I turn my head into his hand as I try to escape his sensual gaze.

"You are too kind. I certainly appreciate everything you are doing for me." I tell him in attempt to break our growing tension. "You are quite welcome." He tells me before we proceed up the spiral staircase. "So tell me, have you named your horse yet?" Elfred asks. "Yes! I named her Lila." I tell him proudly. "I think that is the perfect name for her." He states. "And your saddle, it fits comfortably?" He inquires. "Oh yes, no problems at all." I tell him.

When we approach the top of the stairs, we both hesitate awkwardly. "You know the castle can become awfully lonesome at night. I would be happy to extend my company if you'd like?" He says alluringly. I give him a coy smile, "I'm flattered, but right now all I want is to take a nice long hot bath and get a good nights sleep." I reply. I see Elfred bite his bottom lip to refrain from saying what's really on his mind. "As you wish," he says and then offers a tender kiss to my hand, "till tomorrow my Dove."

He tells me. "Goodnight, Elfred." I say with a parting smile. I then turn to enter my room and find all the candles in my room lit and a tub full of water with rose petals floating atop. I quickly turn back around, but Elfred is already gone.

I find myself smiling idiotically at his romantic gesture. I make my way over to the tub and test the water. It's actually warm so I quickly grab the satin robe from my closet and undress to get in the bath.

I will never take a bath for granted again, I think to myself as I sink to the bottom of the tub and rest my head on the edge. I lay this for awhile until the water becomes lukewarm. When I open my eyes I become startled by Fraeya's looming presence.

"Fraeya!" I say as I frantically sit up and try to cover my exposed body. "Pardon for the intrusion, but I wanted apologize for my horrendous behavior during dinner." She says apologetically. "Uh, it's fine. I get it." I say, hoping my agreeance would get her to leave. She takes a seat on the edge of the tub, which only makes me more uncomfortable, so I scoot to the back of the tub. "I was very curt, and you have been nothing but nice to me. That is not how one should treat their friend." She tells me.

"Really, it's okay. Could we maybe discuss this in a moment, like when I'm not naked?" I suggest. "Oh don't be so modest. It's not as if you're married." She tells me as she stands up and hands me a towel. "What does that have to do with anything?" I retort as I take the towel from her. "Elves are very sensual in nature. So, we find no shame in showing our true form or pursuing our sexual desires. Once an Elf is married though, they should never expose or engage themselves with anyone, but their partner." She tells me as she doesn't break eye contact with me. I turn my back to her to stand and quickly wrap the towel around me before hiding behind the partition.

"Aside from being hypersexual beings, we are also exceptionally romantic and passionate lovers. And while we may hold multiple lovers during our life, we only claim one mate in our entire lifetime. This is the Elf we share our deepest love with and develop a possessive bond for, hence the reason they are united by matrimony. It is of the highest importance that neither Elf break this bond, otherwise it will corrupt the innocent Elf's spirit and cause them to do awful and vile things. At which point, they will be executed and the guilty one will be stripped of their powers and exiled from Elfspond. Same goes for any Elf who tempts, or shows themselves to a mated Elf." Fraeya finishes saying.

"Um… okay." I say in bewilderment. Where is all this coming from I wonder? "Are you and Elfred mates?" I ask curiously as I now step out dressed in my robe. She purses her lips and crosses her arms, "No." She replies flatly. "It is prohibited for anyone to make advances on the Wise Elf. However, should the Wise Elf make advances on someone, it is an honor that is greatly accepted and not easy to forget." Fraeya adds. I take a hard gulp. Is she trying to hint that I should be eager to jump into bed with Elfred?

"What are you implying?" I ask her directly. "Nothing. I came to apologize and then stumbled upon an educative moment." She tells me. "Uh huh." I say leerily. "I do beg for your forgiveness. I let my temper get the best of me tonight, but it does not resemble how I truly feel. Elfred is quite progressive in his ways, but not all Elves are that way, and I am still struggling to adapt." She tells me sincerely. "I appreciate your apology. I understand it can be hard to share something you deem sacred with someone you find undeserving. So, I do admire you for going out of your comfort zone to help me." I tell her. She gives me a smile and says, "I wish I was as level headed as you." "Now if you'll excuse me. I should be off to bed. I shall see you tomorrow for tea after your lessons." Fraeya tells me. "Alright then. Goodnight." I reply. "Goodnight" she tells me as she does a slight bow and disappears into thin air.

What a strange encounter. I walk over to the balcony and admire the shades of deep purple and magenta that fill the sky. The stars and moons shine brightly over the land. It's still weird to see two moons almost overlapping one another, but mesmerizing at the same time. I decide it's time for bed so I head over to my closet to find some PJs to wear. After a couple minutes of searching I give up and decide to ring for Ariti.

Ariti then appears seconds later. "How may I help you?" She asks. "Um, what I supposed to sleep in?" I ask her. She closes her mouth over her lips to keep from laughing. "Elves are not a modest species. We typically sleep in the nude, as clothes are very constricting. In fact, wearing tight clothes is said to ruin the skin. Which is why we usually wear loose clothing." She informs me. I let out a groan. "Why doesn't this surprise me?" I say rhetorically. "Alright, well thank you Ariti that was all." I say. She gives me curtsey and then disappears.

I walk over to my bed and look around the room to make sure I have no other surprise visitors. Here goes nothing, I think as I quickly take off my robe and slide under the satin sheets of my bed. I then close the curtain of my canopy, and even though it's sheer, it still gives me an added sense of privacy. I let my head fall back onto the pillow and it's only a matter of minutes before I'm out.

*

"Now, without looking at the scroll, tell me what are the conditions of exile." Cicero commands. "Okay, I know these! Breaking a mate bond, persistently not abiding by the laws, taking more than giving, abusing nature and or one's powers, and umm…" I say as I try to remember the last answer. "Being born out of wedlock." Cicero answers. "Right." I say defeatedly, "I guess that one is hard to wrap my mind around. I mean it's not like it's the child's fault." "You are not wrong Aislinn. While it's not the child's fault, it serves as a deterrent, because Elf's should know better than to reproduce with someone other than a mate. Could you imagine if we had a child with every one of our lovers? We would not have enough room or resources in the world." He tells me. Good point, I think. "Yeah, but that's the risk you take. You can't just decide whether you get pregnant or not." I say arguably. Cicero gives me a perplexing look as he rubs his chin. "I am not sure how well versed you are in regards to Elven copulation, but creating a child is indeed a conscious effort between two Elves. When we indulge in our sexual affairs we make the decision to have a child by choosing the nature of our love making. When we are merely fulfilling our needs for sexual gratification, the sex is rough, wild, and intense. Sometimes even a group affair. On the other hand, making love to create a child, is much more passionate and intimate. This is when Elves deepen their bond to the highest extent and the female makes themselves vulnerable for impregnation, allowing the male to choose whether to do so or not." Cicero tells me. "Ah. I see." I say awkwardly before continuing, "But what if an Elf mates with someone other than an Elf? How will they know then?" I ask.

Cicero gives me an appalled look. "Aislinn what you speak of is treason." Cicero states, "which is punishable by death. An Elf is forbidden to mate with anyone but another Elf. We can seek pleasure amongst other species, but for an Elf to mate or have a child with another species is not only treason in Elfspond, but treason across the entire Realm. The last time this occurred was nearly 200 years ago and the deities had not only the Elves, but the child executed as well." He tells me. "That is awful! Why is it such crime?" I say in astonishment. "While most other species are gifted with limited abilities and powers, nature has so graciously gifted Elves with many powers, talents, and abilities. Even though we are not immortal, the deities still consider us a threat. And much like the the story of Ragna and Malakhi, the deities fear that if an Elf reproduces with another species, it may unknowingly create a superior species. That is why we do our best to seclude ourselves from the rest of the Realm and abide by our laws and regulations set forth by the deities. Other species label us as conceited and condescending, but in reality it is our means of self preservation."

Man, today is only my first day of lessons and my head is already spinning. I could really go for a Tylenol right about now, or a coffee. Damn I miss coffee. Cicero, which I've learned, means historian, is my personal tutor. He is 283 and definitely knows a lot of information. So far we have covered, Elven customs and traditions, laws and regulations, and how to identify and address the different Elf classes. There's the Elite, which consists of: the Wise Elf, the members of the Wise Elf Council, including past and present members, the mates and children of any of the above members, and any Elf over 300 years old. Then there's the Supplemental's which is basically like the general community, therefore, the hired hands, guards, bakers, blacksmiths, schoolmasters, and so forth. Lastly, there are the Free Spirits, who are minimalists that are self taught and simply live off what the land provides. They have a stronger affinity for nature and do not like to be constrained by materialistic things or ideals.

"I think you are catching on rather quickly Aislinn." Cicero tells me before adding, "I say we call it a day, but it's important you study these materials to prepare you for tomorrow's lesson." Cicero says as he hands me a large, poorly binded book and a scroll. "You want me to read all of this by tomorrow?" I ask. "It is rather lengthy, but fortunately for you, you do not have to learn the spells in depth. Focus mainly on the names and what the spells do." He tells me. "Spells? What good is it going to do me by knowing spells?" I say. Cicero holds up his hands as to signal a yield, "I advised against it, but Elfred insisted that you should at least be familiar with some basic spells should anyone question you." "Fine." I say defeatedly. "Very well. Good work today. Tomorrow we will go over common spells, appropriate timing and use of magic, how Elfspond came to be, and general knowledge that every Vitalisan should know." Cicero says, emphasizing the last topic. "Sounds good, thanks Cicero." "My pleasure." He says while giving me a bow.

Now that I'm done with my class, I have to go meet Fraeya in the courtyard. I could feel Fraeya was sincere about her apology last night, but I just can't help but still feel indifferent, especially since she just barged in on me while I was naked. I mean who does that?

After passing the same guard twice, I decide to ask for help and the guard escorts me to the courtyard. When I finally arrive, I spot Fraeya sitting at a table with two other women. As I approach the three of them, they seem to be enjoying themselves and laughing about something.

"Oh, Aislinn. Hi!" Fraeya says excitedly once she sees me. "Hi." I say nervously as the other two exchange glances after looking me up and down. "Aislinn, I would like you to meet Sarris." Fraeya says as she motions toward the blonde haired one. "And Rosi." She adds, motioning toward the black haired one. Similar to the other Elves, they have long hair, emerald green eyes, and the signature pointed ears. They both stand and give me a slight curtsy. "Pleasure to make your acquaintance." They say in unison, making them seem all the more identical. If not for their hair, Sarris and Rosi would be indistinguishable, as they are even wearing the same purple silk dress. "Likewise." I say as I give them my best curtsy.

"Please, sit." Sarris tells me as she makes room between her and Fraeya. "So, did you enjoy your lessons?" Fraeya asks me once I take my seat. "It's definitely a lot of information, but yes. I find it all to be very interesting." I reply. "I see he has assigned you to do some additional studying." Fraeya adds as she taps the reading materials Cicero gave me. "Oh, yes. I can't believe he wants me to have all this read by tomorrow." I say. "Well what do you expect? Those are just elementary spells, typically an Elf has those mastered before the age of ten." Rosi says in a slightly condescending manner. "Yes, but be mindful, she only found out she is an Elf a few days ago. She was not raised like us." Sarris says reasonably. "I am aware. I just find it baffling her parents could keep her heritage a secret for so long. It's as if they were destining her for failure." Rosi says. Geez, if this is how she talks about me while I'm here, I can only imagine what she would say behind my back.

"Please forgive my sisters brashness. I think it's lovely that you are finally able to be who you are, but you will definitely face some challenges being so removed." Sarris tells me. "It's alright. I understand that I'm at a disadvantage and I know there are a majority who feel that I don't belong here. I can't say that I don't agree, but I certainly appreciate the opportunity to try and prove myself." I say as politically as I can. Sarris flashes Rosi an impressed look and Rosi just crosses her arm to show her irritation.

"I will say, your misfortune has at least brought some good to Elfspond. I don't think we've had a ball since before the last Wise Elf was executed, so what, nearly two years now? I always looked forward to her annual Eclipse Festival Masquerades." Rosi says snobbishly. "I must agree. I think a ball will bring much joy to Elfspond, especially with all the strife amongst the Realm." Fraeya comments. "I know. This whole talk of Neophere is ridiculous. I mean really, eliminating all of the deities and killing everyone besides the Doulos's and his followers. It's blasphemy!" Sarris says heatedly. I let out a gasp and they all three give me a peculiar look.

Everyone had alluded to Stavros's plan to destroy the Realm of Vitalis and create a New World, that he calls Neophere. I just didn't know what that plan exactly consisted of. He is literally wanting to wipe out the Realm so he can rule a world that consists of only people who would support him.

"Why are you acting so surprised? Did your parents not tell you about Stavros's plans to take over the Realm either?" Rosi says coarsely. "Um, yes, of course they did. We just didn't know of his intentions to keep the Doulos's though." I say trying to play it off. "Oh. Yeah that part was shocking when we first heard it too. Ugh could you imagine, a world with horrible, unlawful misfits and criminals just freely roaming about. I guess he would be doing us a favor by killing us off before he freed them all." Rosi says. "Indeed. It would certainly be a world full of corruption and imbalance. We must pray that the deities are able to keep the remaining two Seekers hidden." Sarris says. Rosi lets out a scoff, "Or we should pray for a quick death. It's only a matter of time before that Earth Seeker gets herself caught." Fraeya flashes me a nervous look. "How do you know it's a girl?" I ask Rosi inconspicuously. "I heard it from one of the Elves out at the pond." Rosi says. "In fact, rumor has it she was last seen in the

Land of the Doulos with that ex-lover of yours Fraeya. What was his name again, the Laskaris one?" Rosi adds. I look at Fraeya, "Oh, really? Small world. Unfortunately I can't seem to recall his name." Fraeya says quite convincingly. "Really? Hmm, you'd think you'd recall the name of the lover that almost lost you the spot on the Wise Council." Rosi says questionably with a smirk on her face. "Or one might try to forget their past mistakes." Fraeya replies civilly. "Nevertheless, I hope they don't try to bring her around here. The last thing we need is Elfspond on Stavros's radar." Rosi says.

"Ladies." I hear Elfred say as he approaches from behind us. Sarris and Rosi quickly rise to their feet to give Elfred a curtsy. Sarris then pulls me to my feet and tells me telepathically, "Aislinn, all Elves not on the Wise Elf Council must properly greet the Wise Elf, it's a means of respect." "Oh. Thank you." I respond graciously. I had no idea, no one else had cared to mention that. "To what do we owe the pleasure of your company Wise Elf?" Rosi says in the most pleasant tone I've heard since meeting her. "I was getting ready to take a stroll and thought I would indulge myself with the company of

Miss Aislinn, if she would so kindly oblige?" Elfred says giving me a bow while offering out his hand. I see shocked look spread across Rosi and Sarris's face.

Anything would be better than staying here to listen to another second of Rosi's negativity and bitterness. "It would be an honor." I reply as I place my hand in his. Elfred kisses the top of my hand and then puts his arm out for me. "What should I do with these?" I ask as I motion to the book and scrolls. Elfred waves his hand over them causing them to vanish. "They'll be in your room waiting." He says. I give him a playful smile and then loop my arm around his. With his guards in tow, he then escorts me to what seems to be a garden.

"How was your first lesson?" He asks me. "It wasn't too bad. It's just a lot of information." I tell him. "Yes, yes it is. It's a lot to process in a short amount of time for anyone, but don't be discouraged. You can do this." He tells me encouragingly. "But to go over spells that you know I can't do. Do you really think someone might question me over a spell?" I ask. "The odds are low, but a member of the council may do so to see if you are actually taking this seriously." He tells me. "Very well." I sigh. "And what do think of Sarris and Rosi?" He asks me. I hesitate to respond, because I'm not sure who they are to Elfred and I don't want to offend him.

Elfred gives a chuckle as he looks over at me. "I assure you that you can speak freely around me Aislinn." "Well, Sarris seems friendly and pleasant, but Rosi is rudely forward and unpleasant." I admit. "That is unfortunately, no surprise. Sarris is definitely the more tolerable sister." He tells me. "Are they your sisters?" I ask. "Heavens no, I do not have any siblings. They are the daughters of Calix, my Elf Guard Commander." Elfred says. "Who also holds a spot on the Wise Elf Council." I say proudly. "Very good. I see Cicero is teaching you well." He tells me happily. "I just don't understand how Sarris can be so nice and Rosi, well, not so much." I say inquisitively. "Rosi actually use to be quite pleasant. But after Fraeya was chosen for the spot on the Wise Elf Council over Rosi, she turned hateful." Elfred answers. Now it makes sense as to why she was so cold to Fraeya as well. "Then why would they even hang out if they don't like each other?" I ask.

"That's exactly what I hoped you would ask." Elfred says before continuing, "Elves are a proud species. We do not take defeat easily, but we still recognize that we are all still on the same side. So even though Fraeya and Rosi have their differences, they also understand how vital it is to set their differences aside so they can share or express their knowledge, ideas, or information." Elfred tells me. "Yeah, but if you make friends, you can just do that with people you actually enjoy talking to." I say. "True, but those we enjoy talking to, tend to be likeminded with us. Which is not a bad thing, but likeminded people do not challenge one another and to challenge one another, is to educate one another." Elfred says wisely. "So you're saying that by talking to people we don't always agree or get along with, we may actually learn things from them?" "Exactly!" He tells me enthusiastically. "I guess that makes sense. After all, Rosi did tell us she heard from someone at the pond that, that Seeker from Earth was last seen in Doulos with the Laskaris Fraeya was fond of." I tell him. "Is that so?" Elfred says. I nod my head.

"My oh my. Seems I need to make trip to the pond, so I can gather valuable information every once in awhile." He says. "The pond certainly looks intriguing, does it have any special powers?" I ask dumbly. "Not that we can establish, but it is said that the first Elfs emerged from the pond and so essentially it is thought to be the source of our Elvenhood." "Wow, that's fascinating." I reply. "Would you like to go see it?" Elfred asks me. My face fills with excitement, but then my smile quickly fades. "I wish, but I have a lot of studying to do before tomorrow." I tell him. He taps his chin, "How about instead of reading through the spells, I just go over them with you." He suggests. I pause as I ponder his offer. "Hm. Well what better way to learn than from the Wise Elf himself." I say agreeably. Elfred gives me a bright smile, "My thoughts exactly." He says. "Fetch us our horses." Elfred tells the nearest guard.

As we make our way to the pond I can't help but feel the eyes of every Elf that we pass on me. It's apparent when we make it to the pond that it is used as a social gathering place and a swimming hole. I do my best to keep my eyes to myself as many Elves appear nude, as it's apparent their method of swimming is that of skinny dipping. Each Elf respectfully gives Elfred a curtsy when we pass by and they watch us timidly as we make our way own secluded spot in the clearing.

"Why are they all staring?" I ask as we unmount our horses. "Well, for one, it's not typical of the Wise Elf to visit the pond. And two, I'm sure they have all heard about the estranged Elf trying to reclaim her Elvenhood." I suddenly start to feel self conscious at the realization that everyone here probably despises me. "Oh. Right." I say nervously. "So, why is it so strange for the Wise Elf to come to the pond?" I ask. Elfred looks around the vicinity and lets out a chuckle. "Well, if you haven't noticed, the pond has turned into quite the risqué gathering place. The pond is like an aphrodisiac, our sensuality is greatly heightened when we are around it." Elfred says as he twirls a strand of my hair. I quickly turn away so he can't see me blush.

I look out toward the pond and stare in awe as it's emerald greenness shimmers in the sun. It appears translucent, as I see many fish swimming about, yet I can't see the bottom.

"Care to join us Wise Elf?" An Elf flirtatiously asks, as her and her two friends stand in the nude by the edge of the pond. "Perhaps in a moment." Elfred replies sounding hopeful. The three of them exchange giggles before diving into the pond.

"What do you say? Care to take a swim with me?" Elfred asks. I look nervously at him and then back at the pond. "I...I don't know Elfred." I say as I sheepishly wrap my arms around my body, afraid that my clothes might disappear. "I think I'll have to pass." I tell him. Elfred takes off his shirt and I can't help but notice how lean, but chiseled he is. Elfred then takes off his pants and my eyes grow wide as I quickly look up at the sky. I can feel my face turn red as I try to avoid looking at him. "Suit yourself my Dove, I won't be long." He tells me before walking over to the pond and diving in.

I stand by the horses awkwardly and watch as a a group of Elves quickly gather around Elfred. A chorus of giggles and excited chatter soon fill the air. I'd be lying if I said I didn't feel slightly jealous as I watch some of the female Elves practically cling to Elfred. After a few minutes pass, Elfred sets his eyes on me.

"Aislinn. Do you mind bringing me my clothes?" He shouts. I give a feeble nod as I pick his clothes up off the ground and make my way over to the edge of the pond. I look away as I hold his clothes out to him, but then I feel his wet hand wrap around my wrist as he pulls me into the pond. When I make it up to the surface I take a gasp of air.

"Elfred!" I shout in disbelief. A couple of Elves gasp as I refer to Elfred by his name instead of addressing him by his title. Elfred just lets out a chuckle as he grabs my hand and leads us away from the rest of the Elves. "I can't believe you did that." I say in shock. "What? I couldn't let you miss all the fun just because you are afraid to show your true form. At least this way you have an excuse to be swimming with clothes on." He tells me. I give him a stern look, even though it was considerate of him to respect my modesty. "Well excuse me for having standards. Where I come from, it's important to earn another's love and trust before showing them your true form." I say mockingly. Elfred swims up close to me. "And what is it that I can do to earn your love and trust?" He asks in a seductive murmur.

Between his naked proximity and his tantalizing words, I can't help but feel nervously aroused and I take a hard swallow. After a moment of silence he creates some space between him and I. "Don't fret my Dove. I would never want you to feel pressured. Your affection should be natural and self willed." He tells me. "Yes, I agree." I tell him.

"Ready to learn some spells?" He asks me as a means of changing the subject. I give him an excited nod. He goes to get out of the pond and I follow behind him. As we get out of the water we both try to wring out our soaked clothes the best we can. "See what you did?" I tell him teasingly. He gives me playful smirk as he walks over to me.

With his hair dripping wet and his clothes clinging to his body, he stares intently at me. I hold my breath as he looks me up and down and I immediately wonder how transparent this flimsy dress is. He stops mere inches from me and twirls his index finger between us while he murmurs the words *dynatós ánemos*. A strong wind suddenly encircles us from head to toe and I have to hold down the skirt of my dress so it doesn't blow up. I can't help but let out a thrill filled giggle as the wind fiercely blows our hair around.

Elfred gives a smile as I try to stop laughing. Once the wind dissipates, we now find ourselves dry.

"Is that better?" Elfred asks me. "Much better." I say as I try to smooth out my hair. "Consider that your first spell. It means strong wind." He tells me. "And you direct it by your hand motions?" I ask curiously. "Precisely." He tells me proudly.

We make our way to a nearby weeping willow and take our place under it. We spend the next few hours getting to know one another and going over many different spells. It's not until the sun starts to set that we realize we should probably head back to the castle. I hate to admit it, but today has made me see Elfred in a new light and I shamefully come to the realization that I am developing a crush on him.

"Today was the most fun I've had in over a century." Elfred tells me as he helps me off of Lila. "Well, I must admit, I really enjoyed myself today too. Thank you." I tell him. He gives me his charming smile. "Would you like to accompany me for lunch after your lesson tomorrow?" Elfred asks. "I'd be delighted." I reply.

"Elfred! Where have you been?" Fraeya shrieks as she enters the stables. With his back to her he rolls his eyes dramatically and I can't help but let out a giggle. "Aislinn and I took a trip to the pond." Elfred tells her calmly. "The pond!" She reiterates disgustedly. "Elfred, may I remind you that you are the Wise Elf and as your Advisor, I encourage you to find less racy ways to spend your time." She says superiorly. "Fraeya, your counsel is always welcomed, but I assure you, it was merely an afternoon. It may do you some good to take a trip down there yourself to loosen up a bit." I can see Fraeya bite her tongue. "Yes Wise Elf. I'm glad you at least made it back safely." She says flatly before swiftly walking off.

Elfred turns back to me and raises his eyebrows. "Sorry for getting you in trouble." I say. "I may have to reconsider spending my time with you Aislinn. I am afraid you might corrupt me with your scandalous ways." Elfred says teasingly. We both erupt with laughter. "So I'll see you tomorrow?" I ask him. "I'll be counting the seconds my Dove." He says and then gives my hand a kiss before vanishing.

I walk back to my room in a lovestruck daze as I replay the events of today. Today was the first day since before my birthday that I haven't been stressed and consumed with fear. Elfred has a way of making me feel special and secure. When I arrive to my room, I find Ella waiting for me.

"Aislinn!" She says cheerily as flies over to me. "Ella hi!" I reply. "How are you settling in?" She asks me. "Oh it's been great for the most part. I've found out that not everyone is happy that I am here, but Elfred has made sure that I feel welcomed." I tell her. "Unfortunately not everyone sees the advantages to having you here, but they will come to realize it, it's just important that you feel comfortable staying here." She replies. "Why do you have a book of spells though?" She adds curiously. "Oh, you didn't hear? Apparently since they think I'm an estranged Elf, the Wise Elf Council is only willing to let me stay in Elfspond if I can convince them to let me reclaim my Elvenhood." I tell her. She covers her mouth with her hand. "Oh my. This is quite serious, I wonder if Diona is aware." Ella says. "I have no idea, but I started lessons with Cicero today and now I only have four more days until the ball that they are throwing in my honor, so I can prove myself to them." I say stressfully as all the worry starts to creep back into my thoughts. Ella furrows her brows. "This is certainly a predicament." She says. "And to make matters worse, I think Fraeya hates me now or is jealous that Elfred is paying me so much attention." I say.

I spend the next little bit catching Ella up on what she has missed. Everything from Fraeya walking in on me in the tub, to mine and Elfred's getaway to the pond today. "What do you think?" I ask her. "It definitely seems as if she might be jealous of Elfred's obvious affections toward you." She tells me. "Right? I mean why else would she give me some spiel about lovers and mates. I mean how the heck am I even supposed to tell if an Elf is mated?" I rant. "Oh that's easy. Any Elf with colored hair is mated." Ella answers. "Wait, so all the Elves with blonde hair do not have a mate?" I clarify. "That is correct." "Gosh, that's like majority of them." I state. Ella gives a chuckle, "Most Elves don't mate until way later in their lives. Since they have a long lifespan, they typically seek lovers for the first half of their lives before settling down with a mate." While it makes sense, I can't help but cringe at the thought. I wonder how many lovers Elfred has had in his 172 years. "I see." I reply.

"And what of Jace?" Ella asks. Her question causes a hard lump to form in my throat as the guilt starts to brew. "I'm not sure. I haven't been able to see him since we arrived. Elfred says our imprint emits too much magic and that we shouldn't be within 100 yards of each other." I say sadly. "I'm so sorry Aislinn. Do you know where they are keeping him? I can pass along a message to him if you'd like?" She tells me. Prior to this moment, I hadn't even thought about Jace since we spoke about him in Elfred's office. "That would be lovely, but I don't have a clue." I say shamefully. "Don't worry. You have had a lot on your plate. I'll do some investigating and see if I can find him." She says. I give her a smile, "You are great friend." I tell her.

Chapter 11

The next four days fly by quickly, as my time was consumed with lessons by Cicero and quality time with Elfred. The more time I spend with Elfred, the more smitten I could feel myself becoming with him. However, today is the day of the ball and I am a nervous wreck. My head is spinning with all the information I've received over the last five days, but Elfred has asked me to meet him in the great hall for one last lesson.

"You requested my presence Wise Elf?" I say mockingly as I give Elfred a proper curtsy upon entering the great hall. He gives me an alluring smirk. "Why yes my Dove. I realized we have practiced everything, but our customary dance." He says. "Well then, by all means." I reply as I hold out my hand. He cues the harpist to start the melody as he takes my hand and holds it up and puts our palms together. We start by walking in a clockwise circle three times and then he gently pulls me towards him. His one hand grasps mine while his other hand finds it place on the midst of my back. I let him lead as he guides me forward, then backward as he softly pushes me away from him before spinning me. He stops me swiftly and then tilts me back as he sways me from one side to the other before bringing me back upright. He then swiftly spins me around so that my back is to his front as he sensually runs his fingers from neck down to my navel. He then pushes me away and twirls me once before pulling me back into him, face to face. He stares intently at me and I can see his eyes full of desire. My body betrays me as I start to melt in his arms and I can only hope that the dance is almost over, because I don't think I control myself for much longer.

Once we make it back to the center of the floor, the melody stops and so do we. Neither one of us move for a moment as Elfred stands there holding me in his arms. When I finally snap out of it, I gently break away and give Elfred a polite smile. "Do you think you can remember that?" Elfred asks me. "I don't think I could ever forget it." I tell him. Elfred smiles. "I've been meaning to ask you," Elfred says before continuing, "could I do the honors of being your escort for the ball tonight?" "I would like that very much." I reply with a smile. "Wonderful. I can't wait until tonight." He says.

As I make my way back to my room, I take the path through the courtyard. Just before turning to renter the castle, I hear a familiar voice. When I round the corner and see him, I can't help but shout, "Xander!" Xander quickly snaps his head in my direction. He gives me the biggest heart warming smile I've seen from him. I can't control myself as I pick up my dress and run to him.

When I reach him, I throw my arms around him and give him a big hug. I can feel his strong arms wrap around me as he reciprocates the hug. I get a wave of relief and a wholesome feeling and I'm not sure if it's my feelings or his, but I enjoy the feeling nonetheless. "I'm so glad you're okay, I was worried something happened to you." I tell him. "Who, me? Have you already forgotten who I am?" He says boastfully. I roll my eyes as I give a slight chuckle, "No mister tough guy, I'm just wondering why you didn't come sooner?" I tell him. "After you left, the warriors searched the entire premise and then started to interrogate us. As you know, I cannot lie so things ended up getting a bit messy. We then fled and had to lay low for a couple days. Diona parted ways once it was clear and despite wanting to get to you to as fast as I could, I didn't want to risk someone following me and tracking me here." Xander tells me. My mind quickly flashes back to the figure in the woods that we encountered. Should I tell Xander about it?

"Have they been treating you well?" Xander asks, interrupting my thoughts. "Yes, for the most part everyone here has been great. There are some Elves unhappy that I'm here. But, that could be because the Wise Elf Council is considering letting me reclaim my *Elvenhood*." I say cautiously. "What?" Xander says ferociously. "It's the only way they will let me stay." I whisper. "This is ludicrous." Xander says as he runs his hand through his hair. "And how exactly do they expect you to do that?" He asks in bewilderment. "There's a ball tonight in my honor. All the Elites will be here and they will come to a conclusion based on my performance." I reply. "This was not part of the plan. I need to speak to Elfred immediately." Xander says. "It's not his fault. There's not anything he can do, the Wise Elf Council demanded it." I say defensively. "Aislinn, you are not one of them." He hisses. I give him a scowl. "So that's it then? You are just angry because you don't want me to be classified as an Elf. Would that really be the worst thing?" I reply distraughtly. "I loved an Elf once, I promised myself I wouldn't do it again." He says softly and then turns to walk away.

What is that supposed to mean? I think to myself. "Xander wait!" I say as I catch up to him. "Where are you going?" I ask breathlessly. "I'm leaving." He says flatly. "But you just got here." "Yes, and now that I see you are alive and well, I can return to Valstead with peace of mind." "No. Please stay, you can come to the ball tonight." I plead. Xander remains silent as he avoids my eye contact. "I need you here. I can't do this without you." I tell him. "You know I can't support this." He says as he pushes past me. I feel tears start to swell in my eyes as I watch him briskly walk away.

As I make my way back to my room, my sadness slowly transitions to anger. Whatever, I don't need him. I think to myself. Who does he think he is anyway? He thinks Elves are condescending, but look at how he acts. I aggressively shove the spell book and scrolls off my bed and then fall into my bed face first and let out a scream. My breakdown can't just be credited to my argument with Xander though, I know the pent up stress is fueling it as well. I quickly get up and pick up the mess I made.

I look at the pages the spell book fell open to. Hmph, I wish I could just, "Fotiá" I say angrily as I flick my fingers. I'm instantly startled when a fire to my partition sparks. I look at my hand and then look at my burning partition. Was that me? Did I just cast a fire spell? I frantically look around, unsure of what to do. I quickly flip through the pages as I try to find the spell for water to put my theory to the test. "Neró!" I say as I aim my hand at the fire. I'm equally frightened and relieved when water is casted unto the fire, extinguishing it. Holy shit. I stare at my hands as if I've never seen them before. I can't believe I just cast a spell, two spells actually. What could this mean? I know I should be getting ready, but I have to tell Elfred immediately.

I quickly make my way down the staircase and scurry down the halls, searching for Elfred.

"Have you seen Elfred? I have to speak to him immediately." I say to one of the guards. "Last I heard he was in the council chamber. The Wise Elf Council called a last minute meeting and I'm sorry, but anyone not on the council is forbidden from entering." The guard tells me. "Ugh, of course." I say frustratingly. As I storm off, I pass by his office and come to a halt. I peer inside and decide I can just wait for him here. I take this time to look around. As I glance over the bookshelf, I take account of the different books it holds. Elven history, Realm history, Elven Law, Realm Law, Accounts of the deities, multiple spell books and then all alone locked in a case is an old black book with the word Diablerie inscribed on the front of it. I become entranced by it and put my hand on the glass case. When I do so, I'm pulled into a vision.

I see two Elves and two non-Elves that I haven't seen before. They seem distressed. "We must lock it up, to prevent a being from possessing such dark magic once more." One of the Elves says. "Or we could just destroy the book, so we don't have to worry about it ever again." One of the non-elves retaliates. "We've tried. But the dark magic is too strong. Whoever binded the book put a protection spell that far exceeds our abilities. Even Vasilios could not break it." The other three let out a gasp. "Then we can only pray that another being as evil as Kyrillos does not arise." One of the non-Elves says. "Agreed, but on his death bed, Vasilios told me that the four of us together, could cast a strong enough spell to enchant the book for safekeeping. It can only be undone by saying the spell in reverse, so it is vital we tell no one of the spell. The secret shall die with us." The other three all nod in unison. The other Elf then places the black book on the pedestal in front of them and puts the glass case over it. The Elf who seems to be the leader, takes a knife and makes a cut to his palm, he then places his bloody palm to the glass case. The other three then copy him. "Repeat after me." The head Elf says before continuing, "Take this evil and confine it to this prison, may those unbeknownst of the enchantment access the powers guarded by this incantation."

I am suddenly brought back to reality and the case gives off a forceful push causing me to stumble backwards. I have to steady myself and catch my breath because the flashback drained me. Today is just getting weirder and weirder, I think to myself. I then hear Elfred's voice approaching his office.

"Danae if you must persist on discussing this, then at least come into the privacy of my office. The whole castle should not hear our quarrel." Elfred says angrily. Shit. I look around for somewhere to hide. I quickly duck under his desk and hope that he doesn't decide to sit at it.

"Leave us." Elfred says sternly as I hear him enter the office. I then hear the doors shut and the sounds of footsteps approaching the desk. I can feel my heart thudding in my throat. "You and I both know she does not deserve Elvenhood. No matter what she does tonight or tries to prove, she will never be one of us." I hear an unfamiliar female voice say. "You have not even met her Danae. Are you so simple minded that you have cutoff your voice of reason just because she was not raised as one of us?" Elfred says. "How dare you insult my intelligence and judgement. I am a member of the Wise Elf Council which means what I say should carry some weight." Danae says. "And I am the Wise Elf which should demand your respect." Elfred's voice booms, causing my body to stiffen. "Undoubtedly, but it is the Wise Elf Council who will determine if Aislinn can stay and I can assure you that you don't have the council's support on this matter. She may visit freely, but she will never be considered an Elf or allowed in the castle walls come tomorrow." Danae retorts.

I can feel the tears start to swell in my eyes. I never even had a chance. Now what am I going to do? Who is going to protect me now?

"Unless," Elfred states mischievously. "Unless what?" Danae retorts bitterly. "I marry her." Elfred replies. My eyes widen at his remark. "You can't be serious!" Danae exclaims. "Oh, but I am. The council would not be able to deny her Elvenhood then and the people would be forced to accept her." Elfred says. "This is preposterous! I hope she isn't so naive to accept an engagement for the sake of getting to call herself an Elf." Danae says. "Ah, but you forget how susceptible beings are to Elven charm. I have spent my time ensuring that Aislinn develops feelings for me, so that my proposal tonight does not seem unwarranted. We seem to be building quite the bond." Elfred says. "You are only 172 years old, would you be so foolish to marry now with so much of your life left? Besides, she just reached the Age of Revelation, are you that selfish to deprive her of life's experiences?" Danae states. "What? It would be a win-win for both of us. She will get her Elvenhood and I would get a pure mate." Elfred tells her. "Well, I guess you have it all figured out then. I urge you to reconsider your plan." Is all Danae says.

I can feel the anger boiling inside of me. How could I be such an idiot? I should've known he was using his charm to make me fall for him. All so he could convince me to marry him. For what? A pure mate. Is he referring to the fact I'm a virgin, but how does he even know? I listen as a single set of footsteps leave the room. I can't take it anymore, I spring out from under the desk and take Elfred by surprise.

"Aislinn what are doing in here?" Elfred says shockingly. "How dare you!" I exclaim. "My office is for private matters. You should not be in here unaccompanied." He tells me sternly. "Don't try to overlook the fact that you have been playing me for a fool." I tell him furiously. "Aislinn, you have to understand, I was just acting so that way she wouldn't become suspicious." Elfred says. "Right. Kind of how you have been pretending to have feelings for me?" I question. "You must believe me. My feelings for you are not an act Aislinn." "Oh well of course, because you want me as your, how did you say it, *pure mate.*" I reply. Elfred's jaw clenches as he remains silent. "So primitive. You knew what you were doing all along and it was selfish. You weren't even going to tell me, so that way I would feel pressured to say yes in front of the council." I say with distaste. "Aren't engagements meant to be a surprise? Besides, it's not like my feelings for you are untrue. Is it such a bad thing that

I want to marry you?" He tells me arguably. "It is when you try to trick me into marrying you. I thought you said you wanted my affections for you to be true, yet you have been using your charm on me this whole time." I reply. "That part was a lie. I have not used my charm on you one time. As badly as I want to marry you, I would never force you into it and have you not truly love me. That is not my idea of a good marriage." Elfred says.

I can't tell if my frustrations are with Elfred or myself. If what he's saying is true then I did fall for Elfred on my own, but why am I so mad that he planned on proposing to me. I start to feel that gnawing feeling in my stomach and then it hits me. Jace, Jace is my soulmate and here I've been gallivanting about the castle flirting with the Wise Elf while he is stuck who knows where.

"But you know I am imprinted with Jace. My heart belongs to him." I say. "He is a Doulos. You will not be able to marry or have children with him. What kind of future do you think you two will really have?" Elfred says. The supposed truth behind his words only make me angrier. "And what future do you think we would have? The deities know the truth about me, if we were to marry it would be treason and if we were to have a child, we would both be executed." I say. "Then we don't have to have a child. Our love can make us happy enough." Elfred says almost pleadingly. "There's no denying that I am attracted to you. You have been nothing but nice and affectionate towards me, but I do not love you Elfred." I tell him. I see can the heartbreak spread across his face as my words cut through him like knives. "I care about you a lot, but I cannot marry you." I tell him. The hurt in Elfred's eyes quickly turn to anger. "Get out." Elfred mutters. I have never seen him this upset before and it hurts me to see him this way. "Elfred…" I say as I try to reach out for him. He pulls himself away from me and I think I see tears forming in his eyes. "I said, get out!" Elfred shouts and the doors to his office fly open. He's angry and I'm not even sure what he is capable of, so I decide not to push it.

I quickly make my escape and head back to my room. As I make my way back to my room I realize I'm still holding the spell book. Ugh, I totally forgot to even tell him that I can perform spells. I guess I will just have to wait till tonight. If he will even talk to me that is, but he will have to. He's my escort after all. When I make it back to my room, I see Ariti waiting for me.

"There you are. I've been looking all over for you. We don't have much time to get you ready now." Ariti tells me. "Sorry, I was fighting with Elfred and lost track of time." I say sullenly as I toss the spell book on my bed. "Well once we get you dressed up and looking irresistible, then he will regret ever fighting with you." She says. I give her a warm smile. "Good idea." I reply.

Ariti excitedly retrieves my dress that her and another handmaid have been diligently working on over the last couple of days. "What do you think?" She asks as she holds it out. I admire the one shoulder long sleeve, floor length chiffon emerald green dress. "Wow. It's beautiful! You made this?" I reply. "With some help, yes." She tells me proudly, "Now, let's put it on, I've been waiting all day to see you in it!" I slip on the dress and the one sleeve loosely covers my right arm while the body of the dress slightly hugs me from the waist up and the skirt simply flows down to the ground. Ariti then pulls out a golden braided rope and ties it around my waist. She then steps back and looks me over.

"You look absolutely divine." She tells. "All we have left is your hair." She ushers me to sit as she begins brushing out my hair. "Now for the last piece." She tells me as she pulls out a golden halo with white flowers entwined and carefully places it on my head. "I can't believe you did all this for me. Thank you so much Ariti." She blushes. "It is my greatest pleasure. Let it serve as my way of saying thanks for being so kind to me." She tells me. I give her a big hug. When we pull away she taps her chin curiously. "What is it?" I inquire. "Wait here. I will be back in just a moment." I give her a nod.

She disappears into thin air and a minute later she reappears with two glass jars. "I think you look beautiful just as you are, but how about we really give them something to look at." She says with a mischievous smile. I give her a smirk, "Let's do it." I say. She opens one jar and I see a pink blob. "What is that?" I ask. "It's a special paste to make your lips colorful." "Ah. Okay." I say as I dip my finger in and apply it to my lips. As I rub it in, my lips turn a darker shade of pink. Just like lipstick, I think to myself. "And this, is fairy dust." She says excitedly as she opens the second jar. She holds the jar of a shimmering powder out to me. "What's it for?" I ask dumbly. "May I?" She asks. I give her a nod of approval and she scoops out some of the powder. "Close your eyes." I do as she says and she swipes her finger over my eyelids and wings it out. She then applies a thin layer under my eyes as well. I look in the mirror and have to admit I certainly look very enticing. The fairy dust makes it look as if I am glowing and I can't help but feel like a goddess. "I've never felt so beautiful." I tell Ariti gratefully. She gives me a warm smile. "These materials only accentuate the beauty you already hold." I give her another hug. "Thank you." I tell her. "Now let's get you to ballroom." She tells me.

Ariti accompanies me to the staircase outside the entrance to the ballroom. "Will I see you down there?" I ask her. "Yes. I have to change into my formal wear first, but I will be along the North wall with the other handmaids should you need me for anything." She tells me. "And how will I know when to enter?" I say nervously. She gives a soft chuckle, "The Wise Elf should be meeting you shortly to escort you, but you will enter when the Master of Ceremonies announces your name for your grand entrance." Ariti says. I give a nervous gulp. "Right. Got it." I say.

After Ariti vanishes, I start to anxiously pace the hallway. It'll be okay, I try reassure myself. At least I'm not wearing heels, but I could still trip though, the dress does have a small trail. I shake my head to get the anxious thoughts out of my head. That's not going to happen I tell myself. I need to be focusing on what I am going to say to the council. "Hello I am Aislinn." I say out loud as I give a curtsy. No, that's too simple. "It is an honor to meet each of you. My name is Aislinn Somerfield and I greatly appreciate your consideration." I practice out loud again. Hmm, that could possibly work. I feel my palms become sweaty. I take a deep breathe and let out a long exhale. I look out the window and see that the sun is now practically set, which means I should be announced any minute now. Where the hell is Elfred?

"Aislinn." I hear Ariti say. I whip around and see a worried look on Ariti's face. "Ariti, what is it?" I ask. "Elfred is already in the ballroom." "What?" I ask bewildered. "Is he going to meet me on the stairs?" I ask. She gives me a skittish look and shakes her head no. "He's supposed to be my escort though." I say. "I'm sorry, but it appears that's not the case anymore." She tells me sadly. Great, it's apparent I pissed him off to the point, that this is his way of retaliating. "Whatever, all I'm doing is walking down some stairs anyway. I don't need him." I say trying to pep myself up. Ariti gives me another concerned look. "Is something wrong?" I ask her. "It's just that… by not having an escort it means you are not spoken for." She tells me sheepishly. "And what does that mean?" "Any female without a mate must have an escort to signify that her integrity and honor are spoken for. Otherwise, it means that no one is vouching for you, signifying that you are scandalous and dishonorable." She explains. I can feel the tears start to form in my eyes. This is humiliating. "Wait, can you escort me?" I say desperately. Ariti gives me a frown. "Unfortunately this is an audience of Elites and the Wise Elf Council, so you would need an escort that holds esteem."

"Good evening everyone!" I hear an energetic male voice on the other side of the door say. "I must go, it's time." Ariti says. "No please, don't leave me." I plead. "I am so sorry Aislinn, but I must before they notice I'm gone, I only came up to warn you." She then vanishes. Great, I think I'm going to be sick. I hadn't been paying attention to anything else the voice was saying, but once the double doors open I know it's my cue. I stand up straight and hold my head up high. Elfred can embarrass me all he wants, but I'll be damned if I let it show.

"The guest of honor, Aislinn Somerfield and... erm." The announcer trails off when he realizes I'm without an escort. I step forward to the top of the stairs and when I do so, I feel an arm interlock with mine. I look to my left and I feel like my heart might just burst. "And Xander Laskaris. Captain of the Realms Guard." Xander tells the announcer. "And her escort Xander Laskaris, Captain of the Realms Guard." The Master of Ceremonies announces.

"You have no idea how happy I am to see you." I whisper to Xander. "I can't believe he was actually going to let you present without an escort." He tells me as he guides me down the stairs. We both give the crowd a fake pleasant smile. Some return the smile while others give a scowl instead. "So you heard?" I say. "Heard what?" Xander inquires. Whoops, guess he doesn't know about Elfred's intentions to propose. "Never mind. I'll tell you in private." I whisper. Xander gives me a nod.

As we reach the end of the staircase, many people start to crowd around us. Multiple Elves approach me to introduce themselves. So many that I don't think I will be able to remember all of their names. As we make our way through the crowd I happen to make eye contact with Elfred briefly before he shamefully looks away. "I don't think I can do this." I tell Xander as we get closer to the group of the Wise Elf Council. "Yes you can and I will be right here with you." He tells me as he gives me a reassuring smile. I can't help but smile back.

As we approach the Wise Elf Council I try to speak but freeze, causing the five of them to just stare at me. Xander gives a slight bow and I quickly follow suit by giving a proper curtsy. "It is a great honor to meet you Wise Elf Council." I say. "My name is Aislinn Somerfield and I greatly appreciate your hospitality and consideration." I add. Fraeya and one of the male Elves gives me a polite nod. "It's a pleasure to meet you Aislinn. My name is Calix, Elf Guard Commander." He says. Xander then brings his fist to his heart and taps it twice. Calix does the same in return. Making me assume it must be some soldier thing. I give a slight bow to acknowledge is greeting. "Wow. You look lovely Fraeya." I say hoping she will spare me from any more awkward silence. She gives a tight smile. "You are too kind. Thank you." She says as her eyes longingly fall on Xander.

Elfred then approaches us and he won't take his eyes off of me. "What have I missed?" Elfred says trying to break the silence. I can feel Xander tense up as he tries to hold back his aggravation. "Wise Elf." I say as I give another curtsy to acknowledge his presence. "We were just going over introductions." I reply. Which prompts the next Elf to step forward. "And I am Melanie, Advisor to the Realm." She tells me followed by a polite smile. I give her a nod. And look at the man next to her, prompting him to step forward. "Gannon. The Regional Advisor." He says with a slight bow. Lastly, I look at the lady standing next to Fraeya.

She purses her lips as she looks me up and down. "And I am Danae, the magistrate of Elfspond." So she's the one Elfred was talking to earlier.

"It is a pleasure to meet all of you." I say as I give them all a bright smile. Danae then steps closely to me as she peers into my eyes. "I wish we could say the same." She tells me. "That is enough Danae." Elfred says sternly. Danae flicks back my hair revealing one of my ears. "This has to be a joke, she doesn't even have Elven ears. She would be nothing but a disgrace to the Elven name." She sputters. Xander stands in front of me and gives her an intimidating look, causing her to take a step back. I can feel a hard lump in my throat form as I hold back tears. I've never been so embarrassed in my life. "You will hold your tongue Danae or I shall have you removed." Elfred says. "You wouldn't dare." She hisses. "Try me." Elfred says.

I can't stand listening to the hostile exchange. I quickly make my escape from all of them as I shove my way through the crowd. Doing so I bump into multiple people causing me to channel their feelings. I start to take on feelings of disgust, lust, anxiety, and joy. I clutch my head as I become over stimulated. All my bottled frustration finally erupts. "Na stamatísei!" I scream the spell *to stop*, at the top of my lungs as I begin to cry. As I'am wiping away my tears, I notice that everything around me has gone silent. I look around and see that everyone is frozen in place. I wave my hand in front of the Elf next to me. She doesn't move a muscle. "Hello." I say but it just echoes throughout the ballroom.

I quickly make my way back over to where I left Xander, Elfred, and the Wise Elf Council. I scowl at Danae and as nice as it would be to get a free slap, or two, in on Danae, I won't let her ugliness transgress onto me. I look at Elfred and he has his finger in her face and I can see the anger in his eyes. Even though he is angry, he still portrays a sense of appeal that I have grown attracted to. Despite our fight today, he was still quick to defend me and I hate to admit it, but I actually feel guilty. Elfred had developed strong feelings for me too, so much so that he actually wanted to mate with me and then I basically rejected his feelings. I can't imagine how hurt he must have felt. At the same time though, he left me without an escort and was willing to let me be publicly disgraced.

That is, if Xander didn't show up. I turn to face Xander and this is my first time taking account of his appearance tonight. He's not in his typical Laskaris uniform. Instead, he is dressed in a red and gold royal jacket, with brown tights that fit him nicely, red and gold leather boots that are accompanied by a gold sheath suspended from his belt, holding one of his swords. His blonde hair is slicked over and his stubble is slightly longer, but still not enough to call it a beard. I can see the distraught on his face from realizing that I'm no longer behind him. I reach out to touch his face, but quickly retract my hand. I shouldn't be touching someone without them knowing, that's just weird and wrong. He definitely came to my rescue tonight and my heart flutters at thought of his heroic and genuine gesture. I think it has made me realize that I do have some unspoken feelings for Xander that I have refused to admit until now. It probably doesn't help that Xander is exceptionally attractive. Why the hell are most of the guys here so damn attractive anyway? Maybe Elfred was right, if I'm able to fall for other guys maybe I'm not that in love with Jace after all.

I shake my head. No, he's wrong. I know how I feel about Jace, and nothing will change that. Great, and now that I'm thinking about him, I can't get Jace out of my head. I feel guilty for the way I have allowed my feelings to be so easily captivated and manipulated by others, when I already know Jace is my soul mate. He would be crushed if he knew the feelings I've shared toward these other men, cause I would be if the roles were reversed. I clench my chest as I get a sharp pain in my heart and it brings me to my knees. "Ow!" I cry out in pain. Simultaneously, everything and everyone around me comes back to life. The guest look around confused while Elfred, Xander, and the Wise Elf Council stare at me in shock.

"Aislinn are you okay?" Xander says as he kneels down to help me. "Don't touch me." I say frantically as I rise to my feet. "Did you just…" Elfred starts to ask, but cuts himself off when he realizes how is question will seem to the Council. "Her powers are strong." Melanie mutters in awe. Calix nods in agreement. "How dare you try and sway our judgement by showing out your powers." Danae says. "No, it's not like that. I…I just couldn't stand the fighting. I'm sorry." I sputter. "Danae you know good and well, the average Elf can't even cast that spell on such a large scale." Gannon says reasonably. Danae sneers at me. "I think it would be in our best interest if Aislinn claims Elvenhood. Her powers are strong and could make a powerful addition to the Elvenhood. Especially during these trying times." Melanie states. "Agreed." Calix says.

I look over and see Xander clench his jaw in disapproval. Gannon, Melanie, Calix, Fraeya, and Elfred all look at Danae since she is the only one against it. Danae scoffs, "Fine, since you all are so eager to allow this estranged outsider to claim Elvenhood then so be it. But the second she messes up, she will be exiled." I give her an understanding nod.

I thought I would feel relieved and excited, but honestly, I feel like I could vomit. "If you'll please excuse me, I think I need a bit of air." I say as I curtsy and quickly make my escape. I head straight for the courtyard in hopes of getting some sort of solitude. I stare up at the sky as I ponder this new life that has suddenly became my reality.

"When did you discover you could do the spells?" Elfreds asks, breaking the silence and startling me. I turn around and stare at him for a moment before answering. "Just before the confrontation in your office." I tell him bleakly. Elfred looks away ashamed. "That's what I had come to tell you, before...." My voice trails off. Elfred grabs my hands and looks into my eyes. "Aislinn I am so sorry. It was wrong of me to abandon you tonight. I was just so hurt. These last few days I opened my heart to you and it made me become possessive of your affection. So, when you rejected not only my marriage proposal, but my love and affections for you, it made me jealous and I let the bitterness consume me." Elfred tells me as I feel the sincerity and love radiating from his touch.

"What?" Xander roars as he approaches us hastily. "Xander please, you wouldn't understand." Elfred tells him as he cautiously backs away from me. "Oh I understand clearly." Xander says angrily as he cocks back his fist and punches Elfred, knocking him to the ground. "Xander!" I exclaim. Elfred holds up his hand to keep his guards from detaining Xander. "You profess you love her yet when she rejects your marriage proposal, you leave her without and escort, knowing it would damage her reputation. If you really loved her it should not have mattered. You Elves are disgustingly prideful." Xander shouts. Elfred rises to his feet and wipes the blood from his bottom lip. "You are right. I let my pride get the best of me and I made a foolish decision that I regret tremendously. I hope one day you will forgive me." Elfred says directing his attention back on me. I give him a flat smile, "We'll see." I murmur. He then gives me a slight bow. "I must be getting back to the ball now, but I hope you will rejoin us when you are ready." Elfred tells me. I give him a nod and watch him vanish.

I turn to face Xander and give him a feeble smile. "I knew this would happen." Xander says, still fuming with anger. "Xander, please. He's not entirely at fault." I say as my eyes meet his. "Ah…I see. So your feelings are mutual then?" Xander asks. His question makes me uncomfortable as I don't want to admit my feelings for Elfred when it's apparent I have developed mixed feelings for Xander. "I…well…it's just that it's hard not to. I've spent everyday with him and he has been very nice and friendly towards me. It's not like I planned for it to happen." I tell him. "I don't think anyone plans to fall in love Aislinn." Xander says with his eyes practically searing into mine. "Um, right. I know that. I just meant that developing feelings for Elfred was the last thing on mind." I say nervously. "Right." He says and then we both fall silent for a moment.

When I look up, I catch Xander intently staring off in the distance. "What are you thinking about?" I ask him. He hakes his head. "I just remembered something from the past, but now's not the time to dwell on it. We should be celebrating." He says quickly while giving me a forced smile. "Okay..." I say slowly. "We should probably get back in there before people start wondering where the guest of honor is." Xander tells me. I just nod and he puts his arm out and escorts me back into the ballroom.

Once I make it back in I start to feel uncomfortable as I attract a bunch of stares. I can see Danae giving me the stink eye from across the room and I try to avoid making eye contact with her again. "Care for some wine?" A server asks us as he holds out a silver tray with sparkling flutes of white wine.

"Absolutely." I say as I take one and down it like a shot and place it back on the tray. I grab two more off the tray before the server makes his escape. Xander gives me a shocked look as I take a sip of one the drinks. He takes the second drink from my hand and takes a big gulp. "Hey I was going to drink that." I say. "Not anymore. Trust me, the last thing you want them thinking is that you are a lush." Xander tells me. "And what if I am?" I say quizzically. Xander furrows his brows, unsure of what to say. "I'm kidding. I'm just nervous and was hoping some wine would help take the edge off."

I feel a tap on my shoulder and turn to see an Elf I've never seen before. "Hello. My name is Theo." He says. "Hello." I reply with a small curtsy. "Might I say you look even more beautiful up close." Theo says. I blush, "Why thank you." I tell him. "I was hoping to maybe share this dance?" He asks as he holds his hand out and gives me a pearly white smile. All of a sudden I feel a warm strong hand take its place on the middle of my back as Xander steps beside me. "I'm sorry. I'm afraid we were just about to make our way out there." Xander says. I look over at Xander as he stares the guy down. "Of course. My apologies." Theo says as he gives a bow and then backs away.

I give Xander a suspicious look. "So now I can't dance with people either?" I say becoming slightly annoyed. "No. I truly would like to dance with you he says as he gives me a proper bow and extends out his hand. I give him a smirk. "So, you were jealous then?" I say. He holds his head a little higher. "Of course not. I just really like this particular melody." He tells me matter of factly. I hold back my chuckle as I place my hand in his. Xander then leads me to the center where everyone else is dancing and pulls my body to his.

A warm sensation runs through my body as he stares down at me with his hazel eyes. "So you're a Captain?" I say trying to break the tension, as I rest my free hand on his shoulder. He gives a sexy smirk, as he shakes his head and lets out a chuckle. "Well you know I can't lie." He says. "Good point." I reply. After a couple seconds of silence I ask, "Why did you come back?" Xander lets out a sigh, "I didn't like the way we parted, especially with what's to come." He says. "What do you mean?" I ask. "There's word that Stavros is sending warriors to

Meadows Clearing to implement a lethal raid as a threat in hopes of making one of the Seekers come forward." "What!" I say a little too loudly and gain a couple of strange looks from those surrounding us. He spins me and then pulls me back to him. "It's just another one of his tactics." Xander says. "They're innocent people, they don't deserve to die at my..." My words are cut off as Xander leans in and whispers in my ear, "Careful with your words Aislinn." His warm breath on my ear gives me goosebumps. "Don't worry, the Realms Guard is going down there to provide a line of defense, but it's uncertain how successful we will be." "We? Meaning you will be going too?" I say as I look up at him with distraught. He gives me an emotionless nod. "You said there aren't many of you left, why would you risk all of you going down there? Can't you just stay here?" I ask in a frenzy. He gives a soft smile, "As you've reiterated, I am a Captain, someone has to lead the other soldiers Aislinn. Besides, Meadows Clearing is also the Region I was assigned to look over remember?" I could feel the water works start to form. This means this will probably be the last time I see Xander, he came back to say good bye. Now I feel like I'm going to be sick all over again. "It's not fair. I thought you were assigned to look after me." I say defensively. "I was supposed to see you to safety." He says as he looks around us before continuing, "it's apparent you are safe here and now that you will be one of them, they will protect you. Elfspond has their own militia, now, they are by no means the Realms Guard, but they're good enough." He says boastfully, trying to lighten the mood. I roll my eyes and choke on my laugh as I hold back my tears. "When will you be leaving?" I ask. "First thing in the morning. I am already half a day behind since I came back tonight." He tells me. "Sorry to hold you back, I know how important the mission is to you. But, I am glad you came back, I never would've been able to forgive you for leaving like that." I tell him. "There's no need to be sorry. My duty to the Realm is important, but, so are you." Xander says softly. My heart flutters at his words and I have to break eye contact before I do something stupid. "And I must say, it was very much worth it. You look absolutely stunning, an image that I will never be able to forget." I blush. "Well, you don't look so bad yourself." I say teasingly as he twirls me once more and dips me. As the melody starts to change I realize it's the beginning of the customary Elven dance.

Elfred appears and gives me a polite smile. "I realize we may not be on the best of terms, but would you do me the honor of having this dance?" Elfred asks. I look at Xander as he glares at Elfred, I give Xander a reassuring nod and he steps back. "Sure." I say to Elfred as I hold up my left palm and Elfred puts his palm to mine.

A bunch of people gather around to watch us as we begin our clockwise circles. "I'm really sorry." Elfred tells me through mind transference. "I know." I reply. "I have been a fool to think I am the only one who could hold your affections." "What do you mean?" I ask. "Your heart is split. I never had a fair chance." He says almost sullenly. "I...that's not..." I try to retort defensively as my eyes flash to Xander and then my mind wanders to Jace. He's right. "It's okay Aislinn. The heart is a complicated thing, it doesn't always relay to our mind what it feels, until it's too late. I realize now that even if we were to marry, you would never entirely be mine." He says. "I'm sorry if you feel like I lead you on." I tell him.

"You have nothing to be sorry for. I would like to think our feelings for one another were mutual and neither one of us expected the attraction to grow so strong." "I agree, things are already complex as it is. The last thing I expected was to develop feelings for you. I hope eventually we can get past this because I have enjoyed the friendship that we share." I tell Elfred. "I like the sound of that." He says as and gives me a bright smile before spinning me and bring my back up to him. He sensually runs his hand down my body. Being the traitor it is, I become flush in the face and goosebumps trigger all over my body. Elfred then spins me back out and I stumble back into his arms. "Okay, except we can't do that anymore. I can't think straight when you do that." I say. We both share a small laugh. "Only if you insist." Elfred says.

When the song finishes, an eruption of applause fills the air. "Thank you for the lovely dance." He tells me. I give him a proper curtsy, "It was an honor Wise Elf." I say as I feel the eyes of many Elves on me. "Please come by my office in the morning so we can go over some things." He tells me and I give him a nod.

Speaking of morning, it reminds of Xander and I quickly scan the room for him. I finally spot him towards the back wall talking with Fraeya. I feel a slight twinge of jealousy as I make my way towards them. They both quit talking as I approach them and it makes me feel a little self conscious. "That was quite a performance." Fraeya tells me, offering a smile. "Oh, thanks. I guess it wasn't too bad for just learning it this morning." I tell her. "Really? I couldn't even tell. Maybe it's the chemistry you two share." She says. What the hell is her deal? She has been acting like an ass all night. Xander gives an eye-roll at her last remark. "Uh, maybe." I say unsure of what else to say. "So what were you two talking about?" I ask trying to sound as casual as possible. "Nothing. Just catching up." Fraeya says quickly. I look at Xander he just looks away. I decide not to push it. "Ah. Well, I'm feeling pretty exhausted. I was probably going to turn in for the night." I tell them. "Yeah I bet. Casting a spell like that, with no formal training. It's a wonder you didn't pass out." Fraeya says. I had almost forgot about that, that would explain why I feel so depleted. "Oh, well that explains it then." I say and then look at Xander. "Well, goodnight." I say awkwardly and then turn to leave.

"Wait," Xander says causing me to stop in my tracts. "Can I escort you to your room?" "Sure." I say as I feel my lips curve upward in satisfaction. He holds out his arm and I loop mine around his. We make our way through the crowd and then out into the castle. "I'm going to miss you." I say softly. "Please don't. You have many more things that require your attention." He tells me gruffly. "Well, it's not exactly something I can control." I reply. "Then you will only be causing yourself unnecessary grief." He tells me. "That's not true. I care about you a lot. Do you not care about me?" I ask him. "Well you get on my nerves." He says abruptly and I can tell he is trying to keep from saying more. "You don't mean that." I say, hoping it's not true. "I do. Since I met you, you have annoyed me with your questions. You have annoyed me with your antics and curiosity" He begins to rant and I can feel a lump in my throat form. How could I be so naive to think he actually cared about me.? "You are annoyingly kind to everyone you meet, annoyingly selfless, annoyingly intriguing, and annoyingly beautiful and I can't stand it." Now the lump in my throat starts to sting even more as his rant takes a complete turn. I try to hide my smile, "So you do care." I say with a tone of relief. "I do. Despite telling my heart numerous times not to, you have broken down it's guarded walls." I give him a big smile as the tears start to fall. He stops and I feel his thumb wipe the tear from my cheek. "Please don't cry." He says softly. "Will you come say bye before you leave." I ask him as we make our way up the staircase. "I will." He tells me. We both pause for a moment once we reach my door. Knowing neither one of us want this moment to end. "Are you scared?" I ask him, trying to mask my own feelings. "Not really. It's my duty, it would be an honor to die protecting the Realm." He tells me. "Oh." Is all I can manage to say. "Sorry, I know that's not what you want to hear." "It's okay. I should know better. Even though, I want to be selfish and ask you to stay." I tell him. He gives me a slight smile as he gazes into my eyes. "Can I be selfish?" He asks me. I give him a weak nod. Xander then pulls me to him, as his lips crash down onto mine. His strong arms wrap around me giving me gentle squeeze and I loop my arms around his neck. As I kiss him back, his kiss becomes that much fiercer and I can feel the attraction, the lust, and the feelings between us intensifying. Xander breaks away and I look up at him with yearning eyes. "What's wrong?" I ask. He rubs my bottom lip with his thumb. "Nothing. I just think it wouldn't be fair to either of us to take things further." He tells me. "Right." I say as I look away bashfully. "Goodnight Aislinn." Xander says as he backs away slowly. "I'll see you in the morning." I tell him eagerly.

Chapter 12

I feel a soft kiss to my forehead and I can't tell if it was a dream or reality. I stretch and blink a couple times before I open my eyes fully. I sit up in bed and find a scroll laying on the bed. What is this? I pick it up and unroll it.

Dear Aislinn,
I hope you can forgive me for not waiting till you awoke. I wanted more than anything to hear your voice one last time, but I don't think I would be able to stand seeing you cry again. I would much rather have our last memory together be a happy one. I am forever glad my life was touched by yours. I wish

you nothing but happiness. May the deities allow us
to cross paths once again.
P.s. I can still feel the warmth of your lips on mine.

Love,

Xander

I find myself grazing my lips as I start to cry. How could he leave without saying bye? He's probably right, it was for the better. I roll the letter back up and put it under my bed. I quickly get up and get dressed and rush down the stairs. He couldn't have gotten too far. That must have been the kiss I felt. "Xander!" I shout repeatedly as I make my way up and down the halls. Of course I don't find him anywhere.

As I round the next corner hurriedly I run into Elfred. "Have you seen Xander?" I ask frantically. Elfred gives me a frown, "I'm afraid he's already left." I can feel my heart break a little. "Oh." I say weakly as I start to cry. Elfred embraces me and it makes me cry harder. "I'm so sorry Aislinn." He tells me comfortingly. When I finally stop crying, I pull away and wipe my eyes. "Perhaps, we can use this time to discuss matters going forward?" Elfred says. "Alright." I say bleakly.

I follow Elfred to his office and when we make it inside I slump down into one of the chairs. I feel numb. Hell, I feel worse than I did when I found out Brad was cheating on me. "I have something for you." Elfred says, bringing me back to reality. He retrieves something from his desk. It's a large square box. Oh no, please don't be a ring I think to myself. "I had planned on giving this to you yesterday, but after the turn of events I thought it would be best to wait." Elfred says he crouches down next to me. No. No. No. He opens the box and reveals a necklace. I give him a confused look. "A necklace?" I say and it comes out more as a question. "This isn't just any necklace." He says before continuing. "This necklace is actually an amulet, charmed to suppress your powers while you wear it. I thought it could help hide your powers until you are able to control them." He holds the necklace out to me as I admire the large emerald green teardrop pendant connected to a silver chain. "It's beautiful." I say. "May I?" Elfred asks, motioning to put the necklace on. I give him a nod and he loops the necklace around and secures it. I suddenly feel a slight wave of pressure lifted off my chest. Wow, is it already working?

"Wow. Thank you, this is very thoughtful and much needed." I tell him. "Will it suppress my spell capabilities too?" I ask him. "Yes, it will suppress all of your magical powers. Which, is what we need to discuss." He tells me. I give him and agreeable nod.

"So it is apparent you can cast spells, but you also possess the skills of a Seeker." Elfred states. "Does that mean I'm part Elf?" I ask. Elfred quickly shakes his head. "Highly unlikely since mating outside the Elven species is deemed as treason. The deities would have killed you at birth." "Then what am I?" "You are most likely duobred. A rare species that possess powers from both parents. One, being obviously a Seeker and the other being a Sorcerer or Sorceress." "Wow. So do you think at least one of my parents may still be alive?" "It's possible, but there will be no way of knowing until this whole ordeal is over with." He tells me. A spark of hope ignites within me. I may actually get to meet one of my biological parents and that thought alone perks me up. "Alright, that's just more motivation." I tell him. He gives me a smile. "And now that we know you are capable of magic, we can start teaching you properly, so you will at least be able to control and perform magic properly." "That sounds good." I say excitedly. "The Wise Elf Council also feels you should have some more formal training before your induction ceremony so you don't pose a hazard to anyone." Elfred says. I give an awkward half chuckle, "Sorry. I had no idea I could do that. I was just so overstimulated." I say. "I know. I don't blame you. We just need to be cautious going forward. You definitely hold more power than the average species, so you need to be careful not to have anymore emotional outbursts. The more emotion behind your spells, the stronger the magic emitted will be." "Got it. Hopefully, this will help too." I say as I put my hand over the emerald pendant. "My thoughts exactly." He says. "So, how long do I have? When will my induction ceremony be?" I ask. "Seven days." Damn how can I learn 21 years worth of magic in seven days. "That's it?" I say nervously. "Rest assured, you don't have to know everything by then. Elves learn new spells throughout their entire lifetime. We will cover basic everyday spells that you would commonly use, defense spells, remedy spells, and so forth." He tells me. "Alright. Fair enough." I say.

A knock at his door interrupts us. "Enter." Elfred says. One of the guards enter the room. "The Wise Elf Council is demanding your audience." He says. I shoot Elfred a nervous look. "Very well. Tell them I will be there momentarily." The guard bows and then leaves. "Do you think it has anything to do with me." I ask. "Possibly, but some of our patrol did notify us that they've spotted some of Stavros's men in our Region and we must discuss military tactics should worse come to worse." He tells me. I give a hard swallow to show my alarm. "Don't worry I would let you know if you were in immediate danger. They have only entered the perimeter. Now if you'll excuse me, I mustn't keep them waiting." He tells me. I give him a nod and I go to follow him out of his office.

"Aislinnn…" I hear a voice hiss, that stops me in my tracks while sending shivers down my spine. I look back into the office, but there is no one to be found. My eyes then land on the Diablerie and I have a strong urge to go over to it. "Miss Aislinn." The guard says, bringing me back to reality. I get the heebie-jeebies just looking at the book and it makes me shutter once more. I look at the guard, "I must

ask you to step out of the office so I can shut the door." He tells me. "Right, sorry." I say as I emerge from the office and make my way back to my room. Could the book have been calling to me? In the flashback I had, the Elf had said it was powerful... and evil. I'm curious what kind of spells the book must hold in order for them to want to destroy it. They would have to be pretty wicked and the person who used it had to have been awful. Kyrillos, I think was what they said his or her name was. I wonder if that's whose voice called out to me. At some point I will need to tell Elfred about this, and the vision I saw.

"Aislinn!" A cheerful Ella says as I enter my room. "Ella, hi! I've missed you." I tell her. "I've missed you too, and I come bearing good news." She tells me excitedly. "What is it?" I ask. "I found where they are keeping Jace. They have him on the far East side of the castle. He is assisting in their infirmary." My heart nearly skips a beat at the mention of Jace's name. "Really? Are they treating him well?" "He said that a few of the Elves have been rude to him, since he is a Doulos, and make fun of his so called, limited powers, but not all of them are like that. He didn't appear to look poorly treated and he said he has actually enjoyed being able to heal again." "Oh that's such a relief to hear. I was so worried they would just lock him up and mistreat him. " I say. "I understand, but that is not the case. Now, I can't vouch that it doesn't happen to other Doulos's they come across, but fortunately Jace has you." Her last few words fall heavy in the air and I give a broken half laugh. "Yeah I guess you're right…" I say as I turn around, trying to hide the guilt on my face. Damn, if only Jace knew what I've been doing this whole time.

Should I tell him about developing feelings for Elfred or about kissing Xander? Geez, I sound like a tramp. I've only been here a little over a week and I've already had a more interesting love life than I have in my whole, 25 or should I say 21, years of living. It's not like we are officially dating or anything, but I still can't help but feel like I've been cheating on Jace. Ugh, what did I get myself into.

"Is everything okay?" Ella asks, interrupting my self pity party. "Oh, yeah, sorry, I just have a lot on my mind. I'm glad he is doing well for the most part, I just wish I could see him though." I say glumly as I twirl my pendant between my fingers. That's when the thought hits me. "Wait, maybe I can!" I say a little too excitedly. Ella cocks her head, waiting for me to respond. "This necklace, Elfred gave me. It suppresses all my magical powers, so it should suppress our imprint too." "Which means you can be around him without your powers emitting too much magic!" She finishes. "Exactly!" I tell her. "Oh this is wonderful! He was just asking when he could see you next." She tells me. "I have to check with Elfred, but if that's the case, as long as I have this on, I should be able to be around him." I tell her. "Oh I certainly hope so! He was telling me how he thinks about you every second of every day and that he cannot wait for the moment he gets to see you again." Ella says. Yep, the guilt is definitely hitting home. "How sweet. I've missed him too." I say simply. "He certainly is so dreamy and he is just the sweetest!" She tells me as she clasps her hands together dreamily. I just let out a soft chuckle. "Should we go ask Elfred?" She asks me eagerly. "He's in a meeting with the Wise Elf Council right now." I reply. "Oh, I almost forgot to ask. How did everything go? I tried to come last night, but they wouldn't let any non-elite member on the castle grounds due to the ball going on."

I spend what feels like the next hour telling Ella the course of events leading up to her visit. Aside from the kissing Xander part that is. I don't think Ella would think badly of me, I just feel like it's not something I should go around telling people about. I couldn't imagine if word got back to Fraeya, yikes. For now, it will just be our secret, and Jace's when I tell him. I feel like I owe it to him.

"Wow, so you are a sorceress too? I can't believe you are a duobred, there's only a handful of those." I hold out my hands and shrug my shoulders, "I guess so." I tell her. "Remind me not to get on your bad side." She says playfully and we both let out a laugh. "Show me what the Wise Elf Council's faces looked like again after they unfroze." She says. I mimic each of their faces and she splints her stomach with a long chuckle. "At the time I was so scared and shocked, but now that I look back at it, it was actually pretty funny and I felt powerful." I tell her. "I bet, a duobred's magic is quite powerful. At least you are able to cast spells, that'll help with your

cover. It would be kind of hard to play off if not."
She tells me. "I know. I guess I did get pretty lucky."

A light knock at the door interrupts us. "Come
in." I say. Luckily it's just Ariti. "Ariti, hi. I'd like to
introduce you to my friend Ella." Ella's glow
becomes a little brighter as I introduce her as such.
"Hello, I am Ariti, Aislinn's handmaid." She replies.
"And friend." I add giving her a smile. Ariti gives a
big smile in return. "She helped make me the most
beautiful dress for last night. I felt like a goddess." I
tell Ella. "Oh I wish I could've seen you." Ella tells
me. "You are too kind." Ariti says bashfully before
continuing, "I do come bearing some information."
My face suddenly falls serious, "What is it?" I ask.
"Elfred wanted me to inform you that he has
arranged for your training to begin today. You should
report to the library immediately." She tells me. I
give her a sharp nod as my paranoia kicks in. Why
the sudden urgency? "Very well. I'll be on my way
down." I tell Ariti. "Would you like to come?" I ask
Ella. "And see a duobred wield her new powers? I
wouldn't miss it." She tells me.

When we make it to the library, Elfred and
Cicero are both waiting for me. I notice Elfred is

more tense than usual. "Everything okay?" I ask. "There's word Stavros's men are going to start their encroachment on Elfspond. I figured it would be best if you were well versed in some defense spells in case worse comes to worse." Elfred tells me. I give a hard gulp followed by a nod. "Got it." "Cicero will begin by teaching you the spells with their proper enunciation and forms of casting and then you will follow it up by undergoing some hands on practice." He tells me. "Alright." I say as I turn to Cicero. He raises two fingers in the air and swoops them down and points at the table in front of us. This triggers multiple books to leave their shelves and pile on the table. "Shall we get started?" Cicero asks me. I give him an amazed look as I nod my head.

We decide to leave the necklace on as I practice the enunciation and hand movements, to prevent any accidents from occurring. It's probably a good thing too because I'm having a hard time pronouncing a few of the spells. I supposedly keep pronouncing págoma, the spell for freeze, wrong and saying it more like the spell for choke, pnigomai. Whoops. I made the comment that if they're choking they are still technically stuck in place, but Cicero did not find that as amusing as me and Ella did. After what felt like hours of going over spells, I was then instructed to go to the private courtyard for my hands on practice.

Elfred and Fraeya are waiting with a few of the guards. Elfred approaches me and uses telepathy to communicate, "It's time to take your necklace off, but do it subtly." He tells me. "Why?" I ask him. "I don't want people knowing you have an amulet. They are a rarity." He puts his hand on my shoulder, "Don't be preposterous, you will do fine. This is just your first duel after all." He tells me as a cover. "Duel?" I shriek outloud. "What better way to practice and learn than to have a mock duel?" He says sincerely. "I don't think I'm that ready." I say arguably. "That's the point. It'll help better prepare you. Besides this is just a spell duel, wait until we practice sparring." My eyes become wide and Elfred just laughs. "Are you serious?" I ask "Absolutely. You are going to be an Elf, therefore you must undergo the training of one, especially more so now that we have potential invaders." I just give him a deer in the headlights stare. "Milo, will be your dueling companion today." Elfred says as he motions him to come forward. When Fraeya turns to watch Milo come forth I swiftly slip off my necklace and give it to Ella to hold on to.

I feel awkward as we stand a few feet a part, just staring at each other. "So what am I supposed to do?" I ask confused. Milo will try to come at you and I want you to cast some different defense spells. I give a nod and direct my attention back on Milo. "Begin." Elfred commands. Milo comes at me fast and I just dodge him and stumble out of his way. "What the hell? I wasn't expecting him to go full crazy on me." I say. Fraeya lets out a snicker, "So you want him to take it easy on you? Shall we inform Stavros's men to be sure to attack you in slow motion?" She says. I give her a scowl. "No, I just wasn't expecting him to come at me like that." I reply. "Exactly, you never know when someone may try to attack you or take you by surprise. You have to be ready at all times. I know it seems strange when it's unprovoked, but you want to be confident in your ability to cast a spell." Elfred says. "Let's try again." Elfred says.

Milo resets and then comes at me again. "Na stamatísei." I say as I hold up my hand out in front of me. Milo stops in his tracks for about three seconds and then resumes control. "You need to be more forceful. It will make the spell stronger and cause him to be stopped longer. Remember the more emotion behind it, the stronger it will be." Elfred instructs. I give a nod and prepare for Milo's next attack. This time I am more forceful with my speech and I am able to stop him. "Much better." Elfred comments. "How long will he stay that way?" I ask. "Until you break the connection of the spell by calling it off or leaving the vicinity." He replies. "That's it?" I ask, "I didn't do either of the those at the ball." I add. Elfred and Fraeya exchange a puzzled look. "I mean it can also be broken if you get injured or if a more powerful being is immune to it and reverses the spell." Elfred states. "Oh, well that makes sense, I got a sharp pain in my chest." I reply. Elfred cocks his head, "From what?" He asks quizzically. I bashfully look away, not wanting to talk about my complicated love life in front of everybody. Luckily Elfred catches on, "We will discuss this matter later." He tells me. I give another nod. "Now just hold out your hand again and say akyró. It will nullify the spell." I do as he says and

Milo resumes his composure. "Now, let's try a different spell." Elfred commands.

We spend the next couple of hours practicing spells and I think if it wasn't for dinner being ready we would have kept going. I feel drained, but that's supposedly normal since I've never really practiced magic before. It will get better the more I get use to using my powers. Elfred let Ella stay for dinner and then afterwards we proceeded to his office so we could talk.

"Tell me what happened at the ball. When the spell broke." Elfred says. "I don't know. I had come back over to you all once I realized everything had stopped. No one was moving or talking. I rushed back over to the group and saw you all there. I was in shock looking at you and Xander. And then I started thinking about Jace and that's when I just got this sharp pain in my chest that brought me down to my knees and then that's when everything around me went back to normal." Elfred taps his chin. "Hmm, interesting. I must say I don't know what that means, but the fact it caused you physical harm would explain why it allowed the spell to break." He explains. "Speaking of Jace, we were wondering if the necklace would also help decrease the magic from our imprint?" I ask. Elfred turns to look out the window. "Yes, it should." He says flatly. "Does that mean I could possibly spend time with him now?" I ask. "I suppose." He says gloomily as he continues to stare out the window. I can tell his feelings for me are still strong and it's hard for him to let go.

Ella gives me an excited smile. "I can't wait to tell him!" She says. "But, if he becomes a distraction, I will send him back to Diona." Elfred says sternly trying to assert his dominance. "That won't happen." I say. "Good, because nothing should detract you from your training. This could be a matter of life and death." Elfred says. "I understand. Will I have training everyday?" I ask. He turns to look me in the eyes, "Yes." He replies. "Alrighty. What time?" I ask. "Well you have a lot of catching up to do, so I will have Ariti fetch you in the mornings and you will go until it's time for lunch. I will also set up random duels or spars so that you learn to be ready at all times." Elfred says. "Okay..." I say. It's apparent that he is not happy that I'm wanting to spend time with Jace and is trying to make it nearly impossible to do so. "Very well. I suggest you get some rest though, tomorrow is going to be quite draining for you." "Yes Wise Elf." I say, showing my aggravation. His brows furrow and I motion to Ella for us to leave.

"Ugh, I don't why he is being such a hard ass." I say frustratingly to Ella once we emerge from his office. "Yes you do." She says giving me a sassy side eye. "Okay, I do, but come on. He has to understand, I am fated to Jace though." I say. "I know, it doesn't change the fact that he has feelings for you though. It's not everyday you see an Elf under 200 wanting to marry. Especially the Wise Elf who can have nearly any Elf they want." I let out a groan, "I thought it would be a nice feeling to feel special, but at this point it is exhausting." I say. "You do have a lot of weight on your shoulders Aislinn, but Elfred is right, you do need to focus on your training, so you are well prepared incase one of Stavros's men attacks you." She tells me. "I know." I say as I give a sigh. We both pause in the foyer before we part ways. "Shall I pass along the good news to Jace?" Ella asks. "Yes. Tell him I will hopefully see him tomorrow, probably some time in the afternoon." I tell her. "You got it!" She says.

By time I make it back to my room, I am so tired I just plop down on the bed. When I slide my hand under the pillow I feel the scroll from Xander. I retrieve it out from under my pillow and find myself smiling like and idiot. My smile quickly fades once I realize it's probably the last memory I'll have of Xander though. I place it on the stand next to the bed and then roll back over to go to sleep.

Aislinn...Come here...

I blink my eyes rapidly as they try to adjust to the darkness. "Huh? Ariti is that you?" I say. It's still dark out, surely I'm not training this early. I groan as I sling back the covers and slip on my robe.

Come to me Aislinn...

My body goes cold and stiff when I hear the same familiar hiss. Now that I'm awake I recognize the voice from Elfred's office. The Diablerie. Is a book really talking to me? I think to myself. Crazier things have happened I guess. I look around my dark room and I instantly get goosebumps as I become scared. I get an uneasy feeling as I debate what to do. Whatever that book consists of is evil and I want nothing to do with it, but I also feel oddly drawn to it at the same time. Does this mean I am evil? In the

265

vision they said they hope no one as evil as Kyrillos rises again. I assumed that would be someone like Stavros, but why isn't it calling to him?

Release me Aislinn, you know you want to…

"No! I'm not evil!" I shout.

Don't fool yourself. We are the same, you and I.

"That's not true!" I shout back. My door flings open causing me to scream, but it's just Ariti. "Aislinn what is wrong? Are you okay?" She asks me frantically as she rushes over to me and looks me over, unsure of whether to touch me or not.

I can teach you everything you need to know and answer all your most desired questions. All you have to do is release me…

"Did you hear that?" I ask Ariti, giving her a distraught look. She gives me a frightened look and then cautiously looks around the room. "Hear what?" She asks and it's apparent that I have scared her. "I need to talk to Elfred right away." I tell her. "It's the middle of the night Miss Aislinn are you sure it can't wait?" She replies meekly. I know there's no way I will be able to get back to sleep without getting at least some answers. "No, I can't wait any longer." I tell her. "Alright, follow me." She says.

She leads me down the stairs and through a couple corridors. We then take a secret tunnel and finally arrive in front of a large door that has two guards posted outside of it. They instantly come to attention once they see us. "Halt. What is your business here?" The one on the left asks. "Miss Aislinn is requesting an audience with the Wise Elf. She says it cannot wait until the morning." Ariti replies. The guards look at me and I see the one on the right give a slight smirk as he looks me up and down. I suddenly become aware that I'm wearing nothing but my robe and how inappropriate this may look. "It's important." I add trying to justify my curt actions. "I'm sure it is." The one on the right says sarcastically. "Wait here." The one on the left says as he enters Elfred's room. The three of us stand there silently and after a couple minutes the guard remerges and tells me, "You can go on in." I give a nod and quickly walk past them into the room.

When I enter the room I take notice of how elegant and huge it is, it gives off a very victorian-esque vibe. As I look around the room, I become startled when Elfred appears perched in the doorway leading to his bedroom. He is shirtless and his hair appears tousled and I can see the sleepiness in his eyes. How did he just wake up and still look so damn good? I cross my arms over my chest, hoping to distract from the fact that I'm wearing such scant clothing. "To what do I owe the pleasure of your company at such a late hour." Elfred says. "I was woken up by something." I say. Elfred raises an eyebrow and I realize how silly that sounds. "Not something, someone…well, I think. They are communicating to me and I don't think I should be listening to them and it's freaking me out." I say as the panic starts to resurface. "Who is it Aislinn?" I give him a skittish look as I bite my lip, "The Diablerie." I finally say. Elfred's eyes grow big. "The Diablerie has been communicating with you?" I nod my head. "How do you know it's the Diablerie? How long has this been going on?" He questions. "I just have this uneasy feeling that is drawing me to it. It just started today. The first time was when we were leaving your office it called out my name. Then it just woke me from my sleep and told me to come to it and release it." I say. "This can't be good." Elfred says as he starts to pace. "What does this mean? Is it Kyrillos?" I ask. Elfred's head snaps up at me. "How do you know that name?" He asks baffled. "The other day in your office, I touched the case and I saw a flashback of two Elves and two Sorcerers in the office. They mentioned the name and how Vasilios was killed in the battle of Kyrillos and that they couldn't destroy the book, but could put a spell on it and the only way to undo it is to say the spell in reverse." I tell him. Elfred gives me a terrified look. "Please tell me you didn't hear the spell." I give him a feeble nod. "Damn it Aislinn!" He says angrily as he walks off to sit on one of the chaises.

After a moment, I go over to him and sit next to him. "Elfred, what is it?" I ask. His demeanor is quite unnerving. He lifts his head up from his hands and I can see his eyes are glossy from holding back tears. "Kyrillos was the last demigod to exist. He's the reason the deities do not allow Elves to mate outside their species. He was the son of a powerful Elven woman who mated with a deity that had taken control of a sorcerer's body. Kyrillos was corrupted by evil and when he realized how powerful he was, he developed the need for more power. He wanted to rule over Vitalis as it's king, the deities of course disapproved, so, they sent Galen, the god of peace to hopefully settle things." Elfred says. "What happened?" I ask. "Kyrillos killed him. It sent the whole realm into a frenzy. This only built Kyrillos's confidence. The deities went into hiding and let Kyrillos rule over the Realm as he demanded. It probably would've worked out if he wasn't a greedy, merciless tyrant. From what the history books say, it was the longest, darkest, five years in Realm history. They realm rallied together and started building a realm wide militia against Kyrillos. His own men even started turning against him when they found out he was taking advantage of their wives and killing those who refused. When the deities caught wind of the uprising it was actually Zeus who came down to help destroy him." "But who was Vasilios exactly?" "Vasilios was one of the Great Mages who fought along side Zeus to help defeat Kyrillos. Once the battle was over, they knew they needed to destroy his spell book. The Diablerie was rumored to be passed around amongst those with the most vile thoughts and intent. Basically those who practiced dark magic. Totally corrupting whoever owned it and allowed them to possess the darkest and most evil magic the world holds. I'm sure there's many spells that even I don't know or have the capability to cast." He explains.

"I'm confused. If they destroyed Kyrillos and the book is enchanted. What does that have to do with me?" I see the distress trickle onto Elfred's face. "The book is cursed. Immediately after they defeated Kyrillos, Vasilios tried to destroy the book, but when he tried to do so it poisoned him and everyone who tried to destroy it after him. They tried ripping the pages, burning the book, spells, everything, but nothing worked. The more they tried, the quicker it killed them. Before his passing, Vasilios came up with the idea to place a protection spell around it since there wasn't anything they could actually do to the book and didn't want to chance it falling into the wrong hands again. Unfortunately, after placing the spell on it, the evil spirits enchanting the book began to taunt those capable of freeing it. Calling out to them, filling their heads with paranoia and evil, irrational thoughts, keeping them up all night. Essentially driving them mad, causing three of them to kill themselves. The fourth one had become corrupted by its power and was going to release the book, but luckily he was caught before he could. He begged the guard to kill him and put him out of his misery, that it wouldn't stop unless he freed the book or he died. The guard granted his wish and executed him. They thought it ended there, but unfortunately the Elf had been having nightmares and would chant the spell in his sleep. His daughter had heard him chanting it at night and so the torture passed on to her. When she showed up to the castle acting erratic and demanding to let her inside they had no choice, but to execute her on site. After that it was ordered that anyone who possessed knowledge of the spell should be executed instantly as it posed a threat to Realm security. Since then it has been assumed that no one else knew of the spell, until now that is. The book preyed on your power of psychometry. It knew you would be able to see the past and jbtain the spell, and now it haunts you." Elfred finishes. We both sit in silence.

My head is spinning as I try to process the information. As if things weren't bad enough. "You shouldn't have been in my office unaccompanied. You knew it was off limits." He says angrily. My mouth falls open with shock. "You can't be serious? That's how you're going to treat me after giving me that kind of news." I reply. He gives me a tense look as he looks over at me. "I'm sorry. You're right. How did you even get into my office? It's guarded at all times." He tells me. "No it wasn't. In fact the door was wide open. I walked right in." I tell him. I see his lip twitch with anger. "Duly noted. That guard will be punished accordingly." He says. I remain silent as we stare at each other.

Elfred tries to stifle a yawn. "Sorry, I know you're tired. I just didn't know what to do or who else to go to. It scared me." I tell him. "Don't be sorry. I'm glad I was the first person you thought of. Please don't tell anyone else of this, including Ella. Remember this is considered a threat to Realm security so we don't want people knowing that you also possess the ability to free the Diablerie." "Okay, but what does this mean for me? Is there anything to make it stop or am I going to end up like the others?" I say as my voice cracks on my last words. Elfred embraces me. "Don't worry. I'll do everything I can to find a solution. Until then, I think it's best we have someone watch you at all times." He tells me. "Even while I'm going to the privy?" I say while pulling away. "What is it with your obsession with the privy?" He says teasingly, getting a small laugh out of me. "But fine, except for when you're in the privy?" He adds. I give him a small smile followed by a nod. "What about while I'm sleeping?" I ask. "I think it wouldn't hurt." He says. "That's kind of creepy though." I reply. "I mean, unless someone's sleeping with you that is." He tells me has he rubs my cheek. "Elfred…" I say bashfully. "What? Didn't you say it woke you from your sleep? It would be wise to have someone watching you in case it does it again." "True." I say as a shiver at the thought of it even happening again. I don't like that cold, dark feeling or how it gets in my head so easily.

"Now, will you be staying with me for the night or shall I call for Ariti and instruct her to sit with you?" Elfred says. I purse my lips at an attempt to hide my smirk. "Nice try." I say as I rise up from my seat. He gives a soft smile and a nod. I make my way back over to the door, but as I reach for the handle I become frozen still with fright.

That's right, come to me Aislinn...

I quickly turn to face Elfred. "Was that you?" I ask. "Was what me?" Elfred says precariously and then it hits him. "Wait, did it just happen again?" He asks. I nod as I let go of the door handle and make my way back over to Elfred. "Actually, could I maybe just stay with you tonight?" I say, hoping I won't regret my decision. He nods excessively as he opens up his arms. I walk into his arms and he wraps his arms around me. I don't get the same sense of security as I do when I hug Xander, but Elfred's touch is warm and inviting. I can feel the compassion and affection radiating from him and it gives me a comforting sense of familiarity. He guides me over to the bed and I tie my robe a little tighter before I slide underneath the covers. As he makes his way to the other side of the bed I watch him slip his pants off and I quickly avert my gaze away.

"Um, do you think you can leave those on?" I ask. Elfred chuckles as he slides into the bed. "Aislinn, relax. I'm far too tired to do anything other than sleep." He says as he fluffs his pillow and then closes his eyes.

I on the other hand do not fall asleep so quickly. I toss and turn as my mind races about everything from the Diablerie to Stavros, and now to a naked Elfred sleeping next to me. I look over at Elfred and watch the gentle rise and fall of his chest with each shallow breath. I catch myself admiring his sharp jawline and the way his platinum blonde hair tucks behind his pointy ear. I still can't believe this is all real. I then become preoccupied with counting each rise of his chest, which eventually puts me to sleep.

Chapter 13

The next morning, I' am still half asleep when I feel the warm rays of the sun shinning through and the weight of Elfred's arm wrapped around me. Suddenly I remember there's only a thin silk robe separating Elfred's naked body from mine and I can feel my whole body go warm. I'm debating if I should get up and try to sneak back to my room or remain still and hope he will get up and leave, when I hear Elfred's chamber doors fling open.

"Elfred, I have urgent news…" Fraeya yells as she brashly makes her way into his room. We both become startled by the ruckus and jolt up in bed.

Fraeya falls silent when she sees me in Elfred's bed and her eyes dart between Elfred and I. I instantly realize how this looks and open my mouth to speak, but she holds up her hand to silence me. "I can't say this doesn't surprise me, but I don't have time to hear anyone's excuses right now. If you will just remove yourself, I must speak to the Wise Elf privately." Fraeya says. "Don't move Aislinn." Elfred commands, "Fraeya, have you lost your mind, barging into my private chambers like this?" Elfred retaliates. "Wise Elf, I assure you I would not do such a thing if it wasn't urgent." "Very well. Then I must ask you to step outside while I get dressed and then we will continue this conversation." Elfred demands. Fraeya gives a nod and then flashes me a seething glare before backing out and shutting the doors to his bedroom.

Elfred lets out a sigh as he gets out of bed and walks around to his wardrobe. "I apologize. This doesn't usually happen." Elfred says to me. "It's alright, I just feel embarrassed." I say as I rise up and straighten my robe. "Don't be. No one should think badly of you, this what Elves are known for anyway." He says. "Yeah, but we didn't' even do anything." "I know, I will put an end to any rumors I hear." He tells me. "Okay, thanks. I should probably get going though." I tell him. "Yes, you don't want to miss your training. I have already summoned Ariti, so she should be waiting for you. From now on, unless you are with someone she will be with you at all times." I simply give him a nod and then exit the room.

As I pass through the leisure room, I feel the heat of Fraeya's eyes on me as she watches me walk to the door. "Just so you know, nothing happened between us." I say and then quickly leave the room. When I emerge, Ariti is waiting for me as expected and walks me back to my room. I quickly get ready and then we head to the courtyard.

When we get there, Calix and two Elves standing at attention, are there waiting. "Where is Cicero?" I ask confused. "Today is agility and combat training." Calix tells me. "Wait, what?" Calix gives a smile, "Did Elfred not tell you? There's more than practicing sorcery to be an Elf. The training curriculum consists of: intellect, strength, agility, sorcery, combat, and archery." Calix tells me. "I know that. I, uh, just didn't think I would have to learn how to fight. I don't really like violence." I reply nervously. Calix gives a soft chuckle, "Well, Miss Aislinn, you may be special, but you are not exempt from the Elven curriculum. And unfortunately these are violent times we are living in, so it's best you be well prepared." I give a nod to show my understanding, as it's apparent I don't have a choice.

After a demonstration of what Calix called *simple* moves, he pairs me with one of the soldiers to practice with. The soldier tries to come at me, but I just quickly move out of the way. I hear Calix sigh and turn to see him shaking his head. "You have to stand your ground. An Elf does not run from battle, but faces it head on." He tells me. "I wasn't running. I was dodging, there's a difference." I reply matter of factly. Calix gives me a smirk, "Very well, but if you keep *dodging,* then I'll have no choice, but to tell Alonzo here, not to hold back." I give a nervous gulp as I turn back towards, who I now know is named Alonzo. I take my defensive stance once more.

As he approaches me and takes his first swing I put my right arm up and block his hit as I bring my left fist up and deliver a soft punch to his chest. Alonzo lets out a chuckle, "You can hit me harder than that." "What? No way!" I reply. "He's right Aislinn. You need to be exerting yourself fully. That way you can see what it's like to be in real combat." "I just feel bad. You haven't done anything to me, it's not right for me to hurt you." I reply. Alonzo looks at Calix and Calix gives him a nod. Alonzo looks back at me and I can tell I'm going to regret my words.

Alonzo pushes me to the ground. "Get up." He barks, I quickly get up and he pushes me back down. "I said get up." He shouts. I get up and before he can push me back down I dodge him. "So you're just going to runaway like a coward?" He says as he inches toward me. Geez, all I said was I don't want to hurt the guy and he's acting like I just made him sign away his first born. He throws a punch, followed by another, but I put both arms up to block it and then quickly bring my arms down to block the blow headed for my ribs. I don't see his left hook till it hits me in the jaw, causing me to fall to the ground. "Get up." He says sternly. "Give me a second, you just punched me in the face." I say angrily. "You think your real opponent is going to *give you second?"* Alonzo says mockingly. "You would be dead right at this moment. Now get up." He says. I stand up, fueled with anger. If it's a fight he wants then it's a fight he will get.

Alonzo comes at me once more and I block his swing and grab his arm with my free hand and twist it back. He uses his free hand to break my grasp and I quickly deliver a punch to his ribs. I follow it up with a punch to the side of his face, causing my hand to throb, but it only empowers me. He lands a punch to my chest causing me to stumble back, but this time I charge him and throw a couple punches, only landing two or three. We then start exchanging punches and blocks, and right as he tries to throw a heavy punch, I dodge it and swiftly move behind him and swipe his foot out from under him, putting him on his back. I feel impressed with myself as the stunned look lingers on Alonzo's face. "Get up." I demand mockingly and he does so. I half expect to be met with blazing force, but Alonzo gives me a big smile.

"Excellent!" Calix says, reminding me that this is all just training. I can't believe I got so wrapped up in it. It gave me an adrenaline rush. "I'm so sorry." I say to Alonzo. "Don't be, that was the most fun I've had in awhile. I'll admit though, I'm not use to being taken off my feet." Alonzo says. I can't help, but beam with pride at his last comment. "Now let's see how you do when we add weapons into the mix." Calix says. My eyes grow wide, "You can't be serious?" I question. "Very serious." He says as he holds out two swords.

Alonzo takes one of the swords and Calix holds the other out to me. I give a nervous look between the both of them. "Take it Aislinn." Calix says firmly. I grab the sword and it feels out of place in my hand. "Hold it closer to the handle. It will give you better leverage." Alonzo instructs. I do as he says and it helps the sword feel more secure in my hand. "Have you not wielded a sword before?" Calix asks a bit bewildered. I shake my head. He lets out a sigh, "Well then, we must first practice how to properly hold and wield it before you can successfully fight with it." Calix states.

After about two hours, I finally start to get comfortable with combat by sword. That is until the Diablerie invades my mind. *I have the power to*

*solve all your problems Aislinn…*the voice hisses.
The intrusive words distract me, allowing Alonzo to
strike me. "Owe!" I say as I drop my sword and grab
my arm. The blood starts to seep between my fingers
and run down my arm. Alonzo drops his sword and
quickly takes off his shirt and wraps it around my
arm. "I'm so sorry Aislinn, I thought you were
paying attention." Alonzo says. Calix now
approaches us, "You were doing so good. What
happened?" Calix asks. I open my mouth to reply,
but then pause, remembering Elfred told me to keep
it a secret. "I, uh, just got distracted." I say as I start
to sway. Calix peers at me, "Hmm, very well, this
will conclude today's training. Now, Alonzo get her
to the infirmary." Alonzo scoops me up to carry me.
"Oh, this isn't necessary. I can walk." I tell him.
"Don't be silly, it's the least I can do." I start to feel
dizzy as the throbbing in my arm becomes more
prominent and decide not to argue.

  Your weak, but I can make you strong. "Just shut
up." I say angrily. "I didn't say anything." Alonzo
says in confusion. Shit, the Diablerie is already
getting to my head. I didn't even realize I spoke out
loud. "Sorry, I just hear a loud ringing." Which is

only a half lie. "Ok, hang on, we are almost there." He says calmly.

"Can I get some help? She's got a deep cut to her arm." Alonzo says as he busts through the doors to what I assume to be the infirmary. "Lay her on the open cot." I hear a voice command. Alonzo carefully lays me down on the cot. "Thank you." I tell him. "Don't thank me, I'm the reason you're here in the first place." He says apologetically. "It's alright, it was an accident. It's my fault for being distracted." I say. Alonzo gives a soft chuckle. "True. I'm sure you'll be getting a lecture before your next lesson." I give a small laugh, but it causes my arm to hurt more than it already does. "Anyways, you're in good hands now, so I'll be on my way. Good work today kiddo." "Thanks." I say and then watch him disappear out the double doors.

"Aislinn!" I hear a worrisome Jace call out. "Jace!" I shout and try to sit up, but fail. Jace rushes over to my cot and kneels down next to me. "What happened?" Jace asks. "I, uh, became distracted during training." I reply shamefully. Jace cocks an eyebrow. "I have a lot to catch you up on." "Ah. Well let's see the damage." Jace says as he starts to unwrap the now soiled shirt, causing me to wince. "Alright, hold still." He says as he places his hand over my upper arm. "No!" I say as I put my hand over his, "I don't want to hurt you." I add. Jace gives me a soft smile. "Better me than you." He says as he moves my hand off of his. I feel a tingly sensation where my cut is and I look down to see the edges of the cut coming together and eventually the blood ceases to ooze. I glance to Jace's right arm and see the blood start to seep through his shirt.

Once Jace is done, I don't even have a scratch or scar to show for it. I see Jace grab a roll of gauze and start to wrap his arm. "How long will it take you to heal?" I ask him. "For something like this, it'll be healed by the end of the day." "Good. I hate to put this on you, literally." I tell him. "It's okay." He says as he takes a seat at my side. I try to sit up once more, but become lightheaded. "Easy now, my lady. I healed the wound, but my powers don't replenish the blood you lost." I give him a big smile. "What?" He asks curiously. "Nothing, I just missed hearing you call me that." I tell him. "Well, my lady, I must admit I was looking forward to seeing you today, but I didn't imagine it would be like this." He teases.

"Trust me, this was not what I had planned." He gives me that sexy smile that I had been missing, "Really, and what exactly did you have planned?" He asks. I let out a bashful giggle as our eyes linger on each other.

"Jace are you okay?" A beautiful Elven woman asks as she places her hand on his shoulder. "Oh I'll be fine." He says before turning his attention back on me. "Here let me at least clean it up." She says as she rolls up his sleeve. My face scrunches up as the jealousy consumes me. Who does the chick think she is? I watch angrily as she takes her time cleaning his arm and wrapping it with a fresh bandage. "There, much better." She says as she gives him a bright smile. "Thanks Anastasia." He tells her. She then walks off without even as so much looking at me. It takes everything I have to keep from asking Jace about this, *Anastasia*. Jealousy never wears well, and nevertheless, I have no room to talk. I was almost proposed to by Elfred and was caught in his bed this morning, and not too mention, my complicated feelings and kiss I've shared with Xander. Geez, I really need to get my shit together before they brand me with my own scarlet letter. I need to be upfront with Jace about everything that has gone on up to this point, but we just reunited and don't want to ruin the moment.

"Shall I fetch you some water?" Jace asks as he starts to get up. I hold his hand tighter, "The only thing I want is you to stay right here with me." I reply. He gives a broad smile as he takes his seat again. "Very well. Perhaps you can fill me in on current matters with you." He says. I give a nervous swallow. "Yes, um, I can do that…" Jace perks an eyebrow, "I'm sensing some reluctance?" He questions. I give a long exhale, "Not necessarily. It's just some of the things I need to tell you, are going to be upsetting." He gives a confirmatory nod.

I spend what feels like an eternity catching Jace up on everything from my brief romance with Elfred, his intended proposal, his stand up at the ball, my studies, my meeting with the Wise Elf Council, my ability to perform sorcery, my acceptance into Elvenhood and how I must train to prepare for the induction, and lastly my conversation and kiss with Xander. By time I finish, his eyes are downcast and his face expressionless. "Is there anything you'd like to say?" I ask meekly. "I'm not sure there is a purpose of my input, other than to say that it does pain me to hear about some of the events." Jace replies blandly. I can sense he is trying to maintain his composure, but I can feel the jealousy radiating from him. "I'm really sorry, it was not my intent to hurt you. Everything has just been kind of a whirlwind lately and I think my heightened emotions have made me more vulnerable." I tell him. "I'm not faulting you Aislinn. I dare not imagine what it is like to be in your place. I am just preparing myself for what this means for not only us, but you in general." "What do you mean?" I ask dumbly. "Once you are considered an Elf you cannot mate outside your species. While that's not a concern now, long term, you and I, or erm… shall it be, you and Xander, will not be able to marry." It kills me to hear the uncertainty in his voice, but I'm the one who put it there. "Surely once things return to normal…" I say carefully before continuing, "I won't have to keep up with the facade of Elvenhood." Jace gives me a grim look, "Unfortunately, that is not the case. Did the Wise Elf not explain the induction ceremony?" "No, he hasn't, we haven't had much time to discuss formalities." "I see. Well, long story short, there is a blood oath performed. Should it be broken, it will kill you." "What?" I shriek, drawing the attention of others in the room. This whole ordeal is just becoming more and more of a headache and why is everything out to kill me? "Remind me again what's so great about being an Elf." I whisper. Jace lets out a soft chuckle, "Depending on your stance, the cons could outweigh the pros I guess." He replies.

I try to stifle a yawn, but I have no such luck. "I'm sorry, I really should be letting you rest." Jace says. "Shouldn't you be resting too?" I ask. "It would accelerate the recovery time, but I'd rather stay here and watch over you." He tells me. I scoot to the opposite side of the cot and pat the open space next to me. "Then let us both rest." I say. Jace looks around the room cautiously. "A lady and a Doulos in bed together. They will surely talk." He says. "Aren't they anyway?" I retaliate. He gives a sexy smirk, as he takes his place beside me on the cot. The moment his arm wraps around me, I feel whole. As if nothing else matters. "Speaking of gossip, did you know there's a rumor that you were caught in the Wise Elf's bed this morning." Jace says. My eyes grow wide as I let out a nervous laugh. "Right, about that. It's not a rumor, it did happen, but we didn't do anything except sleep. I even wore my robe the whole time." I say. "And him?" I clear my throat, "And, he did not." I say leaving it at that. "I guess I'm just confused then, of why you would do it. Especially if you say you no longer have feelings for him." I wish I could tell him about the Diablerie, but Elfred swore me not to tell anyone. "I promised I would not say. Maybe once we have more privacy." I tell him. "Alright then." He says softly and his warm breathe on my neck triggers goosebumps. It seems the necklace has done a good job of keeping the impulses and strong feelings at bay, but there is no denying the attraction we still share.

I'm not sure how much time has passed, but a sharp, "Ahem" awakens me. There at the foot of the bed stands Elfred with a displeased look on his face. I sit up and it awakens Jace. Jace quickly gets up and bows to Elfred, "Wise Elf," he says without making eye contact. I hate seeing Jace in such a submissive manner. "Calix said I would find you here. I'm sorry to hear about your injury, but it looks as if it is not anything to worry about now." He says. "Yes, thanks to Jace, it's as if it never happened in the first place." I say looking down at my unblemished arm. "Indeed, and I hate to interrupt your…rest, but I figured it would do you good to eat and thought perhaps afterwards we could discuss some private matters?" "Yes, except, could we can include Jace? It feels bad keeping secrets from my soul mate." I say. I notice Jace shift uncomfortably as Elfred clenches his jaw to hide his disapproval. "Why of course, what a splendid idea." Elfred replies as if his answer is coerced.

After a nearly silent and uncomfortable dinner, the three of us make our way into Elfred's office. "Before I lock us in here, I feel I should state that the matters we discuss in a force of solitude is of the utmost security. Should you speak to anyone about the matters discussed within could lead to a fatal outcome for not just Aislinn, but all of us." Elfred says sternly with his attention directed on Jace. "I am aware of the consequences and assure you that I would never do anything to hurt Aislinn, regardless of our circumstances between each other." Jace says as a dig towards Elfred's recent actions. "Excellent. Aislinn, I'll need you to take your necklace off as it will counteract the force of solitude." Elfred says. "Right." I say as I take the necklace off. "I'll also be interested to see which is stronger the power of Elven charm or that of an imprint." Elfred says spitefully. I shoot a stern look to both Elfred and Jace. "That's enough, you two. We have important matters to discuss." They both give me a civil nod and Elfred shuts his doors.

"I find it best you tell him about the Diablerie so, he will be able to follow the conversation going forward." Elfred tells me. "Wait, the Diablerie? You mean to tell me it's not just a myth." "I'm afraid not." I say sullenly as I direct my gaze at the grim book poached upon it's pedestal. "I had a flashback of when it was enchanted for safeguarding and now that I possess the spell to release it, it will taunt me until either I release or I die." I say. "That's it? There's no other options, just release evil havoc onto the realm or death?" Jace says a bit perturbed. I look to Elfred for support. "I have my most trusted historians working on the matter, as neither of those are options. However, we must be covert in our efforts as this is deemed a threat to Realm security." He says. "Have you found anything out yet?" I ask hopeful. "Yes, it's not much, but maybe it'll at least buy us some time till we can figure something out." Elfred says. "Well, out with it." Jace says. Elfred retrieves a piece of paper from his desk. "This is a journal entry from one of the enchanters, the entry is two days before his death." Elfred hands me the piece of paper and Jace takes his place over my shoulder to read it.

The thoughts are becoming more frequent and more persistent. Yet to no avail, the voice draws chills and I get sick to my stomach each time. The thoughts wake me from my sleep and keep me up, I haven't had a full nights rest in over ten days. I've noticed when I am busy and my mind is preoccupied I am safe from the thoughts, but I am growing weary. There is not a Sorcerer or Seeker who can find a solution to my predicament. My hope is growing thin, I only pray that I do not end up like my comrades.

I throw the paper down on Elfred's desk. "How is that supposed to help?" I ask frustratingly. "It let's us know that as long as you're preoccupied, it cannot communicate with you." Elfred says matter of factly. "Did you even read this?" I shout. "He said it made him weary, he couldn't even sleep! How am I going to stay busy or even function with no sleep?" I say. "It hasn't gotten to that point yet has it?" Jace asks. "No, but who knows how long I have." I say. "We will figure something out Aislinn." Elfred says. "And until then?" I retort. "Someone will be with you at all times and your training should keep you fairly busy." Elfred replies. "Then how come it was able to get to me while I was training today? That's why I got distracted and got cut." I say. A puzzling look falls on Elfred's face. "Yeah, that's what I thought." I say angrily. "Maybe it actually preys on vulnerability, not so much solely when you aren't busy, but moments that you are vulnerable to its powers." Jace comments. "That," Elfred says as he shakes his finger, "is actually not a bad thought." "That doesn't make matters any better. It's not like I can exactly control my vulnerability." I say. "Yet. You can't control it, yet." Elfred says. I throw my hands up in aggravation, "Not everything can be controlled Elfred." I tell him. Jace walks over to me and gives my shoulder a reassuring squeeze. "No it cannot, but in this case, it's worth trying." Jace tells me.

It doesn't have to be this way Aislinn, just release me and all your problems will be over…

I shoot a nasty glare at the Diablerie. Oh the choice words I have, but there's no use. I'd be talking to a book and there's no telling if it would even listen. "Did it just say something?" Jace asks. "Yes." I sigh. "You're emotional right now, understandably, which makes you vulnerable. She should probably call it a night." Jace suggests. "Agreed. It probably doesn't help they are in the same room. Tomorrow we shall practice creating a force of solitude so we can discuss matters elsewhere." Elfred says. I give him a nod as I put my necklace back on. Elfred then opens the doors to his office to indicate our dismissal. When I make it to the doorway, I notice Jace still standing in the same spot.

"Can I help you with something?" Elfred asks Jace. "Your Wise Elf," Jace says with a slight bow, "I was wondering if I could have permission to stay with Aislinn. You said yourself someone should be with her at all times and I was hoping that someone could be me. That is if she doesn't have any objections?" He says as he looks back at me. I try to suppress the smile forming, as not to dissuade Elfred and shake my head quickly. Elfred purses his lips as he briefly ponders the proposal. "I suppose I can allow it, as long as it doesn't distract her from her training and studies." He says gruffly as he turns to look out his window. "Of course Wise Elf." Jace says giving him another bow, even though Elfred's back is to him. Jace turns to face me and I give him a big smile and when he smiles back at me, every worry starts to fade away. "Thank you Elfred." I say appreciatively. Elfred partially glances over his shoulder without saying a word and I know he's not happy about the matter.

"Shall we?" Jace says as he sticks his arm out and I interlock mine with his. "We shall." I say as I lead the way to my room. We make small talk about about my training process and as we approach my room I hear some commotion coming from inside. Surely Ariti isn't tidying up, I've told her plenty of times to leave it to me. As I open the door, I'm met with Fraeya's glowering stare.

"What are you doing in my room?" I question. As she swiftly emerges from the other side of the bed, I now see the scroll from Xander in her hand.

"Fraeya…" Is all I can say before a hard smack hits me across the face. I grab my face in shock as Jace quickly steps in front of me. "What the hell is your problem?" I ask. Fraeya holds the scroll up and waves it in the air irately. "You! You are my problem." She says angrily and then continues, "You just have to have them all don't you?" She shouts. "What do you mean?" I ask confused. "Of course. Just play miss innocent while you have every male fawning after you, with no regard to how it affects others." She rants. I knew she would be upset about Xander, but sheesh this is a bit extreme. "I'm sorry, I know you and Xander had a connection at one point, but…" "Just shut it." She interrupts, "You have Elfred wrapped around your finger so tight that now what we had is nothing but a forgotten tryst. While at the same time you've been stringing along Xander. *I can still feel the warmth of your lips on mine, love Xander.*" She dramatizes mockingly, as she reads his words off the scroll. I see Jace become uncomfortable with the situation.

"You shouldn't be snooping through my things, it's an invasion of privacy!" I say angrily. "Besides, it's not like I asked for any of this." I shout. "Of course not, it's just so natural for you. In fact, here stands another victim to your ways." She says as she looks Jace up and down. "Well aren't you just scrumptious." She says as she runs her finger down his chest. I can feel the anger boiling inside me as she does so. "Stop it Fraeya." I yell. She gives me a mocking pout, "Awuh, are you jealous?" She asks. I grit my teeth. She then swiftly pulls Jace into a kiss and he quickly pushes her away as she gives me a smug smirk. I can't hold it back, the anger conquers me and I lunge for her. We both fall to the ground as we wrestle about. She pulls my hair as she delivers another smack to my face. That's it, I finally cock back and punch her square on the nose, causing it to bleed. Right after I do so, I feel Jace's arms wrap around me and pull me up off of her. He must have gone to fetch a guard because one of them is helping her up and escorting her out the room. We both sneer at one another as she exits the room and I slam the door shut when she does so.

I immediately turn to face Jace and I feel a wave of embarrassment overcome me. "I'm really sorry you had to witness that. I don't know what overcame me." I tell him. "It's alright. I can't say I wouldn't want to do the same if it were me." He says. "Right, about that." I start to say. "Really, it's alright. What's happened is happened and I'd rather not hear about the victories of my competition." He tells me. I give a frown, "I hope you don't think badly of me." I say. "Never." He tells me as he lifts my chin so I can meet his soft gaze. "In fact, I'm flattered to even maintain the affections of someone so highly regarded." He tells me. I smile. "Now you flatter me." I say, as I break away from his gaze. I don't trust myself the longer I look into his eyes. "I understand, things are complicated for you right now, but I assure you, my feelings for you are patient. That is, if it is me you chose." He says. "You are my soul-mate I don't think there's an option not to choose you." I say. Jace gives a flat smile and I realize how that must have sounded. "I didn't mean it that way. I just mean you are literally perfect for me and to me. I would be a fool not to choose you." I rant. "It's okay Aislinn. It should not be a brash decision. I think you have some serious feelings to sift through before you can truly make a sound decision." He tells me.

He's exactly right, there's no way I can make a clear decision when I have some many mixed emotions and feelings running a muck in my mind. I do know that when I'm with him though, I feel at peace. I feel complete, like that part of me that's always felt like something is missing, is now full. I look into his eyes and it's like I'm in a trance, as I get stuck imagining our potential future.

"I just wish things weren't so complicated. There's so much pressure on me and I just feel trapped here. I just want to leave." I say frustratingly as I sit on the edge of the bed. Jace takes a seat next to me as he lets out a sigh. "I can't begin to imagine what your going through Aislinn, but I promise to always be here for you. I understand feeling trapped, but sometimes if you find a new perspective, it can make things more bearable." He tells me. "You know, it's almost annoying how positive you are all the time." I tell him teasingly. He offers a half laugh, "I guess I have my mum to thank for that." "Really? She must be a bright ray of positivity then." I say. "She was." He says followed by a nostalgic smile. "Oh, I'm so sorry Jace. I didn't know." "It's alright. How could you know?" He says rhetorically. "What happened if you don't mind me asking?" "She was a healer who worked for our local villages infirmary. One day at work she had just got done healing a massive gash and was sent home for the day as her powers were spent and she could no longer be of use. Me and my sister were down playing by the ravine, even though we were told dozens of times not to. It had just rained the day prior so the rocks were slick and my sister slipped and fell. She was wasn't responding and just kept bleeding. I ran down for help and ran into my mum." He pauses as I see him try to get a handle on his emotions. "Oh no." I whisper. "She didn't even hesitate, she followed me instantly. When we returned to my sister, she had grown even paler and the water just kept washing away more blood." Jace continues. I grab his hand for support and instantly see a vision.

A young boy, Jace I believe, standing next to a beautiful woman, his mother, kneeled down next his sister. *I love you my sweet boy.* His mother says tearfully as she cups his cheek with her hand before quickly directing her attention back on his sister and scoops her up. Eventually the blood stops flowing and his mother grows paler and paler until she finally stops moving and just slumps over. *Mum,* a young Jace shouts. *Mum!* He cries as he tugs on her.

I'm kicked back to reality and it's a good thing too, because I feel like I shouldn't be witnessing such a private moment of Jace's life. "Sorry, I, I didn't mean to." I say. "It's alright. It was kind of nice getting to hear a voice again." He says thoughtfully. "What about your sister?" I ask carefully. She lived, but it took her about three days to wake up. At first dad was relieved when she awoke, but he slowly turned bitter towards her, as if she didn't feel guilty enough. The older she got the more she favored mum too, so by time we were 16, he couldn't stand the sight of her and kicked her out." "That's awful. Where did she go?" I reply. "I'm not sure, I haven't seen her since. She asked me to come with her, but since that day I've always regretted telling her no. Dad merely became a drunkard, so, not like I had much of home anymore anyway. I guess part of me felt bad for him, mum was the love of his life. Another part of me did blame my sister, but I've grown to realize it was an accident. She didn't ask for it and mum wouldn't have done anything differently, as long as Elizabeth got to live." "I think you're right." I tell him reassuringly. "And thank you for sharing that with me, I'm sure it wasn't easy to relive." I add. "No, it wasn't, but I have this inclination to share everything with you." He tells me. "I know what you mean. I feel the same way with you." I tell him. "Good. I want you to be able to confide in me." He says.

Jace then for the first time takes account of my room. "Wow I can't believe this is your room." He exclaims. "I know it's amazing." I state. I watch as he walks over to the balcony and goes onto the terrace. I get up and make my way over to him. We both stand in silence as we look up at the sky. "I don't think I want to be an Elf." I say softly. Jace looks over at me. "And why is that?" He asks. "Because there's so many rules and stipulations. What's the point in pretending to be something I'm not, if I'm not even happy doing it." I say. "You would be safe and protected though." He counters. "Yeah, but you said yourself we would not be able to mate if I'm an Elf." I reply. "I'd much rather love you from afar than to risk losing you forever." He tells me. "How about we just runaway?" I say erratically. He gives me a sweet smile. "I'm afraid you forget what I am." He says as he holds up his arm showing his Doulos tattoo. "They will always be able to track me. Plus, fleeing with the knowledge you possess, the Wise Elf Council will surely have every bounty hunter on you." I give a frustrated growl. "So I'm trapped." I say woefully.

No you're not. I can solve all your problems… The Diablerie hisses. "Pft, yeah right. You are one of my biggest problems." I scoff. "Oh." I hear Jace say in a hurt tone. "Oh my gosh, I wasn't talking to you." I say frantically, as I grab his hands and squeeze them tight. "The Diablerie?" He questions. I nod. "I'm sorry this is happening to you, on top of everything else." He tells me. "Thanks. I just can't help but feel like I'm doomed all around." I say. "Don't say that. You have a bunch of people on your side." He says. "I think what you need for now, is some sleep. You've had a long eventful day." He says as he ushers us back into my room.

Jace takes a seat on the chaise lounge and begins taking off his boots, so I use this time to go to the bathroom and change into my robe. "You know, I was thinking while you're at training, I could go by the…" His voice trails off as I emerge from the bathroom. He quickly averts his gaze and clears his throat, "By the infirmary to help." He finishes stating. "Is something wrong?" I ask. "No, not at all. You just, um, look very lovely." He stammers as tries to keep himself from gazing up. I can't help, but blush at his sweet innocent demeanor. "Thank you. And I think it would be a good idea if you go to the infirmary tomorrow, I know you enjoy helping." I tell him. "Yes, very much so. I'm glad you can see that." He replies.

I slide into bed and watch as Jace stretches out along the chaise lounge to get comfortable. "Are you not sleeping in the bed?" I ask slightly baffled. Everyone else here has seemed to have no regard for privacy or personal space, but Jace is different, I should know that by now. "I didn't want to insinuate or insult you my lady. It's ok, I don't mind sleeping where I'm at." He tells me. "And I don't mind sharing." I say almost provocatively. He stands up and walks up to the foot of the bed and rests his hands along the top frame as he towers over the edge of the bed. "Are you sure?" He asks as he stares into my eyes. I give a slow nod, not wanting to break eye contact. He comes around and slides in bed next to me and we both sit in an awkward silence for a brief moment. "Shall I blow out the candle?" Jace asks. "Oh, sure." I say.

I don't know why I'm so nervous, it's not like he's going to try anything. Plus, I'm the one who suggested it. As the room falls dark, Jace makes himself comfortable in bed and I follow suit. "Goodnight Aislinn." "Goodnight Jace." I reply and the room becomes silent. To no surprise, I can't fall asleep now and I wonder if the same is for Jace.

I then start to think about all the times Dad would somehow know when I couldn't sleep and would come check on me since he couldn't sleep either. Cue the homesickness. I roll onto my side, incase Jace is still awake so he can't see the tears. I feel a gentle hand on my shoulder, "Aislinn, are you okay?" Jace whispers. I let out a sniffle as I roll towards him. "Not really. I miss home." I cry. Jace kisses my forehead as he wraps his arms around me. "Tell me about something that you miss." He says. "My dad. He always knew when I couldn't sleep so he would come in with a warm cup of milk and he'd sit and talk with me for a bit. Afterwards, I'd be able to fall right asleep." I say. "It's nice you and your father share such a lovely bond." Jace says. "It is." I reply. "Can you educate me on something?" "Sure." "What is warm milk?" He asks and I can hear the curiosity in his voice. "Oh right. So, there's this liquid that comes out of cows that you can drink." I start to say. "Oh, so cow extract." Jace says matter of factly. I crinkle my nose at the distasteful wording for milk here. "Um, yeah. And if you warm it up, it makes a soothing drink that typically helps you sleep." I tell him. "Hm, what an interesting remedy. I don't think that's been tried before." He says. "Probably not." I say as I let out a small laugh followed by a yawn. "If you're afraid to sleep, I will stay awake to watch after you." He tells me soothingly. "No, it's okay. I think I might be able to sleep now." I say. "Alright then." He says softly as his comforting gaze lingers on me. I give him a kiss on the cheek and quickly turn onto my opposite side. He wraps his arm around me to hold me close and I feel at peace.

Chapter 14

"Very good. Let's do it one more time, except I want you to initiate it." Elfred says. We've been practicing constructing forces of solitude since I finished my lesson with Cicero. "Alright." I say wearily as I hold my hands out once more. I concentrate on making the connection with Elfred as we recite the spell telepathically. Just as we get the shield up, I see Fraeya briskly approaching us. "Great." I murmur. Elfred dissipates the force of solitude and turns to see who I'm referring to. He gives me a perplexed look. "Long story." I say.

"Wise Elf." Fraeya says. "Fraeya, how can I help you?" He replies. Fraeya shoots me a glaring side eye, "There's word Stavros's men are setting up camp by the Waterfall." She says. I see Elfred's face turn serious. "Very well. We should reinforce the defenses. Call Calix in for a briefing." "Yessir." Fraeya says and turns to leave. "What does this mean?" I ask. "It means they're testing their boundaries. Seeing how we will react. If we attack first, then it may seem like we are trying to hide something, but if we ignore them, it may delay their raid." "Raid?" I say alarmingly. "It's only a matter of time Aislinn. They are scowering the Realm in search of a Seeker and they aren't going to stop till they find one of them." Elfred states.

I start to pace about as the panic arises. "This is not good." I say. "No. No it is not." Elfred states. "What else can we do?" I ask.

You can release me Aislinn, I can make you powerful. More powerful than Stavros...

"Just shut up, you're not helping!" I shout. I notice Elfred give me a disgruntled look. "Sorry, it was the Diablerie." I say. Now his face switches to that of concern. "We shouldn't be discussing these matters then. It's only going to make you more vulnerable." Elfred states. I let out a manic laugh. "Oh, ya don't say? Elfspond is on the brink of a raid, of which I may or not be taken captive and all the while I have an evil book taunting me. I'd say the days of not being vulnerable are a thing of the past." Elfred's brows furrow, as he tries to think of a response. "Yes, well I reckon you are right. Perhaps we should just prepare for the worst and hope for the better." Elfred says. I give him a peculiar look as his mood turns somber. "Are you okay?" I ask curiously. "Well, as you mentioned, everything is falling apart and my Region is about to be invaded and there's nothing I can do about it. I have worked effortlessly to try to keep you safe as possible, but it seems my efforts have failed. I have failed my Region, I have failed the deities, and I have failed you." Elfred says. Now I feel bad, I didn't mean for him to feel like a failure. "Elfred, none of this is your fault. You couldn't have prevented any of this, this is all my fault. In fact, things would probably be better off if I were dead." I state. "How dare you say such a thing?" Elfred roars angrily.

"Woah, what's going on here?" Jace says as he steps in between me and Elfred. "Aislinn here, thinks the Realm would be in a better place if she were dead." Elfred states. Jace whips around to face me. "Why would you say such a thing?" He says and I can see the hurt in his eyes. "It's true. There wouldn't be a worry about being captured and I wouldn't have to listen to the stupid Diablerie." I say. Jace pulls me into a hug and squeezes me tight. "Please don't talk like that. Think of how much better thing are with you here." Jace tells me. "I must be going now. I suggest you keep an extra close eye on her today." Elfred says. Jace gives him a nod and then takes my hand.

"Come on, it should be just about ready." Jace says as he pulls me along. "What should be ready?"

I ask inquisitively. "You'll see." He says with a bright smile. It's not long before we arrive at the stables, where we are met by Ariti.

"Perfect timing." Ariti says as she hands Jace a basket. "Thank you Ariti. And were you able to get the other." He asks in a near whisper. "I was." Ariti says as she gives a giggle. I give them a suspicious look. "Come along my lady." Jace says as he leads me to Lila, who is saddled and ready for travel. "Where are we going?" I ask. "You'll see." Is all he says again. He hoists himself up on to Lila and then helps me up and hands me the basket to hold. A nice aroma of bread fills my nose. "Jace Galanis, are you taking me on a picnic." I ask. "If I say yes, will that ruin the surprise." "Not at all." I say as I grin from ear to ear.

After about an hour we arrive to an open field surrounded by flowers. In the middle of the field stands a lone twisted oak tree, which is where we take our place. Jace helps me down and then lays down a blanket for us to sit on. After displaying the food Ariti prepared for us, we start to eat. We watch as Lila grazes about the field while we talk about more of our likes and dislikes and who we are as people. We share stories about our childhoods and what we aspired to be. He is sweet and charming, thoughtful and kind, respectful and funny. Oh and of course, he's painstakingly handsome. The more I get to know him, the harder it is to deny that he is anything less than my soulmate.

"So tell me, how did you know about this place?" I ask. "Well it's actually along the border of Elfspond and the Land of Kalos." He says. "The land of the good hearted." I interject. "Yes, that's right. Sometimes as a kid, when I just needed to get away from the world, I would come sit under this very tree to read." Jace tells me. "So you're from the Land of Kalos?" "Yes… I was." He says and I can tell he is alluding to the fact he now belongs to the Land of the Doulos. "That makes sense." I say. He gives me a smile, "You think too highly of me my lady." "That's not true, you just don't give yourself enough credit." I reply. "I suppose you are right. It's just hard to be someone when you aren't even deemed as such." He tells me. My heart aches at the thought of the belittlement and mistreatment he has ensued. "You are someone to me." I say softly. Our eyes lock and I can feel our heads drifting closer and closer. Finally, I think to myself. I have been dying to kiss him since I saw him in the infirmary, but I wanted him to make the first move. Especially with my recent love life complications, I didn't want it to seem like I was just going around kissing every man I see fit.

All of a sudden I feel a tickling sensation to my hand. I look down and see a bug on my hand and instantly freak out. I flick my hands up and end up falling into Jace. "What happened?" Jace asks. "Sorry, there was a bug on me." I apologize. "Well I'm not complaining." He says and I finally take account that I'm practically laying on top of him. "Oops." I say as I push myself up from his hard chest. "Is this the bug in question?" Jace says as he sits up and holds it out for me to see. "The very one." I say. "It's just a caterpillar, totally harmless. Do they not have them on Earth?" He says. I try to cover my mouth from bursting with laughter, but there's no such luck. "What's so funny?" Jace asks. "I just feel so silly. I just ruined the moment over a caterpillar." I laugh some more and Jace starts to laugh too.

"My, my, what am I going to do with you?" Jace says jokingly. "Well that depends, what do you want to do with me?" I say flirtatiously. Despite the necklace, I can feel our bond intensifying. I see the yearning fill his eyes as his gaze falls to my lips. "Well?" I say encouragingly. He firmly grips the back of my neck and pulls me to him, kissing me passionately. I lean into him as I kiss him back and he pulls me onto his lap. He wraps his free arm around my waist and squeezes me close as we sloppily exchange kisses to one another.

I feel as if electricity is running through my veins and each kiss delivers a gratifying shock. I run my fingers through his hair as his kisses start to trail down my neckline. Just before he reaches my breasts, I feel him come to a stop. I look down to meet his gaze and I can see it filled with conflict. "What's wrong?" I ask. "My feelings for you are quite strong. So, as enjoyable this is, I'm afraid if we keep going, it will be harder to stop." He tells me. "Right…" I say and hope he doesn't detect the disappointment in my voice. I slide off his lap and stand up to compose myself. "Aislinn, I hope not to have offended you. I didn't want your judgment hindered by lust and have you end up regretting what I deem to be the most sacred bond."

His thoughtful words only make me want him more, but he's right. I've never been with someone intimately before, but with him it just feels so natural. If he didn't stop us, who knows how far we would've gone. This connection we share is intense, but I shouldn't just give myself to anyone, I need to remember the virtues I once held for myself. Jace is a gentleman and it's apparent he values the intimacy sex holds, but how many woman has he been with? I know unwillingly, with Diona, so that's one, but I cannot fault him for that. These are all things we should discuss before we are intimate.

I turn around and give him a warm smile, "No, you are absolutely right. We shouldn't rush into things or take it lightly. We need to be certain, we are the ones for each other." I tell him. "Then that should only leave one of us." He says as he caresses my cheek. I blush, as his confidence in his feelings for me make it that much harder to deny mine for him. "We should probably head back." He says.

As he goes to fetch Lila, I pack up our things. When I stand up, I catch a glimpse of a dark hooded figure standing at the edge of the woods. I let out a gasp and drop the basket, but by time I blink, the figure is gone. Jace rushes over and assess me. "What's the matter?" He asks. I point to the edge of the woods, "There was somebody there." I say as my voice fills with panic. "Come on then." He says. I bend down to grab the things, but he tugs me back up. "Leave it." He says in an authoritative tone, which makes him all the more attractive. Then, in one fell swoop, he mounts Lila and swings me up on her and sends us galloping back toward to castle.

When we make it back to the stables, I can sense some frustration radiating from Jace as he silently puts away Lila's saddle. "Jace, what's wrong?" I ask. "I am fool. It's no wonder I am a Doulos." He says. I stop him and turn him to face me. "Why would you say that?" I ask flabbergasted. "Because I took you out in the open and risked your safety." He says heatedly. "It wasn't intentional. Besides, I wouldn't change a thing about today." I say as I embrace him, trying to channel some reassurance and happiness onto him. "But what if they had come for you? I would only be able to fend off so many." He tells me somberly. "But they didn't. I'm still here Jace." I reply encouragingly. He squeezes me tight and kisses the top of my head. "That you are." He whispers.

We then spend the next few hours in the library. I'm studying more spells while he scans the history books for something about the Diablerie. We keep exchanging glances from across the room and it's apparent the flame from earlier has rekindled. "You aren't making this easy." I say, giving him a smitten look. "Me? Have you ever thought you are the one that's distracting me?" He counters. I laugh, "Oh, is that so?" "Why yes, yes it is. This is quite fascinating reading material I should have you know." He teases back. "Really? The History of Elven Literature. If I remember correctly, it was a pretty boring read." I tell him. "Actually, you're not mistaken. This is dreadful." He says giving a displeased look and tosses the book aside. We both share a laugh. "Should I fetch Ariti to sit with you so you can focus?" He asks. "No, that's alright. I think if I read anymore, my head might burst." I tell him.

All of a sudden the doors to the library burst open, sending me and Jace to our feet. "Jace, come quickly." Elfred commands. We quickly follow

Elfred to the courtyard to find a guard with an arrow to thigh, bleeding profusely. It must have hit his artery. I kneel down next to guard and realize it is Alonzo. I grab his hand to comfort him. "I'm going to have to remove the arrow first." Jace tells him and he gives a nod. He clenches his teeth as Jace twists the arrow and then pulls it out, causing the wound to bleed even more. Jace then places his hands over the wound to heal him. I watch as the blood eases up and the wound slowly shrinks. I see the wound begin to form on Jace's thigh as he grunts in pain. I have to turn my head because it's to heart wrenching to watch him inflict so much pain onto himself.

After a few minutes, I get an uneasy feeling and turn back to Jace and he is pale as a ghost. I look down at Alonzo and see where the arrow once was, is now merely a scab. Jace then slumps over next to Alonzo and the unsettling sight reminds me of how his mother looked after saving his sister. "Jace!" I shout as I crawl over to him. "Jace!" I shout again as I shake him, but his body is limp. How is this possible? I think to myself. I instantly remember how he said he was going to help in the infirmary today. I start to cry as I feel an emptiness start to form in my chest. I look up at Elfred and see him with a shocked stare. "Well don't just stand there!" I scream. Elfred quickly snaps back to reality and calls on the nearby guards. "To the infirmary, quickly." He commands and two guards pick Jace up and start to carry him off. I go to follow them and Elfred grabs my wrist. "Perhaps you should wait awhile." He tells me. I yank my wrist free. "No." I say coldly. I then run to catch up with the guards.

After a few hours I find myself nodding off in the chair next to Jace's cot. He hasn't moved a muscle and his color hasn't returned in the slightest. Elfred tried to get me to come eat dinner, but I refused. I don't think I would be able to stomach it anyway. I try squeezing his hand in hopes of him doing so in return, but there's been no such luck. I let out a frustrated sigh as I sit back in my chair. I feel helpless, there's nothing I can do except wait here. The Elf in charge said it's customary to watch over a healer for two days. If they have not awoken by two days, then it means they have passed on. My frustration quickly turns towards Jace. He should've known he was not healthy enough to treat such a bad wound. "How could you?" I say angrily. "Maybe you are a fool after all." I mutter. I instantly regret my words as I quickly take his hand. "I didn't mean that. I'm sorry, I'm just upset and I don't know what to do." I say tearfully.

I feel a gentle hand on my shoulder and I look up to see Ariti. I rise up and she gives me a consoling hug. "My dear friend, you should try to get some rest. He would not want you up worrying yourself sick." I look down at Jace and then back at Ariti. "I don't want to leave him." I say. "I know, but you can come first thing after your training." She tells me comfortingly. Ugh, the last thing on my mind is training. I give a reluctant nod and then bend down to give him a kiss on the cheek before following Ariti out.

After I take a long bath, Ariti rejoins me so she can watch after me. I toss and turn as I fail miserably to fall asleep. Even though he had only stayed with me one night, the other side of the bed already feels so empty without Jace.

I can bring him back...

"Shut up." I say through clenched teeth.

It's true. You know what you have to do...

"No!" I shout. "Huh? What did you say?" Ariti says sleepily, as I awaken her. "I'm so sorry Ariti, I did not mean to wake you." I tell her. "That's quite alright. I take it you haven't gotten any sleep?" She inquires. "Not at all." I say tiresomely. "Well, I got something that might help." She says as she flings back her covers. "Wait here." She instructs.

She leaves the room and a few moments later she returns with a cup. "Careful, I'm afraid I might have made it a little too warm." She says as she hands it to me. "What is it?" I ask cautiously. " Warm cow extract." She tells me. "You brought me warm milk?" I say with nostalgic smile. "Ah, yes that would be the word Jace said you called it." Keep it together Aislinn.

"Jace asked you to do this?" I inquire. "He did. He knew it was an odd request as, Elves find extracting to be a bit invasive on the cows, but said he would give five coins if I could try and get him some." I want to cry at the sweet gesture, but the ducts are all dried out by now. I sip the warm milk and it's nothing like the milk back home. It actually tastes so much better and I'm not sure if it's because it's just fresher or because of the thoughtfulness behind it. "Thank you Ariti." I say as I take another sip and let it warm my soul.

When I'm finished, Ariti takes my cup and pulls the blanket up over me. "Now get some rest." She says soothingly and then blows out the candle. It's truly a wonder what some warm milk can do, because before I know it I'm fast asleep and dreaming of me and Jace dancing in the moonlight.

The next morning comes way too soon, because when Ariti tries to wake me I just pull the covers up over my head. "Aislinn, I'm afraid you really are going to have to get up now." She says tensely. "Ugh, I don't want to go to stupid ole training today." I groan as I sit up. I now see why Ariti was so persistent. Elfred stands perched in my doorway. "Stupid ole training huh?" He reiterates. "Did I say that? I meant super fun training." I reply. He just gives me a smirk and shakes his head. "Glad to see you in higher spirits this morning." He tells me. "We'll see how long it lasts." I say. "Now to what do I owe the pleasure?" I add. "I will be accompanying you to your combat training today." He says formally. "Okay…" I say. "I also, wanted to check and see how you are doing." He says a little more personably. "Well, I've been better." I say flatly. "Yes, of course." He says and we both stare at each awkwardly for moment. "Very well. I will leave you to get ready and I'll meet you outside." He says and I simply give him a nod.

*

"Come on Aislinn, you practically had this down just the other day." Calix states. "Yeah until I got my arm sliced and Jace got put in the infirmary." I say frustratingly. Calix exchanges a look of concern with Elfred. "I mean how do you really expect me to concentrate?" I say as I throw my sword down. "I told you, you will be notified the second he should happen to wake up." Elfred says. "Why would you say it that way?" I yell. "How dare you raise your voice to the Wise Elf." Calix says in astonishment. I have to gather myself, as I'm reminded that the lax relationship me and Elfred share, is not appropriate in front of everyone.

"I'm sorry, Wise Elf. I did not mean to take my aggravations out on you." I say with a slight bow. Elfred returns the bow to indicate the acceptance of my apology. "Now pick up your sword. I believe I have a solution." Elfred says drawing a curious look from Calix and I. "To what?" I question. "A way for you to take out your frustration while maintaining your concentration." He says. "How?" I ask, but my question is quickly answered as Fraeya appears.

"Yes Wise Elf?" Fraeya says. "Miss Aislinn here is having trouble concentrating on her training. I would like you to take Alec's place." Elfred commands her. "Yessir." She says as she shoots me a nasty smirk. She takes Alec's sword and shield and displays a defensive stance. Seriously, the last thing I need is Fraeya trying to kill me today. "Ready?" Calix says. "And go!" He orders.

Me and Fraeya walk in a circular formation, waiting to see who will make the first move. I should know better than to mind link with her so I don't have to hear her taunting, but I let her do so. "How awful, your infatuation with Jace had to end so soon." She says. "Shut up! You're just jealous that a man can actually care for me without sleeping with him." She gives me a snarl. "Maybe after this I should make a visit to Jace and see if true loves kiss really does work." She says. I let out an aggravated roar as I charge her.

Our swords clink together and she pushes me back forcefully. She takes a swing, but I block it. She then tries to stab me, but I dodge it and quickly realize she is truly trying to injure me. "I never meant to hurt you Fraeya. If you would've told me you had feelings for Elfred then.." "Then what? You would erase his affections for you?" "I don't know. I could've tried." "Pft, please. You just switch from man to man when it's convenient." Well fine, it's apparent there's no talking sense into her, she just wants to hold a grudge.

Even though she keeps trying to stab me, I can't bring myself to do it back. So, I keep swinging my sword, only to keep getting blocked.

Kill or be killed...

I try to shake the Diablerie's awful words out of my mind and regain focus. The small distraction allows her to land a small cut to my leg, and now I'm pissed. I relentlessly start swinging the sword, giving her little time to counter and end up cutting her shoulder. She looks at her shoulder and then at me and I can see the anger fill her eyes. "Sikóno!" She shouts as she raises her hand, causing me to lift up off the ground.

"Fraeya!" Elfred barks. She gives me a smug look, trying to assert her dominance and then throws me to the ground like a rag doll. I rise to my feet as she gives me a twisted smirk, which only makes my blood boil. "Pnigomai!" I shout, casting the spell to choke her. I know better, but she needs to be knocked down a couple inches. She grabs at her neck as she gasps for air. "That's enough!" Elfred's voice booms. I flick my hand to release the hold and she immediately starts sucking in air. I see the astonished look on Calix's face, and I don't even care what he thinks. "Hopefully you two have worked out whatever animosity it is between you two." Elfred states. "She choked me!" Fraeya screams. "Oops. I meant to freeze you, guess I still need to work on my enunciation" I say trying to sound as sincere as possible. "Are we done for today?" I quickly add and Calix gives a very perturbed nod.

I briskly make my way to the infirmary to sit with Jace. It's hard to tell if his color has returned any after staring at him so long, but the head Elf said there hasn't been any signs of improvements, so it's unlikely. I hold his hand as I talk to him. I thank him for the warm milk and tell him about my dream of us dancing. I tell him about my spar with Fraeya and how I couldn't help but feel like I let the Diablerie influence my actions during it. I then squeeze onto the cot with him and run my fingers through his hair. He still smells like that of sandalwood and fresh rain and it's comforting as equally as it is captivating.

I didn't even realize I fell asleep until I feel a nudge. "Jace." I say quickly coming to a full wake. I look at him, but he remains still. "It was me, Aislinn." Elfred says. I look up and see him standing over us. "Oh." I say disappointedly. "It's time for dinner." He says. "I'm not hungry." I say as I lay back down. "It wasn't a suggestion." He says, giving his authoritative tone. I let out an aggravated huff. Time is dwindling. It's already been over a day, if he doesn't wake up by this time tomorrow, then…stop it. I can't think like that, I tell myself. "Come back to me and I'll be yours." I whisper as I give him a kiss on the cheek. "Fine." I say as I reluctantly get up and follow Elfred.

As I sit through dinner, I feel numb. Elfred and Fraeya are quarreling about which tactic should be approached, now that Stavros's men have attacked one of ours. I haven't even thought to check on Alonzo, hopefully Jace's efforts weren't in vain. "Aislinn." Elfred echos. "Huh? What?" I say as I emerge from my thoughts. "I said, do you feel prepared enough in case we went to battle." "Oh... I don't think I really have a choice." I reply. "Now, that doesn't really sound like the same Aislinn I battled earlier." Fraeya says cordially. "Save your civility for those who believe it." I tell her. I see her brow furrow. "I do admit, I have been quite harsh to you, but I do extend my most sincere apologies and hope we can work on becoming allies again." Did I cut off some of the oxygen to her brain earlier. "Um, excuse me?" I reply "Must I really repeat it? It's taking all the pride I have just to apologize." She says. Nope she's good. I let out a small laugh. "Then I suppose we can work on that. As long as you promise not to invade my privacy. Or kiss Jace again." I say. Elfred gives a bewildered look, causing us both to laugh. "Deal." She says.

After dinner, Elfred offers to walk me to room. "Do you think Fraeya meant what she said?" I ask. "I would like to think so. She's always been one of her word." He tells me. "So this was all over a kiss between her and Jace?" Elfred asks. "Um, not quite, but I am not at liberty to discuss the finer details of our feud." I tell him. "Ah, I see." He replies. "I wonder what caused her change of attitude." I wonder out loud. "Well, she's one of our top warriors and you beat her in a spar. It's customary to respect those ranked higher than you." "But I'm not ranked. I'm not even a warrior." I say. "Every Elf is naturally a warrior and the stronger you are, the higher ranked you are." "So, I'll be going into battle when Stavros's men attack?" I say nervously. "Only to protect yourself. You will be hidden away, to hopefully keep them from finding you." Elfred says. "Alright." I say, not sure whether to be relieved or petrified. When we arrive to my door I give him a polite nod and turn to go in. "Also, I thought I'd let you know I instructed Cicero to cut your lesson in half tomorrow so you could spend more time at the infirmary." He tells me. I throw my arms around him and give him a big hug. "Oh thank you." I tell him. "It's the least I could do." He says as he steps back, then gives me an awkward smile before disappearing down the steps.

Chapter 15

The next morning I'm wide awake and have never been so quick to get to my lessons. Today I' am being positive. I feel hopeful and ready to see what the day holds. I am actually able to pay attention and retain the new spells Cicero is teaching me. There's only five I need to keep practicing the enunciation on to cast them properly. As the sun starts to shine through the classroom window, I can tell it's almost high noon and I start to become anxious for when he might release me. It's not till after a couple practice runs of the more difficult spells, that he tells me I can go.

I dash out of the class and head straight for the infirmary. When I walk through the doors, my heart sinks a little at the sight of Jace's still body laying there. My eyes narrow on his hand as I notice it entwined with someone else's. My vision trails up and I recognize the Elf, Anastasia, from the other day. I march right up to Jace's cot and clear my throat to show my displeasure.

She looks up at me with fright in her eyes and quickly rises to her feet. "You don't usually come till later." She stammers. "Not today. Now do you wanna tell me who the hell you are and what you are doing?" I say with frustration. "I'm Anastasia." She says trying to bump arms with me, which I have learned is this worlds form of shaking hands. I leave her hanging and just stare at her, waiting for more answers. "Right. I realize how this may look, but I swear I meant no offense. I just want to pay my respects. While working in the infirmary together, Jace has been nothing but kind and helpful. He's not coarse and prideful like other men. I will not lie and say I did not grow an attraction to him, I mean look at him." She says as she looks down at Jace. I can feel my jealousy starting to kick in. "But I know he is off limits. His heart belongs to you and he made that evident from day one." She finishes telling me. I remain silent, as I'm not really sure how to feel or how to respond. I mean I don't blame her, Jace is a wonderful guy. "Anyways, I will leave you two alone. I hope I did not upset you any further." She tells me as she goes to leave. "Thank you." I say quickly and I can hear her stop in her tracks. I turn around to face her and give her a small smile. "Thank you for keeping him company while I could not be here." I tell her. She gives me warm smile. "He did say you had the kindest heart. I can now attest to that." She says. We both give a polite nod and I turn back to Jace as she leaves.

I sit with him and hold his hand while I tell him about the dinner last night and Fraeya's apology. Next, I go over the lesson and spells I learned today. I tell him more about dad, mom, and Natasha. I tell him how I couldn't quit thinking about him after I met him at the club. I joke how there's no way my dad couldn't approve of him after saving his life. Then it makes me picture a life where I do get to go back home and see them again and introduce them to each other. "Would I even be able to tell them about who we are?" I ponder aloud. I try to avoid dampering the mood, so I retrieve my satchel to show him my surprise.

"So, I remember you saying you liked to read, but I didn't know what genre. So, I have two options I can read to you." I say as I pull them out. "Proper Elven Etiquette." I say mockingly. "Or, Ariti lended me, the Tales From Beyond." I say as I look to Jace, but the returned silence is harrowing. I then hear the doors to the infirmary open and I see Elfred, the Head Elf, and an Elf dressed in all black.

I feel my stomach lurch as I try not to throw up. My face fills with panic as I look down at his lifeless body. I shake him, "You have to wake up now." I say frantically. I shake him more forcefully as they grow closer and I start to cry. "Jace, please wake up." I beg. "Aislinn." Elfred says softly as he tries to pull me away. "No!" I shout as I shove him off me. "Miss Aislinn, I'm very sorry, but it's been two days and we have already waited longer than typical so you could have more time with him." The Head Elf states. "I said, no!" I roar, and the become still. "Just wait, he's going to wake up any second now." I add as I grab his hand and search for a sign, any sign, of hope. After a long moment of heartache, I hear the Head Elf whisper to Elfred. "Wise Elf, I'm sorry, but we need this bed." Elfred picks me up and pulls me from Jace. "No, no, no!" I cry as I wither about in his arms. "Aislinn, please stop." Elfred begs and I can hear the heartache in his voice. I wish I could be strong, so it didn't have to pain him to see me like this.

The Elf in all black approaches Jace. "Stop! Hey stop it!" I shout at the Elf. "What's he gonna do to him?" I ask. "He takes care of the body. I've had it arranged for you to receive his ashes." Elfred tells me. "Ashes? He's going to be cremated?" I say appalled. "It's customary for all Doulos's to be cremated." I finally quit squirming and turn to deliver a swift smack to Elfred. The whole room stops as everyone lets out a gasp. I point at Jace, "He, is more than just a Doulos." I say ferociously. "I understand you are upset, but I am trying my best here." Elfred whispers. "You think it doesn't pain me to see you like this? What should you have me do?" He questions. "One more day, please. Can we just wait one more day? I beg you." I say pleadingly. Elfred looks to the Head Elf, "My Wise Elf, your people need help. There are many waiting for an open bed so they can be treated." The Head Elf states. Elfred looks back at me and I can see the conflict in his eyes. "It won't bring him back Aislinn." Elfred says gently.

But I can... The Diablerie hisses.

My heart feels like it's being ripped apart and I feel helpless. The Diablerie's words echo in my mind as they try to poison my thoughts. No, Jace wouldn't want this. I look over at Jace's still body and then back at Elfred. I see the concern fill his eyes. I feel broken and angry. I let out a guttural scream as I shove everything off the table and knock over the cart. Everyone stares at me and I can't tell if they are frightened or they just pity me. The longer they all stare, the embarrassment starts to settle in, so, I pick up my satchel and quickly run out. "Aislinn!" I hear Elfred call after me, but I don't stop.

I barge into my room and startle Ariti as she's dusting the trinkets. It only takes her a second to realize what's wrong and she holds her arms open. I walk into her arms and begin to sob. She soothingly caresses my hair. "Is there anything I can do?" She asks. "I would like to be alone please." She gives me a sympathetic nod. "I will have to remain right outside though." She tells me and I just give her a weak nod. As she shuts the door, I crawl into bed and just lay there.

I didn't even know I could hurt this much. I feel shattered inside. Is this what it's like to lose someone you love? I remember sitting with Natasha after her mom died and she just cried. I wish Natasha was here, she would know what to do. After what feels like an hour, I run out of tears so I just stare blankly at the ceiling.

A light knock on the door doesn't even phase me. "Aislinn can I come in?" I hear Elfred ask. I don't answer him and just roll onto my side. "Aislinn." He pleads, but I ignore him again. He mind links with me, "Aislinn, please." He says. "Ánoixe." I mutter, which opens the door. I keep my back to him. The bed caves a little as he takes a seat next to me and he places a gentle hand on my shoulder. "I told the Head Elf we will be giving Jace a proper burial, so, it will give you another day so they can make the arrangements." I jolt out of bed. "Really?" I say, eager to get back to Jace. "Yes, the Head Elf was not very happy with me, or you for that matter. He has banned you from entering the infirmary until further notice."Elfred states. "What's the point then?" I give an aggravated growl. "That was the Head Elf's terms." He says. I give him a defeated nod. "Thank you." I tell him sullenly. He gives me a nod, "I'll leave you to your thoughts." He says as he rises up and makes his way out the room.

I go out on my balcony and look up at the night sky. "What am I to do now?" I ask aloud. "You deities are a joke. Told to be so mighty and powerful, but where are you now?" I say angrily. "I know where, you're in hiding because you're scared." I add. "Pft, pathetic. You'll only intervene when it's convenient for you, but mark my words. I'll do your job, I'll kill Stavros." I sputter.

That's right Aislinn and I can help you. I can make you the Queen of the realm. The Diablerie hisses. I clench my head. "Leave me alone! Get out of my head!" I scream as I slide down to the ground.

"Aislinn what happened? Are you okay?" Ariti asks frantically as she busts in the room. I slowly run my fingers through my hair as I try to compose myself. "I think I am just becoming a little delirious." I tell her. "Maybe you should try to get some sleep. Shall I fetch some warm cow extract?" Ariti says comfortingly. "Yes, that would be nice." I say as Ariti helps me to my feet and walks me over to the bed.

The next morning I feel the stares and hear the whispers as I make my way to the garden for today's training. They are gossiping about my tantrum in the infirmary and say that I must be a mad woman to act in such an uncivilized manner. "I don't know why the Wise Elf hasn't banished. I heard she even slapped him." I hear another say as I pass by them. I try to hold my head high, in hopes of maintaining my dignity.

When I arrive to the garden, Calix and Elfred are waiting for me. Today is my first archery lesson and there's a couple different bows and different types of arrows I see laid out. After a brief run through of what the different arrows can do, they have me practice holding different bows and loading them. I already like the feel of the bow in my hands, much better than the sword. I can't help but feel more naturally drawn to it.

"Alright lets practice shooting the targets. You want to aim for the center of the target." I lock my eye on the center of the target, pull back, hold my breathe, and release. "Sometimes if you hold your…" Calix stops talking as my arrow lands right in the center of the target. "Bullseye." I whisper to myself. I turn to face Calix and Elfred and see their look of astonishment. "Are you sure you haven't done this before?" Calix inquires. I give him a nod. "Perhaps it's beginners luck then. Let's try another." He says. I grab another arrow and load it up. I do just as I did before and the arrow lands right next to the other arrow. I actually feel a smile spread across my face as I turn around to see their reaction.

After a few more shots on the same target. Calix has another target arranged, but this one further away and higher up. I land three arrows right on the bullseye. "My goodness she's a natural born archer." Calix comments. "Your weapon of choice shall be a bow. I'll have them begin making you one right away." Elfred notes. "Would you like to try some more challenging targets." Calix asks and I give him an eager nod.

Calix has a few more targets set up and this time he wants me to practice moving from target to target. I nail the first three, but right as I'm about to release my fourth one, I feel an instant surge throughout my entire body. Causing the arrow to go amiss and sending Elfred and Calix ducking for cover. I feel my heart beating uncontrollably and I start looking around frantically. "My word!" Calix exclaims frustratingly. "What is it Aislinn?" Elfred asks with alarm. All of a sudden, I just know. "Jace." I say quietly. "What?" Elfred asks. "Jace, he's alive. I can feel it." I say excitedly as I throw down my bow and make my way past Elfred and Calix. "Aislinn it's been over two days. It's not possible." Elfred shouts after me.

I don't listen. I start running to the infirmary and I can sense Elfred and Calix chasing after me. I run as fast I can, making my lungs burn like they are on fire in the process. The infirmary is over a mile away, but I don't care. I sprint the whole way there and when I make it to the doors there are two guards standing outside. They see me approaching and put their spears in an X to block the entrance. "You cannot enter Miss Aislinn." One guard shouts once I'm only thirty feet away.

When I reach the entrance I stand there huffing and puffing. "Please you have to let me in. He's alive, I'm sure of it." I say with ragged breaths. "Miss Aislinn, we are under strict orders to not let you enter." The other guard says. Elfred and Calix finally catch up with me and Elfred tries to pull me back. "Aislinn, please." He says while trying to catch his breath. I turn to him, "You don't understand." I say as I fall to my knees, "Please Wise Elf, I'm begging you to tell them otherwise." Elfred pinches the bridge of his nose and lets out a heavy sigh as he processes the internal struggle. Before he can say anything, the doors to the infirmary open and the guards lower their spears as the Head Elf emerges. He becomes taken aback by the scene before him. His eyes quickly fall on me. "Let her in." He says. I jump to my feet and throw my arms around the Head Elf, giving him a big hug.

I then slip between the doors and stand at the entrance of the room. I stand in shock, as I almost can't believe it. Jace is propped up while one of the Elves is helping him sip some herbal concoction. I think he senses my presence because he quickly looks to his right. When our eyes meet, I give him the biggest smile I can fathom and when he does so in return, my heart feels as if it's going to burst out of my chest. I run over to his cot and kneel beside him. I take his hand in mine and squeeze it and he immediately squeezes it back. Reassuring me this isn't a dream. He caresses my cheek with his free hand, "You really are the most beautiful woman of all the worlds." He says. I turn my head into his hand, savoring the moment.

"You know, you are making it real hard to be mad at you." I tell him. "Mad? At me? I've been on deaths bed." He questions. I nod my head, "Exactly. How could you do that to me?" I say half jokingly, but also half serious. He gives me a warm smile and I notice that his color is slowly starting to return. "It was not intentional. I saw the man in trouble and knew he did not have much time if I didn't act quickly." He tells me. "But you nearly killed yourself Jace. Do you know if Elfred had not convinced them to keep you another day, you would have been cremated yesterday." I tell him. "Then I am grateful for another day." He tells me. "You don't understand. I thought I lost you." I say as I start to cry. He pulls my head to his chest and soothes me. "I felt so broken Jace and I never want to feel that way again. Promise me you won't ever leave me again." I say. "I promise." He says and then kisses my forehead. "You know, I think it's only fair you pay up to your promise too." He adds. I pull back and look into his eyes. "My promise?" I question. "I think I recall you saying, if I came back to you, you would be mine." He states. I automatically blush, "You heard that?" I ask bewildered. "Oh yes. I heard everything." He says, while exaggerating the word everything. I suddenly become embarrassed about last nights events, but also relieved to know that my visits weren't entirely meaningless either. "I will gladly pay up to my promise." I tell him. "Good. It's what helped keep me fighting." He says. I try to give him a quick kiss, but I should've known that would be impossible.

The moment I feel his warm lips on mine, I can't break away. I cup his face in my hands and kiss him deeply. I don't want to stop, but I have to pull away for air. When we pull away, we stare at one another, realizing something is different now. We don't even have to say anything, it's as if we both come to a mutual realization that we are indeed, each other's soulmate.

I feel the heat of eyes on us, and as I look over my shoulder, I see Elfred and the Head Elf standing at the foot of the bed. "I think it would be wise if we leave Jace to rest now." The Head Elf states, and it feels more like a command than a suggestion. "Perhaps, he can be released to stay with me?" I offer. The Head Elf opens his mouth in protest, but I cut him off. "After all, you do need this bed pretty badly don't you?" I add. "Uh, well, yes. You make a good case Miss Aislinn. Let me go get that arranged." He says and then briskly walks off. Elfred gives a smirk and just shakes his head. I shoot Jace another smile and he gives my hand a gentle squeeze. Elfred then goes to walk off.

"Wait, I need to thank you, Wise Elf." Jace says. Elfred turns around and looks Jace directly in the eyes, "No need to thank me. Aislinn made quite the influence." He says and I can't help but feel a little embarrassed by my outburst yesterday, but it was well worth it. "Yes, but you made the decision, and I know the outcome of it." Jace replies. Outcome? What is Jace talking about? "Yes, well, no need to harp on the matter. Just focus on getting well." Elfred says before finally leaving us.

After Elfred leaves, Anastasia appears with a big smile, holding some supplies. Her eyes flash to me and I give her a polite smile as I step out of the way. She respectfully keeps her distance as she approaches Jace. "Glad to see you awake." Anastasia says. Jace gives a smile. "Thanks and thanks for tending to my wound." He says. I become slightly jealous at the realization she has been touching Jace's thigh, but I remind myself that it is her job. "You're welcome. I know you're a healer, but I wanted to see if the seaweed would help speed up the skin regeneration." She says. "Which is why, I brought some extra." She says as she hands me a package of wet seaweed. "Along with some gauze, incase it starts to bleed and a few herbs to make into tea that should accelerate the healing process." She says handing me the rest of the stuff one by one. "Got it. Thanks." I say giving her a confirmatory nod. "Other than that, the Head Elf said you are good to go." She tells us. "Thanks Anastasia." Jace says. "Yes, thank you." I add.

Once she walks off I put the supplies in my satchel and go over to Jace's side as he slowly sits up. "Ready?" I ask him. He gives me a nod and then stands up. His legs are wobbly, but he holds onto me for balance and eventually becomes more steady. He takes a step forward and I can see him wince with pain. "Okay, maybe this isn't a good idea after all. I don't want you to push yourself too much." I tell him. "I'll be alright. It just burns like hades." He says.

I help him as he hobbles his way through the infirmary. Luckily, Elfred had Lila fetched for us so that saved a lot of time and torture. Getting off Lila, seemed to be the most painful for him, and I can tell all the activity reopened his wound when blood started seeping through his pants. I help him through the castle and up to my room, hoping not to have left any trails of blood.

I lay him on the bed and then pull out the supplies Anastasia gave me. I then fetch a bucket of clean water and some soap. "Um, alright, I need you to pull down your pants." I direct. He unbuttons his pants and pulls them down to reveal his thigh. The seaweed is bloody so I peel it off carefully and place it into an empty bucket. I then wet the rag to wipe away the blood before cleaning it with the soap before rinsing it with water. Next I rip the seaweed into little strips to place atop the wound and wrap it with the gauze to hold it in place.

When I'm done, I look up at Jace. "You would make a fine addition to the infirmary." He says proudly. I give him a blushing smile. "Thank you." He adds. "Is there anything else I can do?" I ask him. "Should I make one of the teas?" I inquire. "Perhaps in a little while, maybe we can just rest for now?" He suggests. "I thought you'd never ask." I tell him. I climb into bed next to him. I hadn't slept good in the last three days and knew I was finally going to be able to do so. I snuggle up next him and lay my head on his chest as his arm engulfs me. Next thing I know, I was out.

Chapter 16

"My word. If I didn't know any better I would think you are a goddess." Jace shouts from across the garden. I laugh as I lower my bow and unmount Lila, making sure to give her a good pat. I make my way over to him. "Not bad, huh?" I say, knowing damn well that I am perfect shot. "To say the least. It's apparent Apollo has blessed you with the skill of archery." His compliment makes me feel all the more confident.

It's been four days since Jace woke up and we have spent nearly every waking minute together. Which hasn't been a bad thing. I could feel myself falling for him, hard, but I'm conflicted on what to do. Fortunately, my induction ceremony got pushed back another week, due to my *horrendous behavior* in the infirmary, but it's only prolonging my fate. I don't want to allow myself to acknowledge my full feelings for Jace. Only because if I do become an Elf, it would make it that much harder to turn him away. Perhaps, the Wise Elf Council will rescind their decision altogether and then I will be left to do as I please. That's wishful thinking though.

"And you're not too shabby with a sword." I say as I approach Jace and Alonzo as they put an end to their sparring. Alonzo and Jace bump arms and I trade places with Alonzo as I pick up one of the swords. I give him a mischievous smile and he just smirks back at me. "I'm not going to spar with you my love." Ugh, I thought his, *my lady* was irresistible, but hearing him say, *my love* gets me weak in the knees every time. He knows it too, because the first time he did it the other day, I nearly collapsed.

I clank my sword to his. "You afraid to get beat by a girl?" I challenge. "On the contrary. I just prefer when you're not upset with me." He replies. "Why would I be upset?" I ask. "Because you'd lose." He says. I give a satisfied grin as I raise my sword and take my first swing, only for him to block it. Our swords start to ricochet as we duel. Jace then swiftly disarms me and my sword falls to the ground. He points his sword at me, "Checkmate." "Afoplízo." I say, casting the spell to disarm him. I say it a little too forcefully and end up knocking him to the ground. "Oh, that's not fair." He states. "I prefer to think of it as an advantage." I reply. He gives a smirk and then tries to get up, but grabs his leg and lets out a groan. I rush over to him. "Jace I'm so sorry." I say, but he gently takes me down to the ground and pins me down into submission. "Hey! You tricked me." I say as I squirm. "I prefer to think of it as an advantage." He says teasingly. I free my hand and give him a soft punch to the chest as we both laugh.

As he looks down at me, I suddenly become aware that he's on top of me and it instantly makes me flush. He's glistening with sweat and his hair tousled in a sexy way and it's getting harder to deny the desire brewing inside. It's as if he starts to feel the same because he clears his throat and quickly gets off and helps me up. As I dust myself off, I notice a group of guards riding into the courtyard. "What could that be about?" Jace says exactly what I am thinking. "I don't know, let's go see though." I say.

When we approach the courtyard, we see one of the guards throw a non-Elven man in shackles to the ground. "Just wait, you egocentric Elves will be the only species completely wiped out." The prisoner says. "Shut your mouth." One of the guards demands. I notice a few of the other guards are injured as they get off their horses. Jace tries to make his way over to them, but I hold him back.

"What are you doing?" I whisper. "I'm going to help them." Jace replies "No, you're not ready." I say anxiously. "I'm fully healed, it won't be an issue. I promise." He reassures. He tries to let go of my hand once more, but I only squeeze tighter. "Please Jace, don't do it." I beg. He lets out a sigh and hangs his head. I can tell it's paining him not to help, but I can't risk losing him again.

Elfred and Calix hastily enter the courtyard and take notice of the prisoner. "Wise Elf. Commander. We have detained one of Stavros's men after their group took us by surprise." The guard says. "Fatalities?" Calix inquires. "Not enough." The prisoner mutters. I see Elfred's eyes flash with a firery vengeance. He raises his hand, causing the prisoner to lift up in the air. It's apparent Elfred is choking him as he does so, because the prisoner looks just as Fraeya did when I did it to her. Elfred then throws the prisoner to the ground. "5 soldiers and 3 bystanders." The guard replies. "And we have four needing urgent medical treatment." He adds. "Fetch a wagon and get them to the infirmary." Elfred commands. But before anyone can move another inch, one of the injured guards falls to the ground, hemorrhaging out. I feel Jace tense up and I just squeeze his hand. "He's losing too much blood!" One of the guards shout. I see Elfred scan the crowd and his eyes land on Jace, his eyes flicker to me and I shake my head in disagreement. Elfred doesn't say anything, and instead directs his attention back on the prisoner. Jace breaks my grip and storms off into the castle. I know my selfish request is upsetting him, and I can't imagine how hard it is for him to stand by when someone needs help.

I decide to let him have some time to himself, so he can hopefully calm down. "Where are your people now?" Elfred questions. The prisoner just spits at Elfred. Elfred looks unphased as he gives the guard a nod. The guard then punches the prisoner in the face a couple times, breaking his nose and making it a bloody mess. "Please don't make me ask you again." Elfred says calmly. I've never seen this side of Elfred before and it's actually quite intimidating. "The prisoner just spits a mouthful of blood at Elfred. The guard cocks his fist back waiting for Elfred's signal. "Very well, don't hold back this time." Elfred tells the guard and I see the prisoner's eyes grow wide with fright. "W, w, wait!" The prisoner cries out, and the guard stops right as his fist is less than an inch away from his face. "He has one of the brigades advancing on your stupid pond as we speak. We were to ride ahead and see what your defenses were like. Once we returned to provide the intel, our plans were to attack by the end of tomorrow." He says. A chorus of gasps echo amongst the crowd. "How many is in your brigade?" Calix asks. "Uh... like a thousand." The prisoner stammers. "It would be unwise to lie." Calix says. "Please, he'll kill me." The prisoner pleads. "I will kill you!" Elfred roars. "Now how many are in your brigade?" He demands. "A thousand on the frontline, five hundred on the bows, and four on the catapult." He states. The crowd erupts with panic. "Quiet." Elfred commands and the crowd hushes. I don't stay to hear anymore.

I slowly back out of the crowd and make my way into the castle. My mind goes numb as I start to walk about aimlessly. I'm definitely going to be taken. Stavros is going to make me his Doulos and use me to get what he wants before he kills me.

That's not true, you can save them and yourself...

I let out an aggravated huff. Now I got the stupid Diablerie filling my head with thoughts I know shouldn't be having. I just want to be with Jace and I can't find him anywhere. I check the dining hall, the library, and the commons area. No luck, so I make my way to my room.

I fling the door open and am met by Jace standing in nothing but a towel. I know I should turn away, but I can't take my eyes off of him. "Sorry. I... I didn't realize...realize that you were bathing." I stammer as my mind becomes mush. I can't stop my eyes from perusing every inch of his exposed body. He chuckles as he runs his hand through his wet hair, which unknowingly flexes his bicep and sends my primal instincts raging. "I'll let you get dressed." I say quickly as I grab the door handle and shut myself outside the door.

Sweet mother of pearl, get yourself together Aislinn. I think to myself. But then again, who knows what the outcome of tomorrow will be. Maybe I should just put my feelings out there in the open, there's no point in holding back anymore. The door opens and I turn around to face Jace. I throw my arms around him and give him a big kiss. I quickly pull away and push my way past him to make my way into the room. "I know you're upset with me asking you not to heal those soldiers." I say and I can feel him tense up as he gives me a stiff nod. "I know that was selfish of me, but dammit Jace, what happens when there's no one there to help you? What if you exert yourself too much and you don't come back next time?" I rant. He opens his mouth to respond, but I just keep talking. "You tell me you care about me and would do anything for me." I say. He comes over to me and takes my hands in his. "You know I do. That's why as hard as it was earlier, I stood by. I would do anything for you, deities as my witness, I would die for you." He proclaims. I give him a horrified look as I shove him away, "Why would you say that?" I shout. "Because it's true. You are everything to me Aislinn, and I, I am nothing without you." He tells me with a burning stare. "You don't understand what your saying." I argue as I try not to become engulfed in those eyes of his. There was so much promise within them. "You don't know what it was like waiting by your side those three days. Begging, pleading, hoping you would come back to me. Desperately trying to figure out how I was going to fill the emptiness that occupied where my heart should be, because I was hit with the realization that I can't live without you." I admit breathlessly. Jace steps closer to me, and I can't will myself to look away. "And I, without you." He whispers softly.

Just as we are about to kiss, there's a knock to my door. "Come in." I reluctantly grumble. Ariti enters and gives us a grim look. "The Wise Elf is requesting to see you in the council chambers." She tells me. I give a nervous swallow and look to Jace. "The council chambers?" I reiterate. The council chambers are restricted to Elites only. "That is correct." She says.

We follow Ariti as she leads us to the council chambers. We come to a halt as we wait for the guards to verify our permission to enter. "I wonder what this is all about?" Jace thinks aloud. I forgot he wasn't there to hear what else the prisoner had to say. "The prisoner informed us that by tomorrow evening, Elfspond will be under attack." I say somberly. He gives me a comforting smile as he takes my hand in his. "We are going to get through this." He says. Damn him and his positive attitude.

The large doors creak as they open and the guards quickly usher us into the council chambers. When we enter we see Elfred sitting at a podium like desk along the opposite end of the wall. To the left, sits Fraeya and Melanie, and on the right is Calix rearranging pawns on a strategy map. Elfred makes his way down from the stand when we enter.

"Ah, nice of the lovebirds to join us." Elfred says while throwing his hands up in the air dramatically. "And why are we here?" I ask bluntly. "Because even though Elfspond will fall, we still have to protect one of the Realms last precious Seekers." Elfred says with underlying animosity. I quickly look at Melanie and Calix and neither will make eye contact with me. "They know?" I shockingly ask. "Well, given the fact Fraeya and I might not make it through tomorrow. I thought we should inform some trusted others." He says, making the atmosphere turn gloomy. "Okay… so what's the plan then?" I ask. "Simple." He says as he makes his way over to a cabinet and pours himself a drink. He takes a big swig and then walks back over to us. "You and lover boy will hide out in my room. You'll be armed with your weapon of choice and there will be a couple guards posted out front should they happen to find the secret passage." Elfred says. "That's it?" I ask. "I'm sorry, is that not enough for you?" He says mockingly. "No…I meant, we are just supposed to hide out while you all are under attack? We can help fight." I say. "Oh my dove, I've always admired your strong spirit." He says as he sensually twirls a piece of my hair. I can sense Jace's jealousy as Elfred speaks his words of endearment while his finger continues to encircle my hair.

"You're drunk." I exclaim. "Ah, and you're so bright." He says. I smack him so hard that he stumbles a little bit. He gives an appalled look. "How dare you! I am the Wise Elf." Elfreds roars, sending everyone into a frozen fright "And I am not one of your Elves." I bark back. "Everyone else out!" Elfred demands as his gaze sears into mine. Fraeya, Melanie, and Calix quickly leave, but Jace remains still. "I said out!" Elfred shouts. Jace looks at me and I give a reassuring nod.

Once everyone is out Elfred throws back the rest of his drink and slams the glass on the table. "You should not be getting drunk." I say. "And why do you care?" He says gruffly. "Because you are my friend Elfred and your Region is relying on you." I reply. "My Region is doomed. I will be the Wise Elf who let Elfspond fall." He says flatly. "You will be the Wise Elf who led his people into an unjust battle. You can either give them hope or you can give them fear." I say. He peers over at me, but remains silent. "I know you have a lot of weight on your shoulders, but no matter what happens tomorrow. You will have done the best you can do, and that is all that your people want from you." I say. He comes over to me and I can see his eyes are filled with sorrow and pain. "I am sorry for the way I spoke to you. I was just angry... and scared." He says quietly. "I know. I'm sorry for slapping you." I reply. "I deserved it." He says pulling me into a hug. I let us embrace for a moment, hoping it will alleviate the looming fear of uncertainty. As I go to pull away he holds me tighter and whispers in my ear. "In my room, under the rug with the chest, is a passageway. The key to unlock it is in the tall silver vase on my nightstand. If the castle should be breached take the passage. It's a tunnel that will lead you to the border of Elfspond and Eternal Keep."

When he breaks away, I just give him a nod. It's apparent this passageway is a secret unbeknownst to others. "Now, if you'll excuse me. I believe I have some tactics to run through with Calix." He says. "Yes you do." I say proudly and he gives me smile. I make my way out the doors to find Fraeya, Melanie, Calix, and Jace waiting in the hall.

"I believe he wants to speak with you three some more." I say. Fraeya and Calix enter, but Melanie hesitates. "As the Realm's Advisor, I feel I should tell you, thank you, for your contribution to protecting the Realm. I know you do not see this place as your home, but the Realm of Vitalis is grateful for your efforts. It's a large weight to bear, with the fate of the Realm laying in your hands, but don't forget, so does the Seeker lineage. May the deities watch over you." She says. I'm a little taken aback, but still politely thank her for the encouraging words.

Once she reenters the Council Chamber, Jace takes my hand and gives it a squeeze. "Are you alright?" He asks. "I'm not sure." I say. We make our way back to the room and it's evident the mood all around is dim. I go to the bathroom and when I come back out I notice Jace standing out on the balcony looking into the night sky. I silently take my place next to him. In the distance, you can tell the news of tomorrow has brought increased business to the local tavern. It's patrons spreading melancholy as their hymns echo throughout the night. I turn to Jace to catch him staring at me.

"What?" I ask. "You look beautiful in the moonlight." He tells me, causing me to blush. "Dance with me?" He says as he holds out his hand. "But this sounds like a sad song." I reply. "Then I shall hold you a little closer." He offers. I take his hand and he pulls me close. I rest my head on his chest as our bodies slowly sway back and forth. I hold back the tears as long as I can so that I can savor this moment.

"What's wrong my love?" Jace asks. "I just hope we have a chance to do this again." I say. He caresses the back of my head. "Me too. Me too." He whispers. We stay that way for a little bit longer before we decide it's time to get ready for bed. As I change into my robe, Jace leaves and soon returns with two cups of warm milk.

"Are you sure about this." He says as he peers into the cup. I chuckle, "It's good. I promise. It always puts me fast to sleep." I say encouragingly and then take a sip of mine. "I sure hope so. I think it will be nearly impossible to sleep tonight." He says. He takes another second of hesitation and then finally takes a sip. "Well?" I say. He doesn't respond, instead he just takes another sip. "This is actually quite delectable." He finally says. We make small talk, trying to avoid any mention of tomorrow's events, as we sip on the milk. By time we finish our cups, we are both yawing. Jace blows out the candle and then snuggles me close. I try to fight the sleep so I can cherish the moment, but the feeling of his warm embrace and the wave of his familiar scent when I inhale, puts me right at ease. "Tell me something good." I whisper. "I love you." Jace whispers back. "I love you too." I feel myself say as I drift off into sleep.

Chapter 17

"Women and children to the burrows!" A guard shouts as he waves them in the right direction. The whole castle grounds has been a mad house, rightfully so. Especially since Elfred opened refuge to the women and children of the village, but everyone has to be checked thoroughly first. The heightened emotions have made it all the more a frenzy. People all around are crying. It's quite overwhelming. I can't even sit idle, not yet anyway, so we have been helping Ariti prepare baskets to hand out to those in refuge. In the distance, I can see Elfred and Calix giving a pep talk to the Elven Soldiers. There's a lot more of them than I realized, so that brings me hope. Afterall, aside from Laskaris's, Elven soldiers are the next strongest force to be reckoned with. Now, I'm anxiously wondering what ended up being Xander's fate.

"Thank you so much for helping with these." Ariti says, bringing me back to reality. "No problem, it's the least we could do." I tell her. "Is there anything else we can help you with?" Jace adds. "No, my tasks are complete as of now." She says and a silence falls between us. "Where will you be going?" I ask. "I am going to visit my parents and then I will take refuge in the burrows." She tells me. I know we have only known each other a short time, but Ariti has become a good friend to me and it saddens me to part ways like this. The uncertainty of who I may or may not see again is gut wrenching. We exchange a long hug before finally parting ways.

All of a sudden I feel weight on my shoulder and look over to see Ella. "Ella, I'm so glad to see you!" I say relieved. "I know, I'm so glad I could find you." She says. "I've missed you." I tell her. "I've missed you too. I wanted to make sure I got to see you, but unfortunately, I can't stay long, I have to start helping the others prepare." She tells me. "Will you not be seeking refuge?" I ask her. She giggles, "No. Us fairies are small and fast, making it easy to evade them. Plus, the Fairies are allying with the Elves to aide in battle." She tells me. "I see. Well, please be careful." I tell her. "And same to you my friend." She says as she sprouts a small pink flower from her hand and hands it to me. I give her a smile and she smiles back before flying off.

I look over at Jace with a somber look. He takes the flower from my hand and tucks it in my ear and gives me a small smile. I can't help but smile back.

Jace has been extra sweet today and I can't tell if it's from us exchanging our first *I love you's* last night, or the circumstances of today. Either way, I'm just grateful to have him by my side through it all. I look up and see the sun is a quarter past high noon. The bridge will be shut soon and that's when are to report to Elfred's chambers.

We make our way back into the castle and decide to stroll about the commons area. "There you are." I hear Elfred say from behinds us. We stop and turn to greet him. "Elfred. I wasn't sure if I would get to see you today." I tell him. "Well of course you would. I would have made sure otherwise." He says and then his eyes shift to Jace. "Plus, I have to give you both your gifts." He says. "Our gifts?" Jace inquires. Elfred gives a proud smile. "Jace." Elfred says as he snaps his finger and a sword appears. Jace's mouth drops open. Elfred holds a dazzling, long silver sword in his hands. It has an emerald green handle with Jace's name engraved on it. "Alonzo tells me you are quite skilled with a sword." Elfred says as he holds out the sword. "I…I am honored Wise Elf, but I will not be able to accept this." He says sadly. "Well it would be disrespectful not to accept, given that I am an Elite. Besides, I have already ran it by Diona and she says she will allow you to have it, as you have rightfully earned it." Jace's eyes light up and Elfred offers him the sword once more. Jace takes the sword and looks over every inch, taking account of every detail. It makes my heart happy to see him get something so meaningful. "Thank you Wise Elf." Jace says giving Elfred a bow, but Elfred does not bow back. Instead he holds out his arm and Jace gives Elfred a cautioned look. Elfred nods and Jace bumps his arm to Elfred's. "I expect you to take good care of her." Elfred says as he now directs his attention on me. "Although, I doubt she will need much looking after." Elfred adds. "Aislinn." Elfred says as he snaps his fingers. An exquisite looking bow and a big case of arrows appears in his hands. "For you." He says and I give him a big smile as I take the bow from his hands. I run my fingers over the bows smooth curve and take notice of the shimmering gold flecks in the wood. "It's made by wood from the Tree of Vitalis." Elfred states. "It's beautiful." I comment. "Wow, the Tree of Vitalis." Jace says intriguingly as he focuses his attention on my bow.

"What is the Tree of Vitalis?" I ask. "It translates to the Tree of Life. It resides in the Garden of the Deities located in Eternal Keep. It's said to be the Realm's essence of life, having sprouted the original deities." Elfred answers. "Wow, this must have been really hard to get." I say. "Typically yes, but after Valstead fell, other regions were desperate for steel. We don't normally trade our Elven steel, but sought it as an opportunity to obtain such a rare material in return." "So this is Elven steel?" Jace says in amazement as he resumes admiring his sword. "Sure is." Elfred says proudly. Jace's eyes go wide with excitement. "Well thank you. These are lovely gifts. I will cherish it always." I tell Elfred. He gives me a charming smile. "Yes, thank you Wise Elf." Jace adds. "Well, I hate to cut this visit short, but I must be on my way. It's time we say our goodbyes." Elfred says. His words are an abrupt reminder of the reality ahead. I give him a big hug, "This isn't goodbye. We will see each other again." I try to say reassuringly, but my voice cracks with emotion. "Whatever you say my dove." Elfred says softly and then vanishes into thin air.

"Raise the bridge!" We hear a guard shout and I give Jace a panicked look. It's time. As we make our way out of the commons area I stop in the courtyard and take a look around me. I try my best to commit the image of the shimmering castle and the engulfed greenery into my mind. This place has been my home for the last few weeks and the thought of it being destroyed is making me emotional.

There's still time, you can prevent all of this…

I shake the Diablerie's taunting thoughts out of my head. As tempting as it sounds, I can't. It would be madness, trading one evil for another. Right? "Miss Aislinn, you and Jace need to come with us." A guard says, snapping me out of it. Jace takes my hand as we briskly follow the group of guards to Elfred's private chambers.

The guards take their post out front after locking us in. Now my panic settles in as I pace about the room. He won't admit it, but I can tell Jace is nervous too, his eyes keep glancing back to the door. "This is daunting." I say. I look at Jace and I can see the struggle on his face as he tries to find some uplifting words. "Do you think we will know when the battle starts?" I ask. "I'm afraid I do not know.

Elfred's plan is to have a regiment meet them outside the castle walls to hold them off from invasion. Should they get past them…" Jace says somberly and his voice trails off. I walk up to him to give him a hug and he embraces me. I listen to his heart beat against my head and it calms me just a little. "I love you." He says. I pull away and look into his eyes, "I love you too." I reply and he instantly kisses me. I melt into his arms, but he holds me tight as he deepens his kiss. He pulls away to let us catch our breath and I can see his eyes fill with seriousness. "Should we make it out of here—" Jace says, but I cut him off. "When we *do* make it out of here." I say matter of factly. He gives me a nod before continuing, "Then I—" Jace starts to say, but is once again interrupted. This time by a large boom, causing the castle to shake.

My eyes grow wide with fear. We quickly make our way to the door and put our ears to it, to see if we can hear anything. Silence. Suddenly, from above us we hear screaming. Jace ushers me back into the bedroom and shuts and locks the doors. "They're here. They're in the castle." I say frantically. I feel as if I could throw up. Jace comes over to me and takes me in his arms. "Shh. It's okay." He says and I can tell he's trying to not only convince me, but himself too. We listen to the rumbling and occasional screams of agony from above.

"For Elfspond!" We hear one of the guards shout. "For Elfspond!" The others echo and their armor begins to clink as they run. We then hear the sound of swords clashing, making it apparent the Neophenian's have breached the Wise Elf's secret quarters. Jace prepares to draw his sword, but I stop him. "We have to hurry." I say, wishing I would've thought to utilize the secret passage much sooner. Jace gives me a puzzled look.

I grab the vase off the nightstand and retrieve the key. "Move this." I say pointing to the large chest at the foot of the bed. Jace picks it up effortlessly and I fling back the rug, revealing the secret door. I twist the key and it opens. "We have to go through here." I say and Jace nods. I sling my bow and arrows over my shoulder and make my descend into the tunnel. Jace quickly follows me, being careful to pull the rug back over the door and then locks it. I hop off the end of the ladder and see a torch hanging on the wall. "Fotiá." I say as I grab it, causing it to light.

"Let's go." I say and we quickly make our way down the tunnel. We jog for what feels like two miles before we finally slow down. Hoping to have gotten some head way incase they discovered the passageway. We stop and listen for a moment, but neither of us can hear anything.

We walk and walk for miles, occasionally stopping for a few minutes to sit and rest. Just as I start to wonder if the tunnel will ever end, I spot a ladder almost 100 feet away. I take off and Jace follows closely behind. Jace offers to go first, as neither of us are sure what lies above. I watch as he unlocks the door with the same key and only lifts the door a little to peek out and then shuts it. "What's out there?" I whisper. "I can't see much, it's dark. There's a bunch of trees and that's about all I can make out." He says as he hops down. "Did you hear anything?" I ask "No. It was silent." He replies. "Good. Then we should be in the clear." I say. "Perhaps, but maybe we should rest in here and then continue our journey when there is daylight. We will be able to see our surroundings much better and we will at least have shelter for the night." He proposes. I know what he is saying makes sense, but I look back towards the dark eery tunnel. "I don't think I will be able to rest at all regardless. I want to put as much distance between us and them." I counter. Jace lets out a sigh and hangs his head in defeat. "As you wish, my love." He says.

Jace takes the lead and I follow behind as we make our way up the ladder. He opens the door fully this time and I cringe when it gives a loud creak. Jace waits a minute to see if the noise has drawn any attention. He then climbs out and then helps me out. We lock the door to the tunnel and I place the key in my satchel. As we look around, it's apparent we are in a forest. To the North I can see a bright golden aura peeking through the horizon of trees. "What's that light?" I ask. "That is the palace." He says. "Like *the* palace?" I reiterate. "The very one." He replies. "I hope I can see it one day." I comment. "But not while it's under siege by Stavros." I quickly add. "I'm sure you will." He says and takes my hand.

We begin our trek through the forest. We walk aimlessly, not really sure where to go, but knowing we can't go back. We come to a halt when we hear some twigs snap. Jace pulls me close to his side as he takes out his sword. We begin to frantically look around. I see a dark flash in my right peripheral and then it quickly dashes to my left. "Jace." I say frightfully as we butt our backs to one another and turn in a slow clockwise circle. "Show yourself!" Jace shouts. Then, right before me appears a giant wolf with golden eyes. "Jace…" I say with panic as I tap his hand. Jace looks over his shoulder and sees the wolf. "Aislinn, don't move." Jace replies to me as he slowly moves in front of me.

The wolf shows it's canines as it growls at us. The wolf steps closer to us and Jace raises his sword up, prompting the wolf to give a deeper growl. I look at Jace and then at the wolf. "Put your sword away." I tell Jace. "No way." He says. "Just trust me." I tell him. Jace reluctantly and slowly sheaths his sword. The wolf then slowly circles us, getting closer and closer each time. He then smells something as he lifts his head and sniffs the air frantically. It tries to approach me, but Jace steps I front of me. The wolf starts to growl again. "It's okay." I say as I slowly make my way in front of Jace.

I carefully put my hand out and the wolf cautiously steps forward as it sniffs. The wolf begins to sniff me erratically and then steps back. It looks me directly in the eyes and then gives me a bow. When it raises back up, it lets out a long howl, followed by a chorus of howls in the distance. The wolf then runs off, disappearing into the night.

"Wow." I say as I turn to Jace and I can see his face transition from that of horror to relief. "What?" I ask. "We just came face to face with a Lykaios and lived to tell the tale." Jace says. "A Lykaios?" I inquire. "They're people who shift into werewolves. No one dares go seeking one. When they are in their wolf form, they are feral and savage." Jace says still in astonishment. "That's crazy. I wonder why it did didn't attack us then?" I reply. "Well, it showed you a sign of respect. Maybe it could sense who you are?" Jace suggests. "That is so cool." I comment aloud. I can't believe werewolves exist, but then again I don't know why that surprises me at this point. I'm starting wonder just how many more of these so called, mythical creatures, truly exist.

I look over Jace's shoulder and see a dark hooded figure looming in the distance. I let out a gasp, "Jace there's someone behind you." I shout. Jace whips around and draws his sword, but the figure is gone. "Are you sure?" Jace asks as he scans the perimeter. "Yes, it was right over…" My words are cut off as I'm grabbed from behind and gagged with a cloth. "Aislinn?" Jace says as he turns around to see me being detained. "Let her go!" Jace says as he let's out an enraged roar and charges toward my captor. They let me go and I suddenly feel dizzy as I stumble about. Did, did they just chloroform me? I watch hazily as Jace and the cloaked figure duel. Eventually my legs give out and I fall to the ground.

"What did you do?" I hear Jace yell angrily as I start to fade in and out of consciousness. I see Jace fall to the ground and the figure takes his place over him. "Stop." I try to yell, but comes out as a mere whisper. My eyes become heavier and heavier. Stay awake Aislinn, I tell myself. Jace looks over at me as he coughs up some blood. His eye's are filled with so much anguish. *I'm sorry* he mouths. I reach my hand out for him, but it expends the rest of my energy. Everything around me goes black.

~

I blink a couple times before I am able to fully open my eyes. I have a throbbing headache that is only worsened by the light. Oh no, I think to myself. I quickly bring myself to all fours as I start to throw up. When I'm finished, I use the stone wall to help me rise to my feet. My eyes aren't seeing double anymore, allowing me to focus as I look around. I appear to be in some kind of cave. I inch along the rock wall as I make my way closer toward the light. As I approach the mouth of the cave, the stone ground begins to transition to sand and I can hear what I believe to be, the sound of waves. I have to shield my eyes from the light as I finally emerge from the cave.

Once my eyes adjust, I quickly take in the scene before me. I am surrounded by a large body of water with waves nearly reaching the top of the cliff I stand on. The water stretches for as far as I can see. I turn around and look up to find a huge over hanging rock that is covered in moss and scattered flowers. A drop of water drips onto my face and it's coolness is refreshing. The atmosphere is much more humid and warmer here.

"Good, you are awake." A man's voice says, startling me. I quickly turn in the direction of the voice and see a cloaked figure standing a little ways down, looking out to the water. I instantly become enraged. "Who are you?" I yell. The man turns around and slowly pulls back his hood. Now, before me stands a handsome man with brown skin, caramel eyes, and his hair is pulled into a braided bun. His eyes intensely lock on mine.

"I am Dru, your brother." He says.